MAR 2018

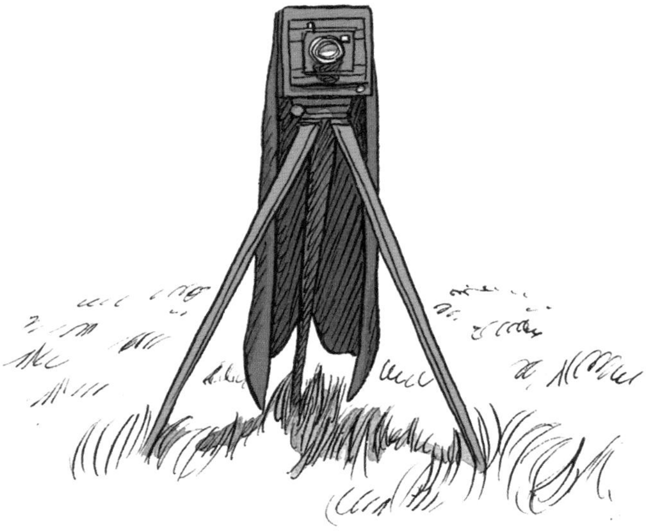

Loo Hui Phang thanks Orlando Pereira Dos Santos, Caroline Chik, Jean-Marc B. and Craig Thompson.

© Casterman / 2016
All rights reserved.

First published in English in 2017
by SelfMadeHero
139-141 Pancras Road
London NW1 1UN
www.selfmadehero.com

Written by Loo Hui Phang
Illustrated by Frederik Peeters
Translated from French by Edward Gauvin

Publishing Director: Emma Hayley
Sales & Marketing Manager: Sam Humphrey
Editorial & Production Manager: Guillaume Rater
UK Publicist: Paul Smith
US Publicist: Maya Bradford
Designer: Txabi Jones
With thanks to: Dan Lockwood

A CIP record for this book is available from the British Library

ISBN: 978-1-910593-40-0

10 9 8 7 6 5 4 3 2 1

Printed and bound in China

FREDERIK PEETERS
LOO HUI PHANG

THE SMELL OF STARVING BOYS

SELF
MADE
HERO

TEXAS

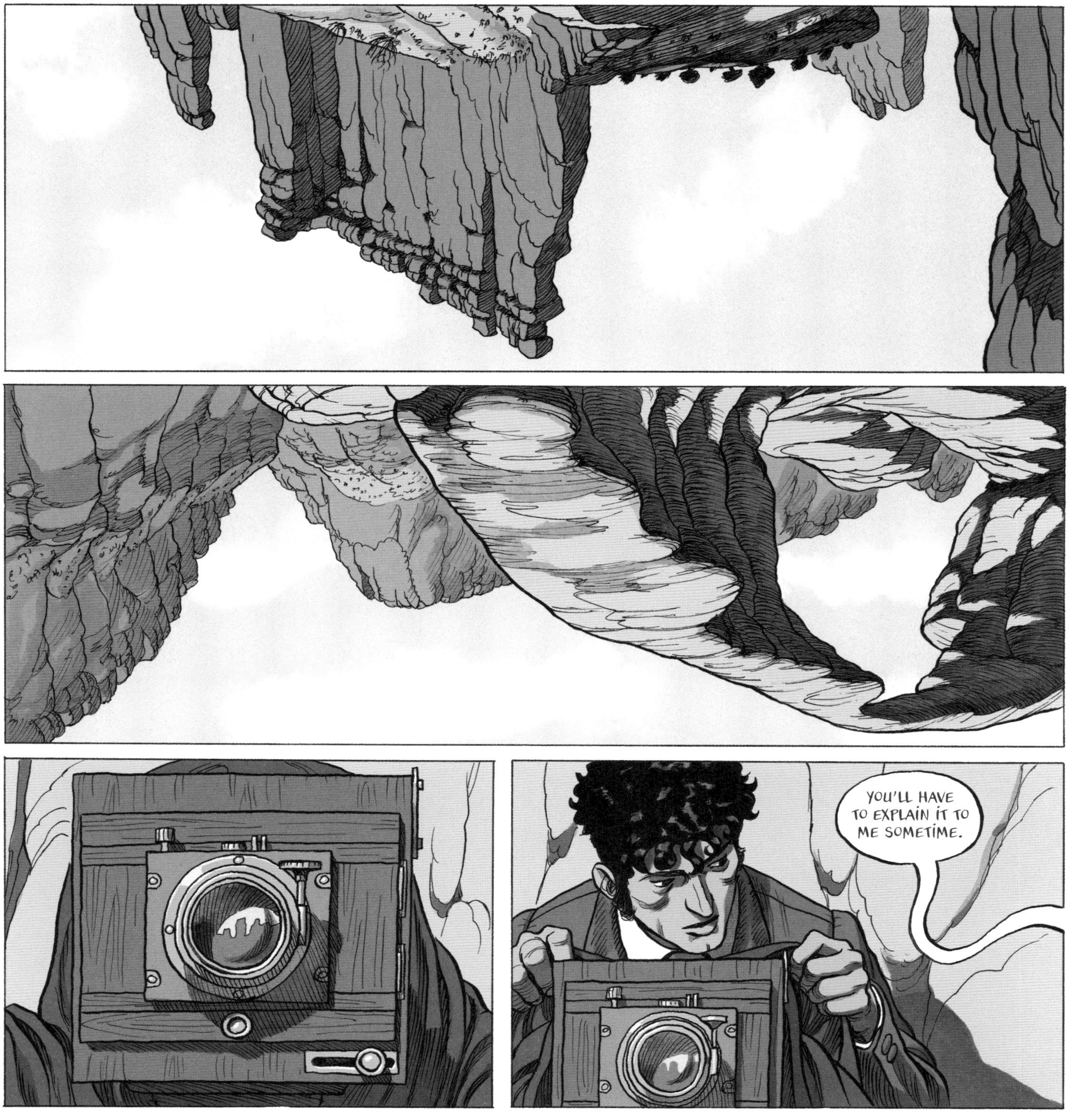
YOU'LL HAVE TO EXPLAIN IT TO ME SOMETIME.

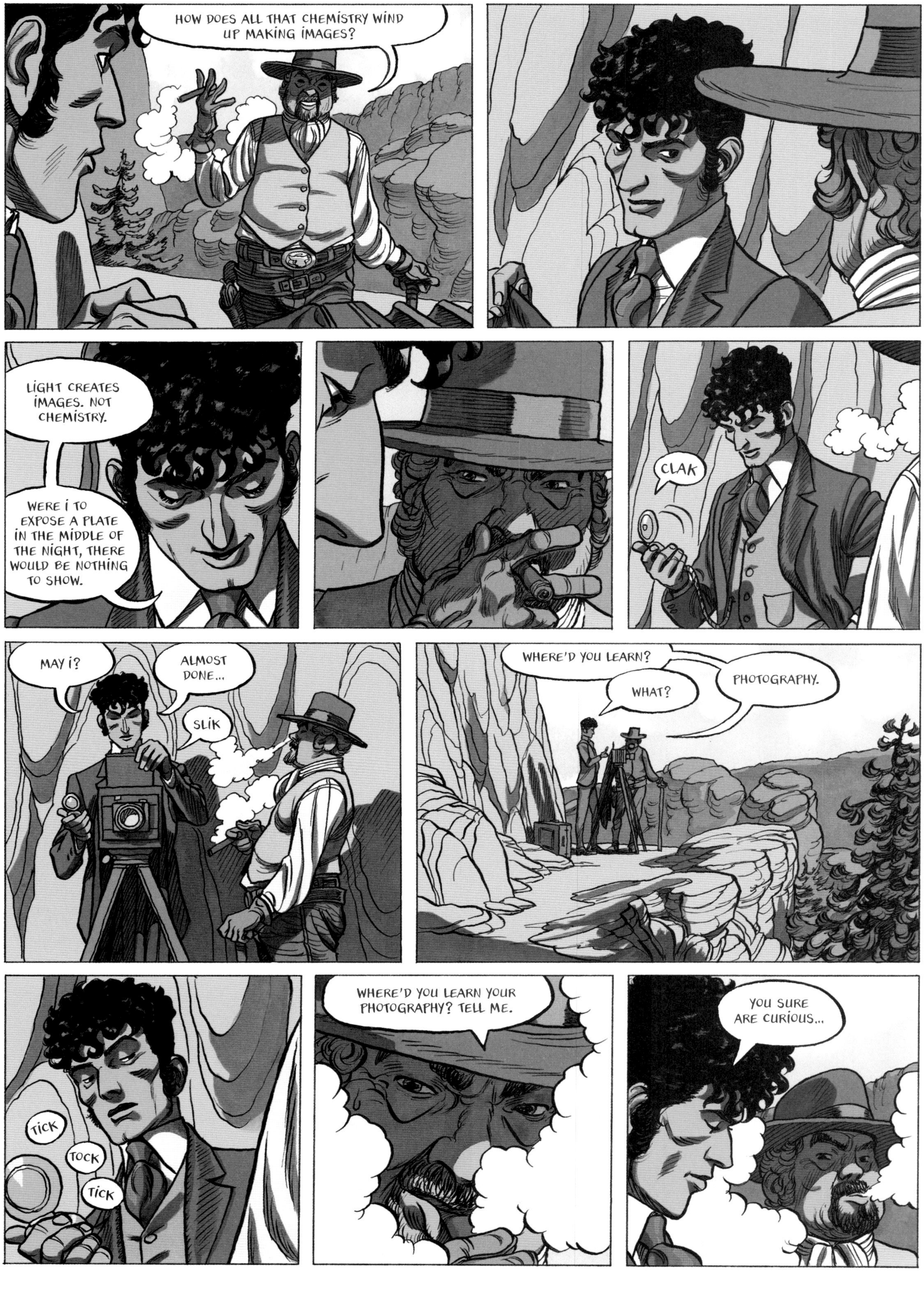

HOW DOES ALL THAT CHEMISTRY WIND UP MAKING IMAGES?
LIGHT CREATES IMAGES. NOT CHEMISTRY.
WERE I TO EXPOSE A PLATE IN THE MIDDLE OF THE NIGHT, THERE WOULD BE NOTHING TO SHOW.
CLAK
MAY I?
ALMOST DONE...
SLIK
WHERE'D YOU LEARN?
WHAT?
PHOTOGRAPHY.
TICK
TOCK
TICK
WHERE'D YOU LEARN YOUR PHOTOGRAPHY? TELL ME.
YOU SURE ARE CURIOUS...

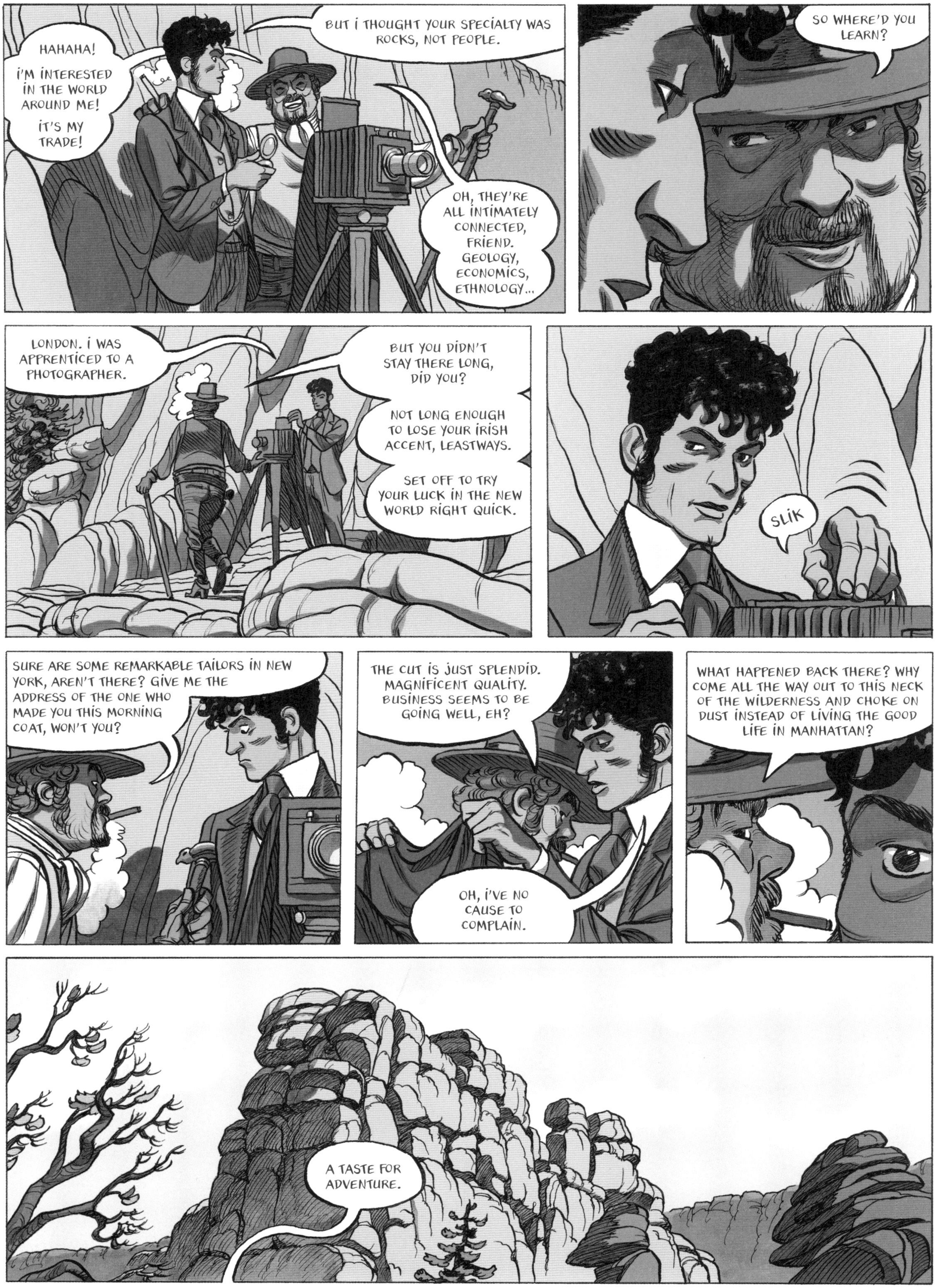

BUT I THOUGHT YOUR SPECIALTY WAS ROCKS, NOT PEOPLE.
HAHAHA!
I'M INTERESTED IN THE WORLD AROUND ME!
IT'S MY TRADE!
OH, THEY'RE ALL INTIMATELY CONNECTED, FRIEND. GEOLOGY, ECONOMICS, ETHNOLOGY...
SO WHERE'D YOU LEARN?
LONDON. I WAS APPRENTICED TO A PHOTOGRAPHER.
BUT YOU DIDN'T STAY THERE LONG, DID YOU?
NOT LONG ENOUGH TO LOSE YOUR IRISH ACCENT, LEASTWAYS.
SET OFF TO TRY YOUR LUCK IN THE NEW WORLD RIGHT QUICK.
SLIK
SURE ARE SOME REMARKABLE TAILORS IN NEW YORK, AREN'T THERE? GIVE ME THE ADDRESS OF THE ONE WHO MADE YOU THIS MORNING COAT, WON'T YOU?
THE CUT IS JUST SPLENDID. MAGNIFICENT QUALITY. BUSINESS SEEMS TO BE GOING WELL, EH?
OH, I'VE NO CAUSE TO COMPLAIN.
WHAT HAPPENED BACK THERE? WHY COME ALL THE WAY OUT TO THIS NECK OF THE WILDERNESS AND CHOKE ON DUST INSTEAD OF LIVING THE GOOD LIFE IN MANHATTAN?
A TASTE FOR ADVENTURE.

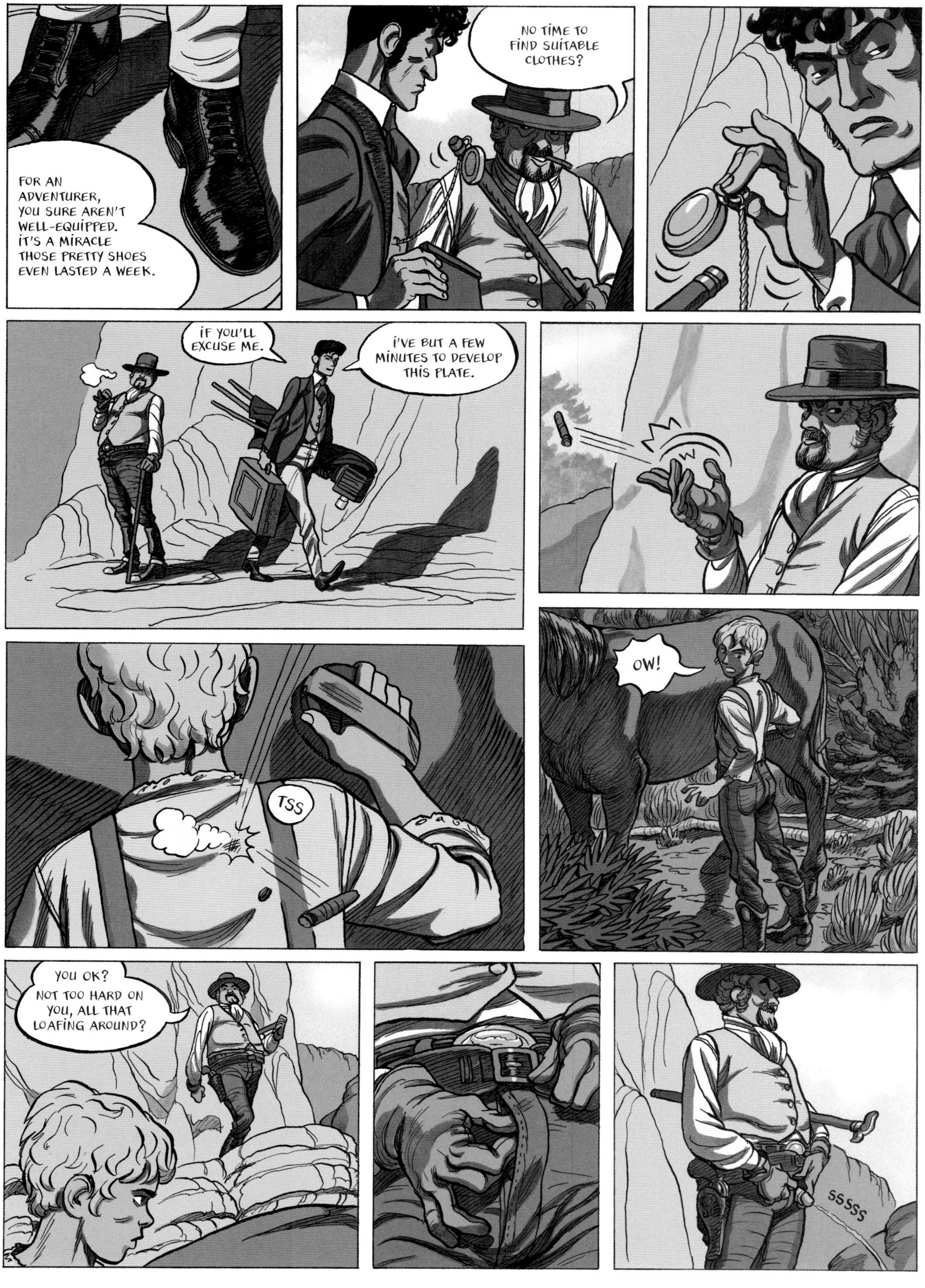

FOR AN ADVENTURER, YOU SURE AREN'T WELL-EQUIPPED. IT'S A MIRACLE THOSE PRETTY SHOES EVEN LASTED A WEEK.
NO TIME TO FIND SUITABLE CLOTHES?
IF YOU'LL EXCUSE ME.
I'VE BUT A FEW MINUTES TO DEVELOP THIS PLATE.
TSS
OW!
YOU OK? NOT TOO HARD ON YOU, ALL THAT LOAFING AROUND?
SSSSS

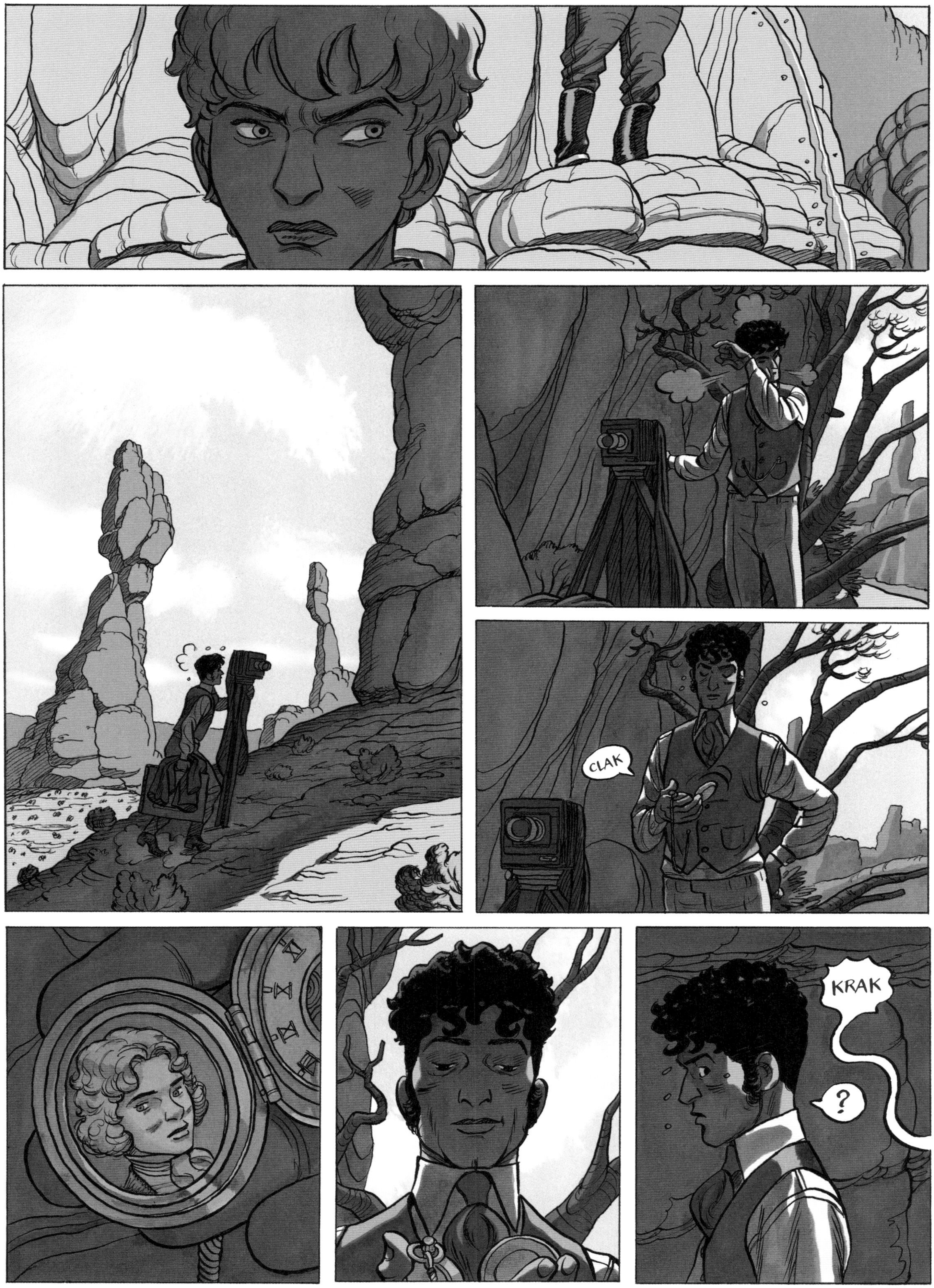
CLAK
KRAK
?

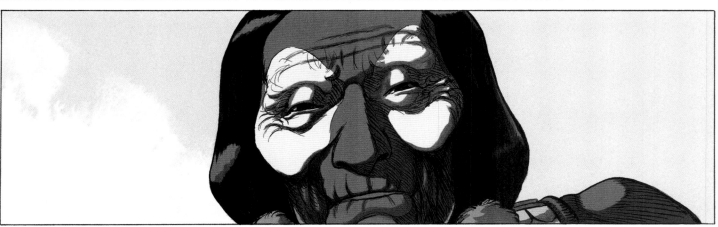

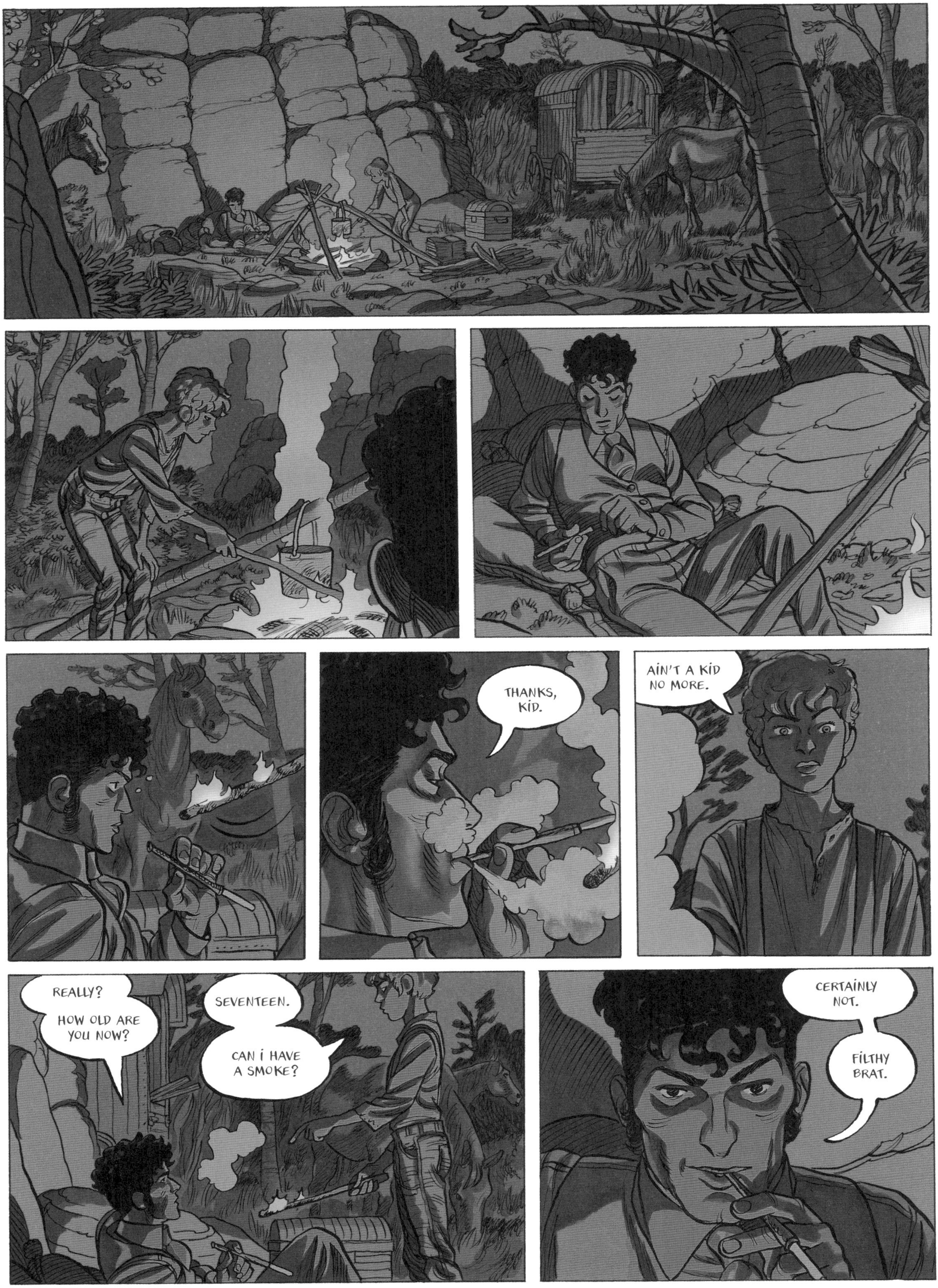
THANKS, KID.
AIN'T A KID NO MORE.
REALLY?
HOW OLD ARE YOU NOW?
SEVENTEEN.
CAN I HAVE A SMOKE?
CERTAINLY NOT.
FILTHY BRAT.

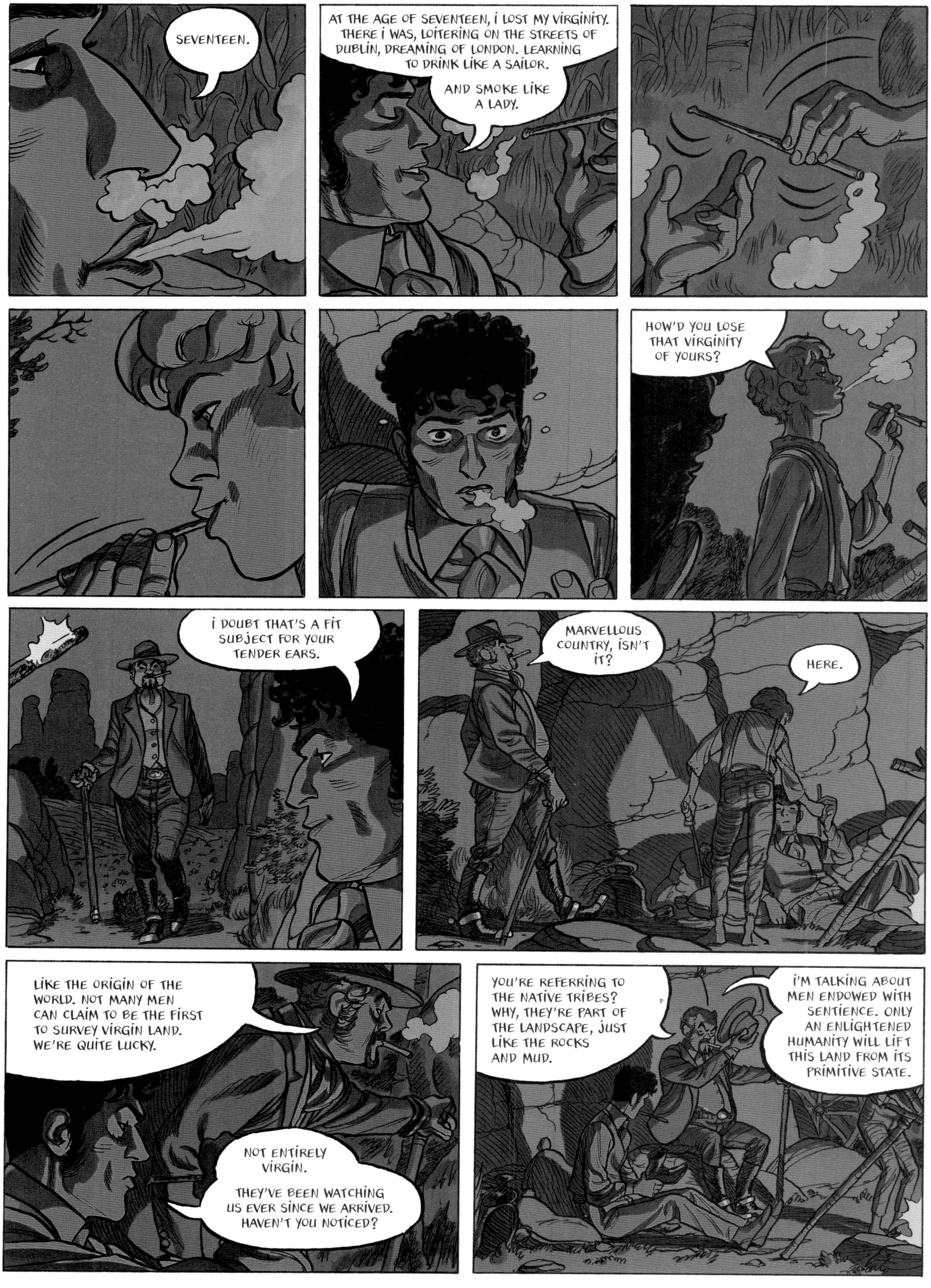
SEVENTEEN.
AT THE AGE OF SEVENTEEN, I LOST MY VIRGINITY. THERE I WAS, LOITERING ON THE STREETS OF DUBLIN, DREAMING OF LONDON. LEARNING TO DRINK LIKE A SAILOR.
AND SMOKE LIKE A LADY.
HOW'D YOU LOSE THAT VIRGINITY OF YOURS?
I DOUBT THAT'S A FIT SUBJECT FOR YOUR TENDER EARS.
MARVELLOUS COUNTRY, ISN'T IT?
HERE.
LIKE THE ORIGIN OF THE WORLD. NOT MANY MEN CAN CLAIM TO BE THE FIRST TO SURVEY VIRGIN LAND. WE'RE QUITE LUCKY.
NOT ENTIRELY VIRGIN.
THEY'VE BEEN WATCHING US EVER SINCE WE ARRIVED. HAVEN'T YOU NOTICED?
YOU'RE REFERRING TO THE NATIVE TRIBES? WHY, THEY'RE PART OF THE LANDSCAPE, JUST LIKE THE ROCKS AND MUD.
I'M TALKING ABOUT MEN ENDOWED WITH SENTIENCE. ONLY AN ENLIGHTENED HUMANITY WILL LIFT THIS LAND FROM ITS PRIMITIVE STATE.

BELIEVE ME, A RADIANT AND PROSPEROUS FUTURE IS OURS FOR THE TAKING. THE WAR OF SECESSION IS OVER. WE'RE THROUGH WITH SOUTHERN CONSERVATISM. THIS COUNTRY NEEDS HOPE. THAT'S WHY THE GOVERNMENT MOUNTED THESE EXPLORATORY EXPEDITIONS.

?

TO SHOW THE BEAUTY OF THIS TERRITORY AND REVEAL ITS NATURAL SPLENDOURS.

MAKING PEOPLE WANT TO COME OUT AND SETTLE THE WEST - NOW, THAT'S DOING YOUR PART IN BUILDING THIS GREAT NATION.

Scandal and Scam

I DIDN'T KNOW I WAS PART OF A PROPAGANDA CAMPAIGN.

AH, BUT A NOBLE ONE, FRIEND!

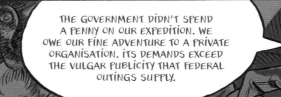

THE GOVERNMENT DIDN'T SPEND A PENNY ON OUR EXPEDITION. WE OWE OUR FINE ADVENTURE TO A PRIVATE ORGANISATION. ITS DEMANDS EXCEED THE VULGAR PUBLICITY THAT FEDERAL OUTINGS SUPPLY.

WE LABOUR TOWARD THE FUTURE OF THE WORLD.

A FUTURE DREAMED BY, CONCEIVED BY AND MADE FOR US.

AT THE MOMENT, WHAT INTERESTS ME MOST IS WHAT WE'RE EATING TONIGHT.

I'M SO HUNGRY THAT I'D SETTLE FOR STONE SOUP.

HAHA!

YOU'RE IN LUCK! THAT'S EXACTLY WHAT MILTON'S MADE US!

GO ON, KID.

GIVE ME TWO HELPINGS OF THAT STUFF.

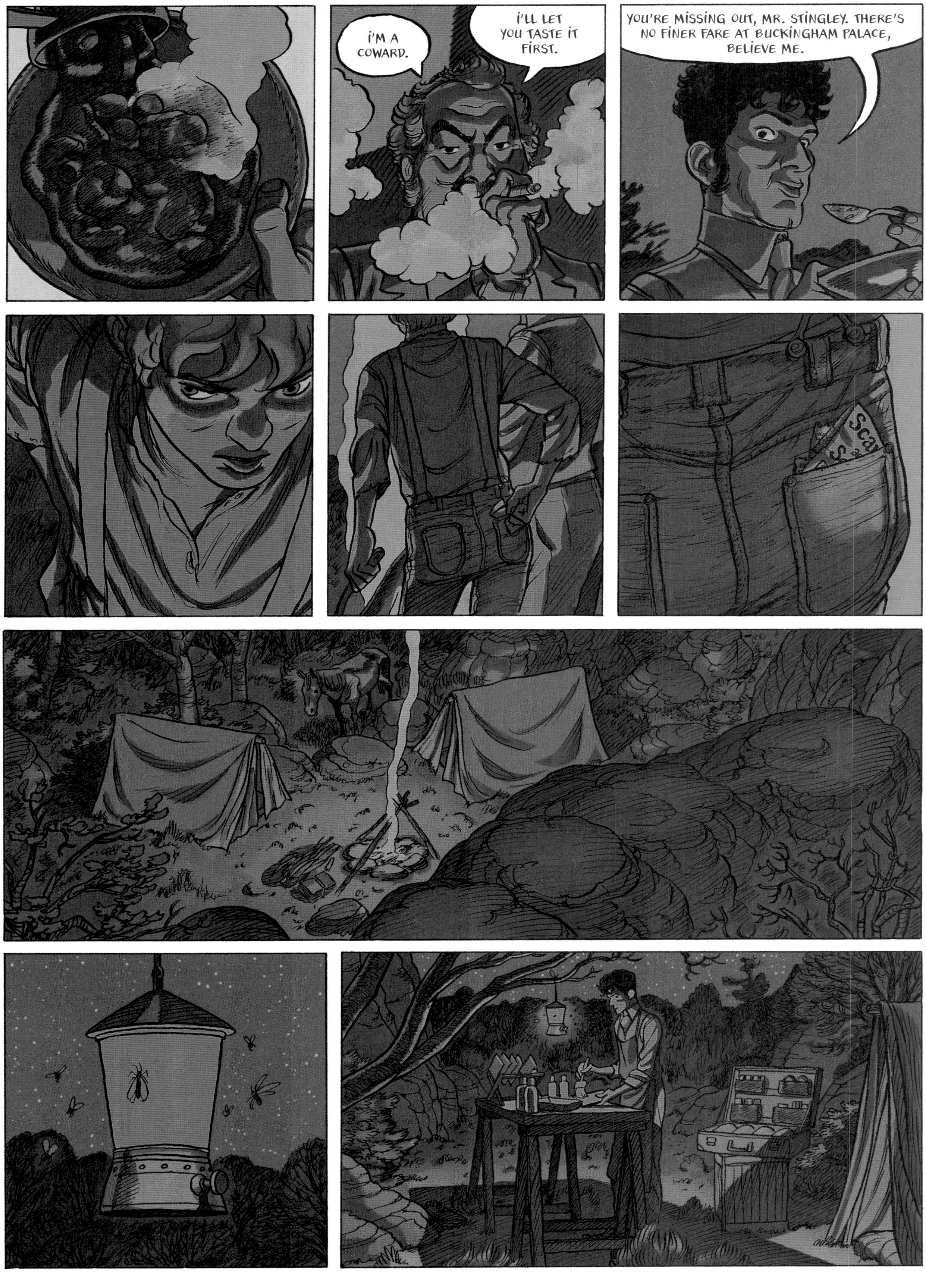
I'M A COWARD.
I'LL LET YOU TASTE IT FIRST.
YOU'RE MISSING OUT, MR. STINGLEY. THERE'S NO FINER FARE AT BUCKINGHAM PALACE, BELIEVE ME.

?!
THIS IS NO TIME TO BE DOING LAUNDRY.
YOU OUGHT TO BE CAREFUL OF COYOTES.
I CAN SPOT ONE BETTER'N YOU CAN, MISTER.
HMF.
FILTHY BRAT.

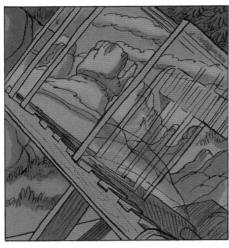

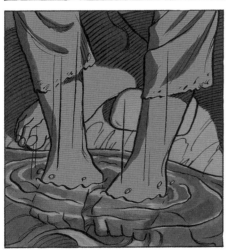

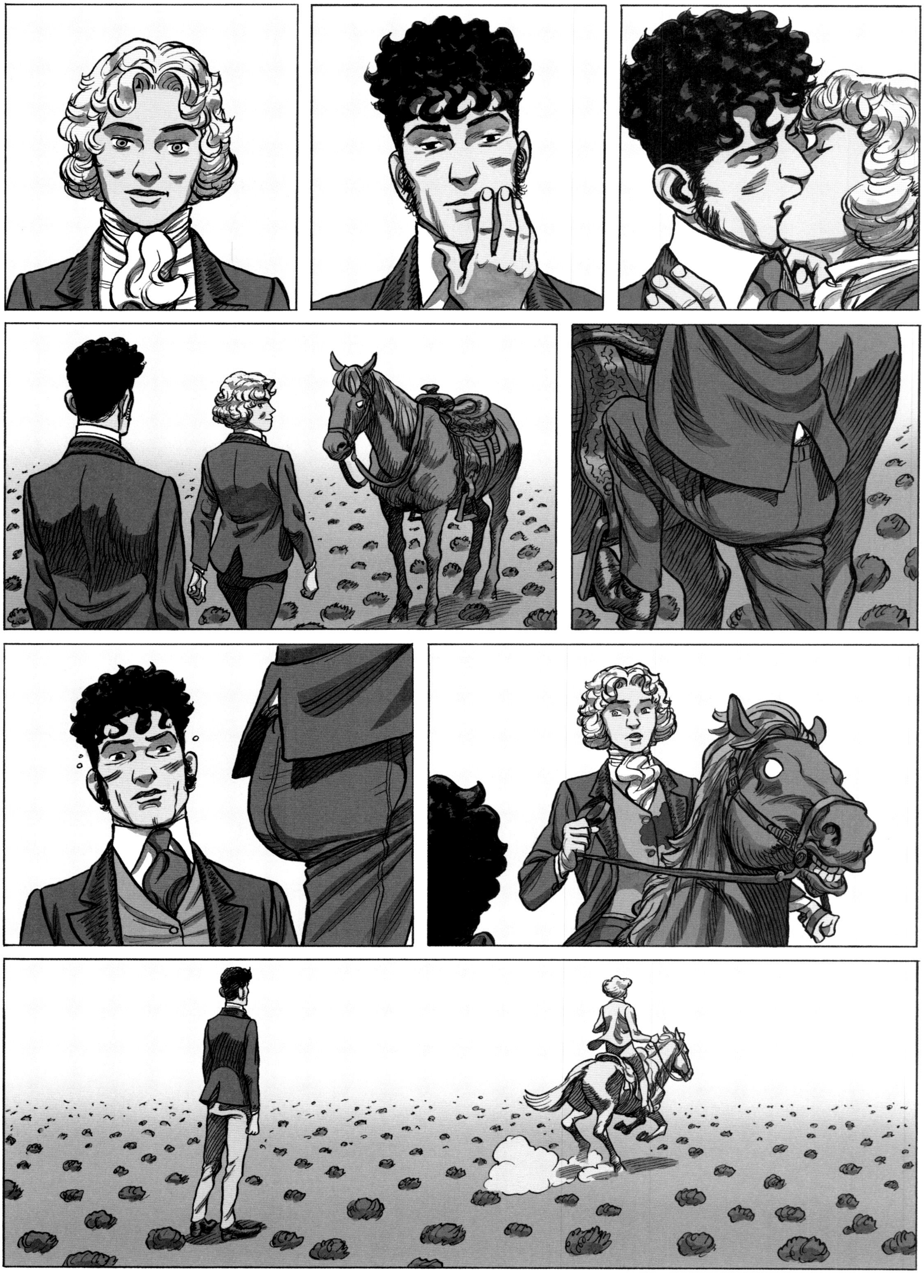

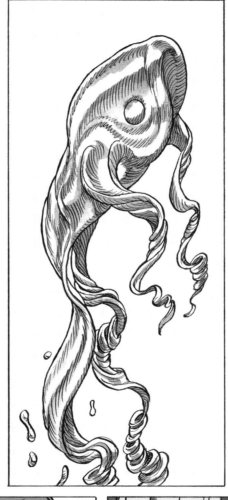
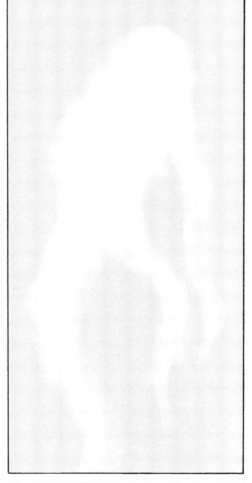

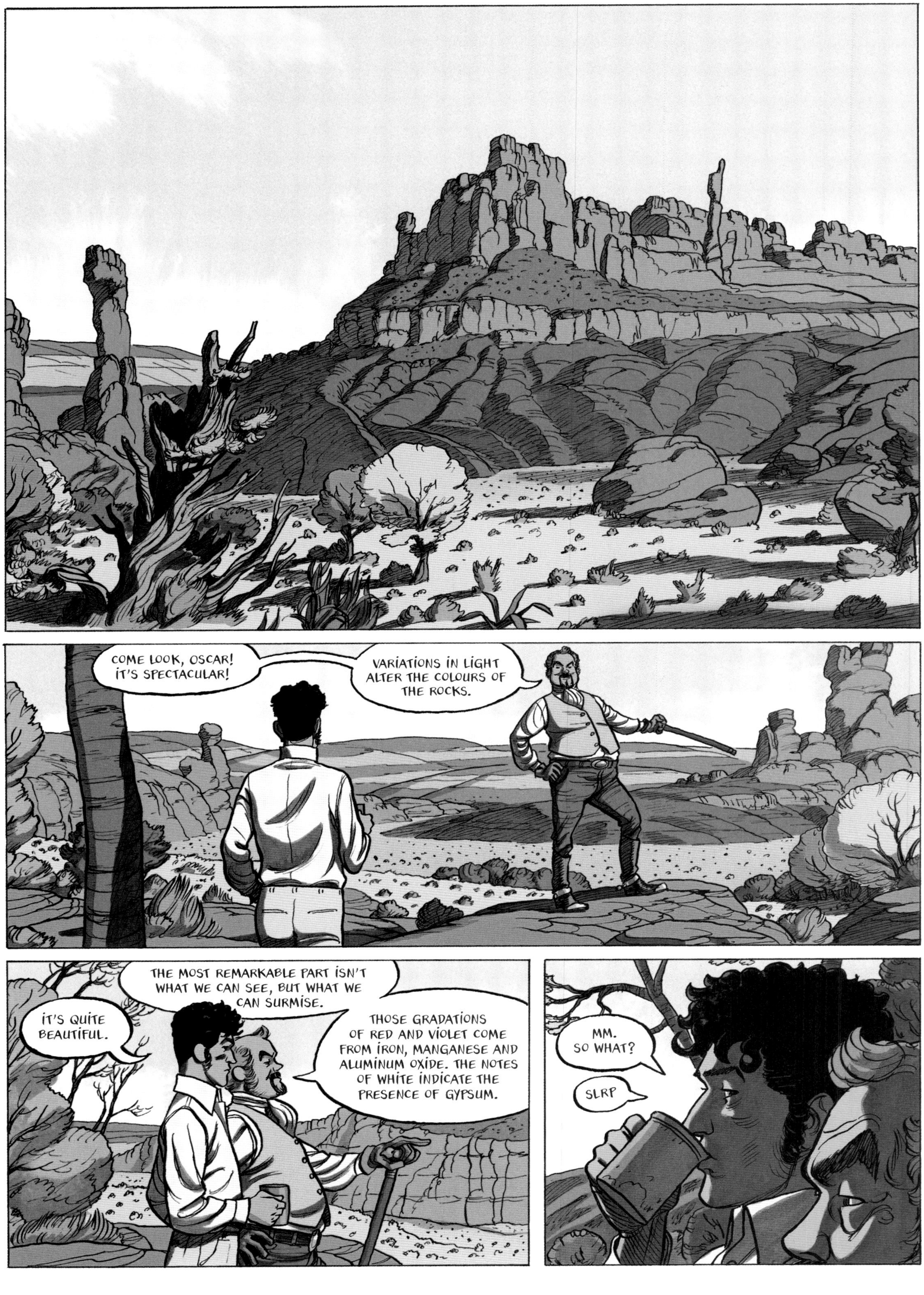
COME LOOK, OSCAR! IT'S SPECTACULAR!
VARIATIONS IN LIGHT ALTER THE COLOURS OF THE ROCKS.
IT'S QUITE BEAUTIFUL.
THE MOST REMARKABLE PART ISN'T WHAT WE CAN SEE, BUT WHAT WE CAN SURMISE.
THOSE GRADATIONS OF RED AND VIOLET COME FROM IRON, MANGANESE AND ALUMINUM OXIDE. THE NOTES OF WHITE INDICATE THE PRESENCE OF GYPSUM.
MM. SO WHAT?
SLRP

THIS LAND IS RICH. WE'LL CLAIM IT, DRILL IT AND EXTRACT FROM ITS VERY BOWELS THE TREASURES HIDDEN DEEP INSIDE.

AND THIS SPECTACULAR LANDSCAPE WILL BE DEVASTATED.

QUITE A PLAN.

YAAWN

COME NOW, FRIEND! THE NATION'S FUTURE MUST TAKE PRECEDENCE OVER AESTHETIC CONSIDERATIONS.

NOT FOR ME. I'M JUST A FOOLISH AESTHETE, I'M AFRAID.

A MAN OF YOUR INTELLIGENCE SHOULD BE ABLE TO SEE PAST MERE SURFACES.

IT SO HAPPENS THAT APPRECIATING MERE SURFACES IS IN FACT MY MÉTIER: PHOTOGRAPHY.

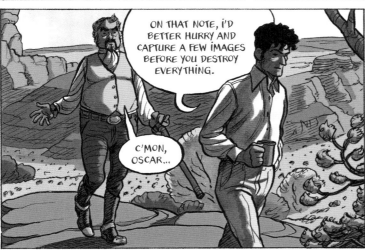

ON THAT NOTE, I'D BETTER HURRY AND CAPTURE A FEW IMAGES BEFORE YOU DESTROY EVERYTHING.

C'MON, OSCAR...

WHAT'S GOING ON HERE?

DID YOU TAKE THE CLOTHES DOWN FROM THE LINE?

STUPID QUESTION. THAT'S NOT OUR JOB.

HALF OF THEM ARE MISSING.

MUST HAVE BLOWN AWAY DURING THE NIGHT.

OR MAYBE THOSE NATIVES MADE AWAY WITH 'EM.

WHAT KIND OF A DUNDERHEAD HANGS LAUNDRY SO FAR FROM CAMP?

SNIF

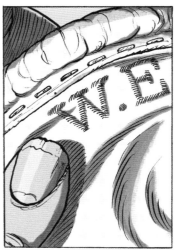

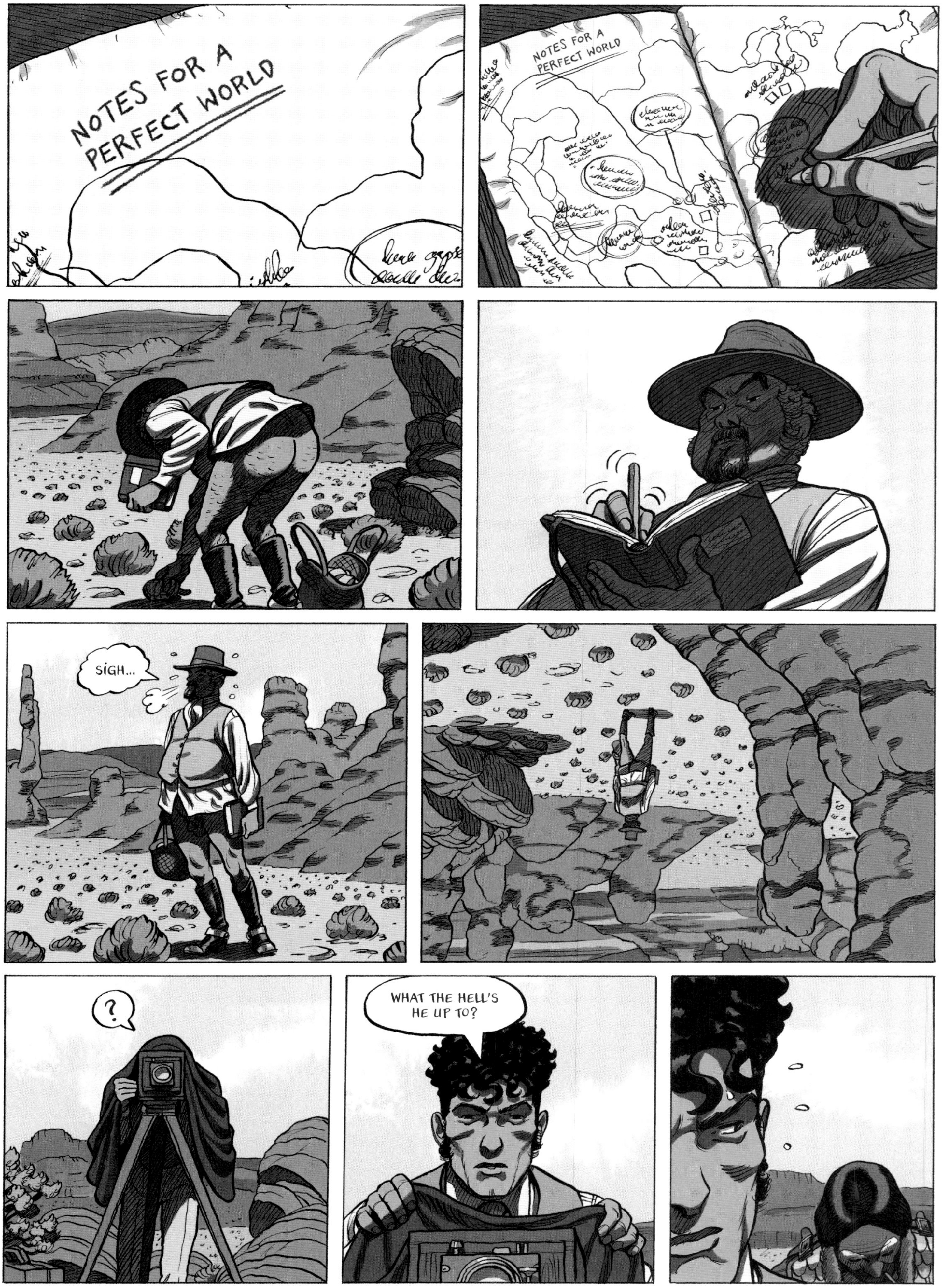
NOTES FOR A PERFECT WORLD
NOTES FOR A PERFECT WORLD
SIGH...
?
WHAT THE HELL'S HE UP TO?

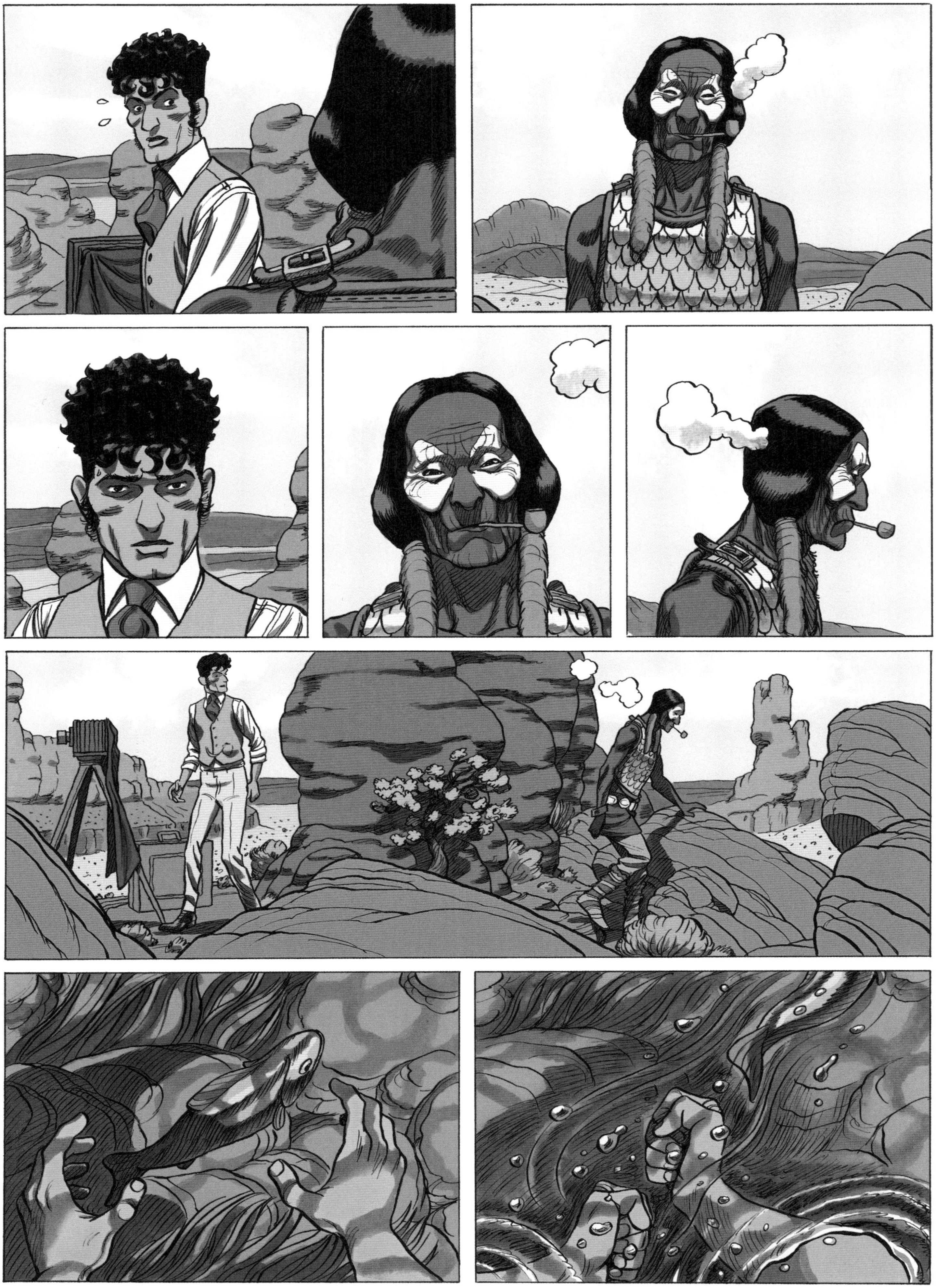

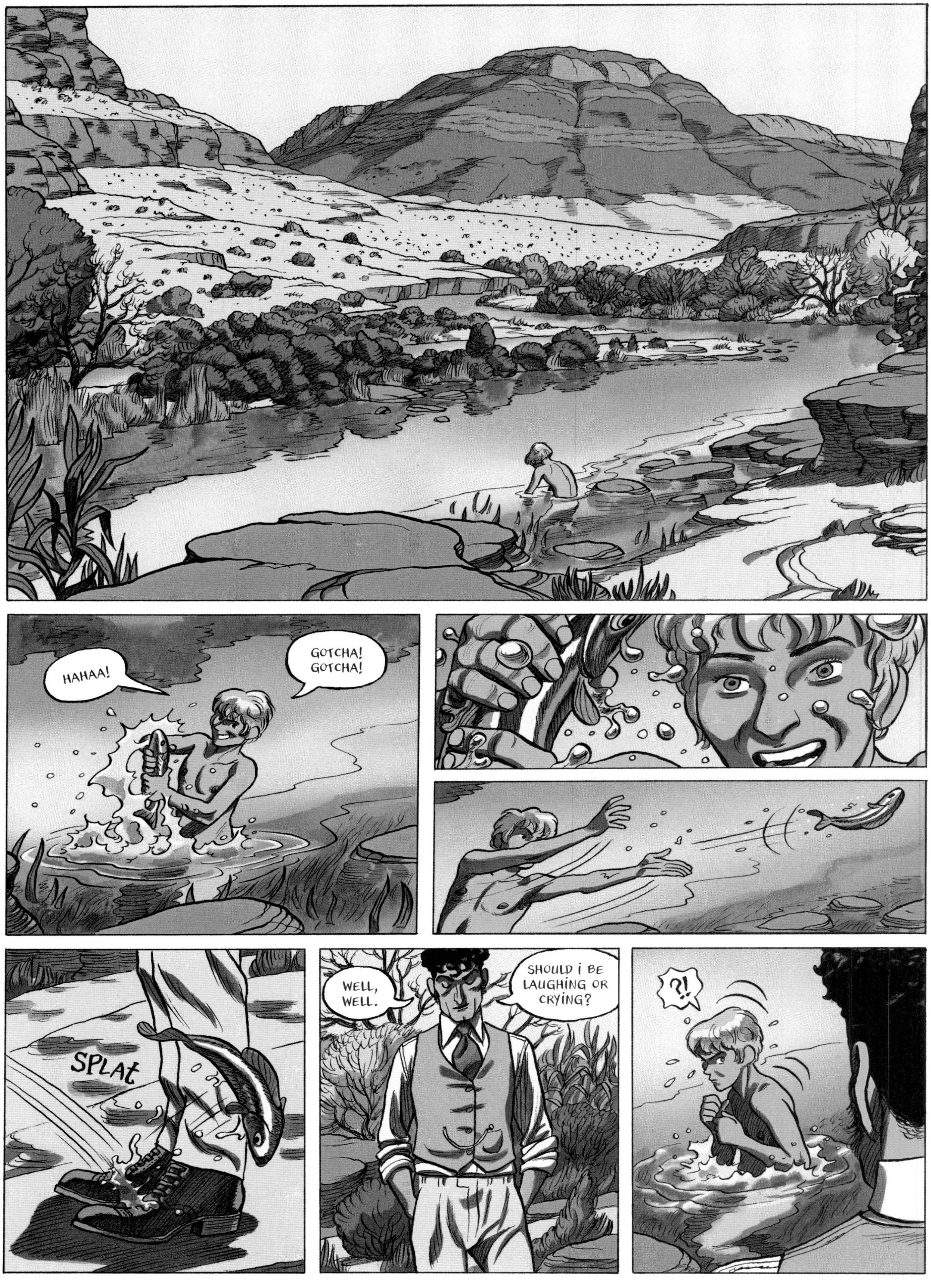
HAHAA!
GOTCHA! GOTCHA!
SPLAt
WELL, WELL.
SHOULD i BE LAUGHiNG OR CRYiNG?
?!

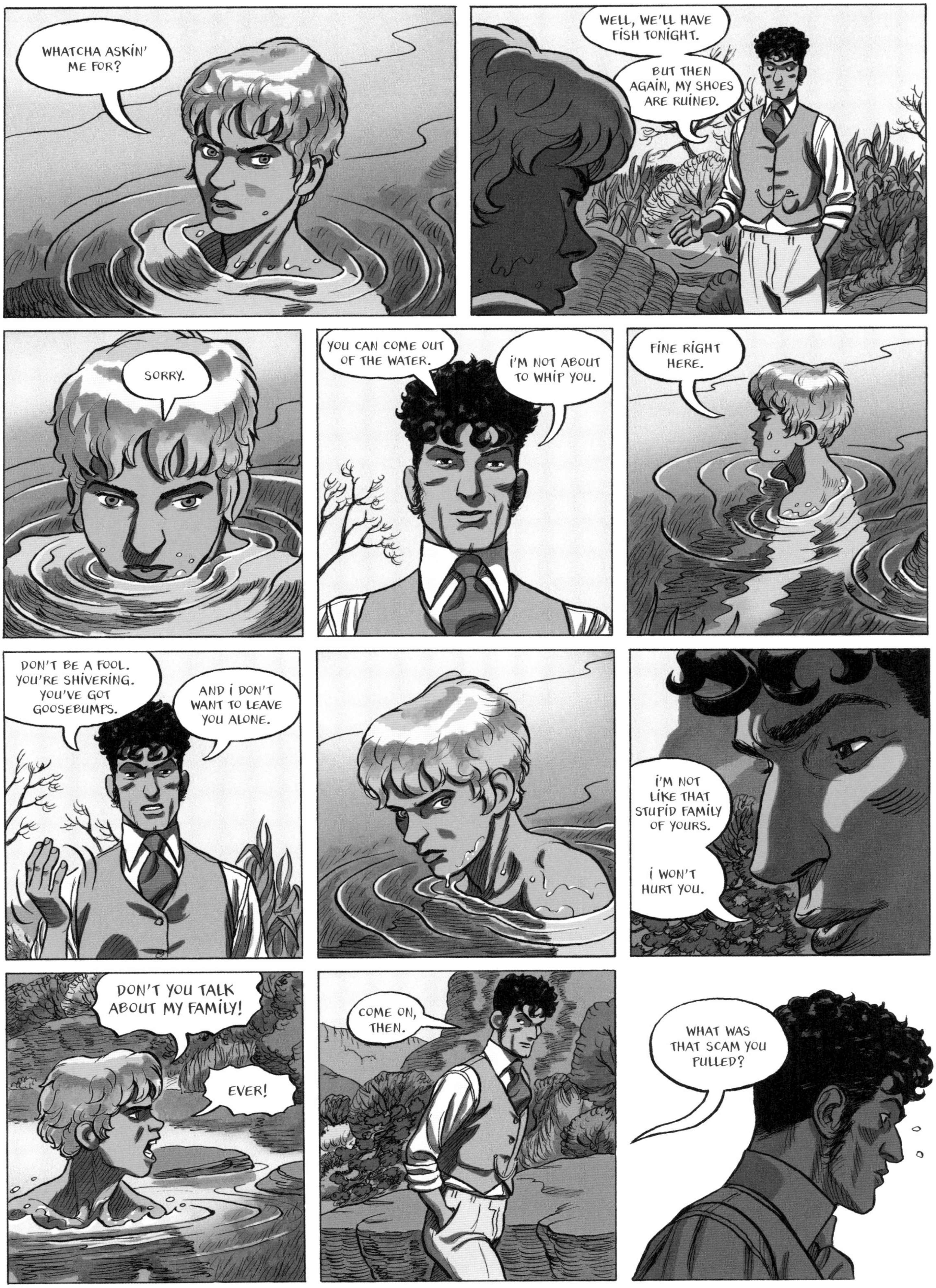
WHATCHA ASKIN' ME FOR?
WELL, WE'LL HAVE FISH TONIGHT.
BUT THEN AGAIN, MY SHOES ARE RUINED.
SORRY.
YOU CAN COME OUT OF THE WATER.
I'M NOT ABOUT TO WHIP YOU.
FINE RIGHT HERE.
DON'T BE A FOOL. YOU'RE SHIVERING. YOU'VE GOT GOOSEBUMPS.
AND I DON'T WANT TO LEAVE YOU ALONE.
I'M NOT LIKE THAT STUPID FAMILY OF YOURS.
I WON'T HURT YOU.
DON'T YOU TALK ABOUT MY FAMILY!
EVER!
COME ON, THEN.
WHAT WAS THAT SCAM YOU PULLED?

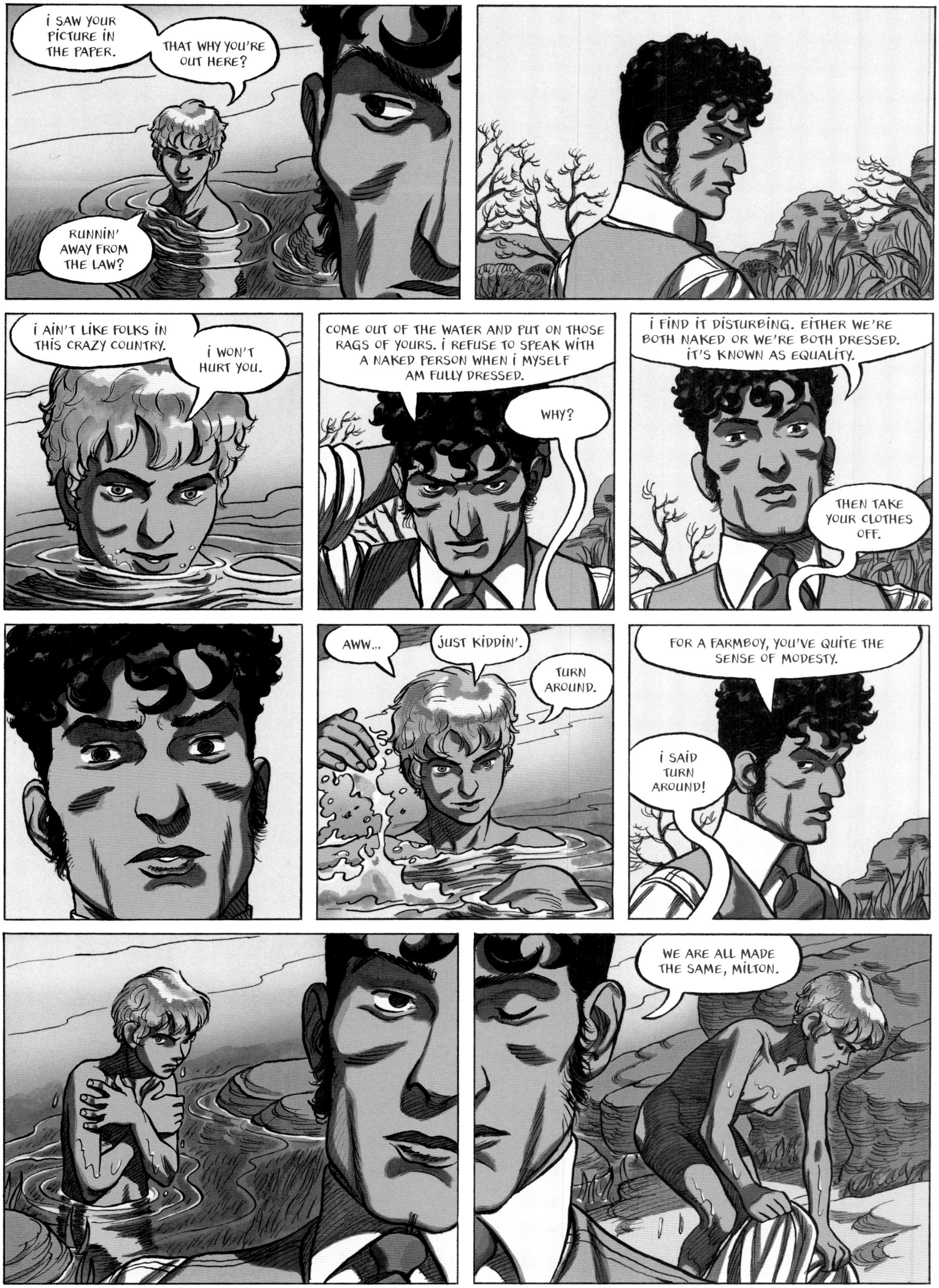
I SAW YOUR PICTURE IN THE PAPER.
THAT WHY YOU'RE OUT HERE?
RUNNIN' AWAY FROM THE LAW?
I AIN'T LIKE FOLKS IN THIS CRAZY COUNTRY.
I WON'T HURT YOU.
COME OUT OF THE WATER AND PUT ON THOSE RAGS OF YOURS. I REFUSE TO SPEAK WITH A NAKED PERSON WHEN I MYSELF AM FULLY DRESSED.
WHY?
I FIND IT DISTURBING. EITHER WE'RE BOTH NAKED OR WE'RE BOTH DRESSED. IT'S KNOWN AS EQUALITY.
THEN TAKE YOUR CLOTHES OFF.
AWW...
JUST KIDDIN'.
TURN AROUND.
FOR A FARMBOY, YOU'VE QUITE THE SENSE OF MODESTY.
I SAID TURN AROUND!
WE ARE ALL MADE THE SAME, MILTON.

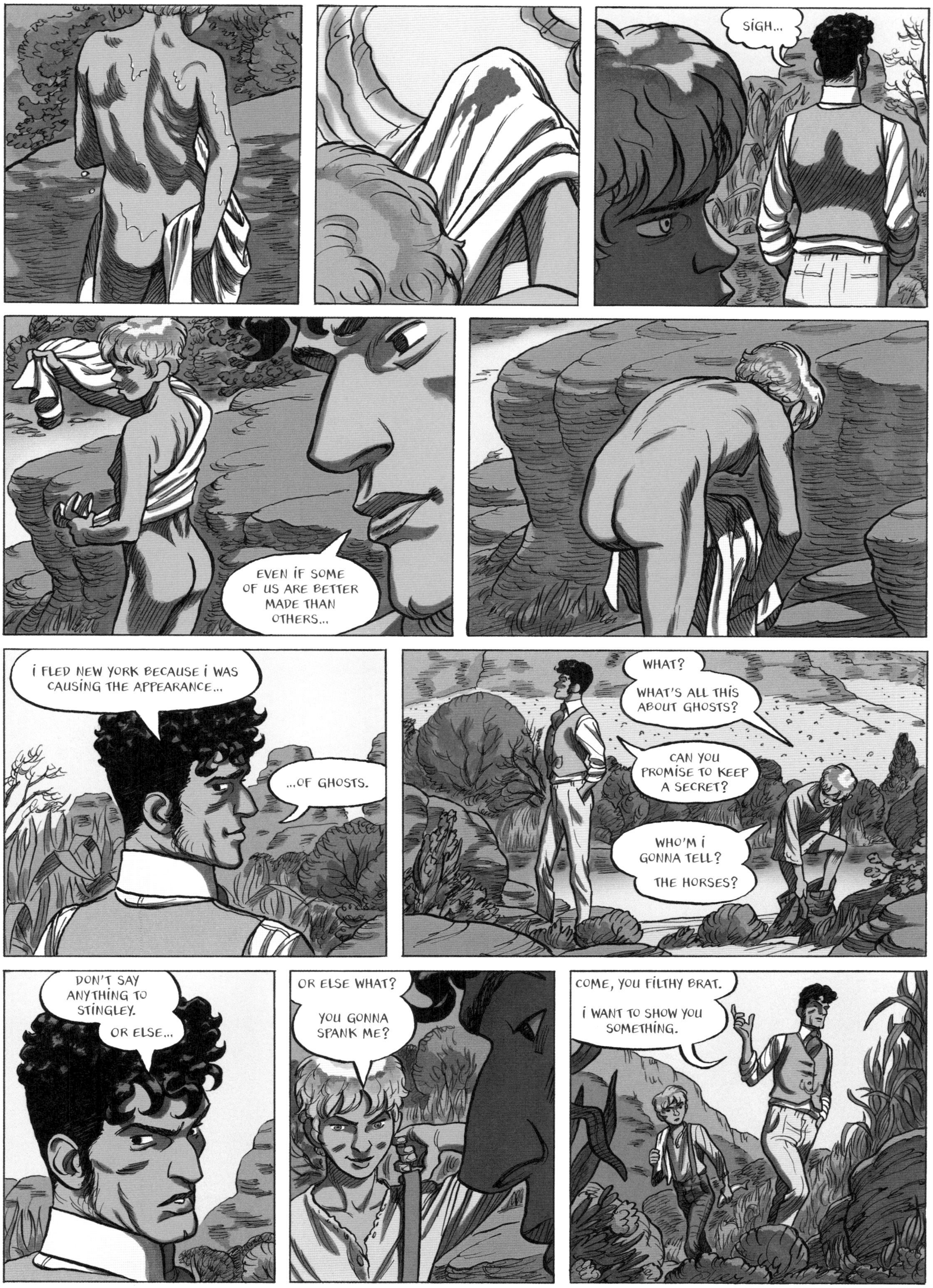
SIGH...
EVEN IF SOME OF US ARE BETTER MADE THAN OTHERS...
I FLED NEW YORK BECAUSE I WAS CAUSING THE APPEARANCE...
...OF GHOSTS.
WHAT?
WHAT'S ALL THIS ABOUT GHOSTS?
CAN YOU PROMISE TO KEEP A SECRET?
WHO'M I GONNA TELL?
THE HORSES?
DON'T SAY ANYTHING TO STINGLEY.
OR ELSE...
OR ELSE WHAT?
YOU GONNA SPANK ME?
COME, YOU FILTHY BRAT.
I WANT TO SHOW YOU SOMETHING.

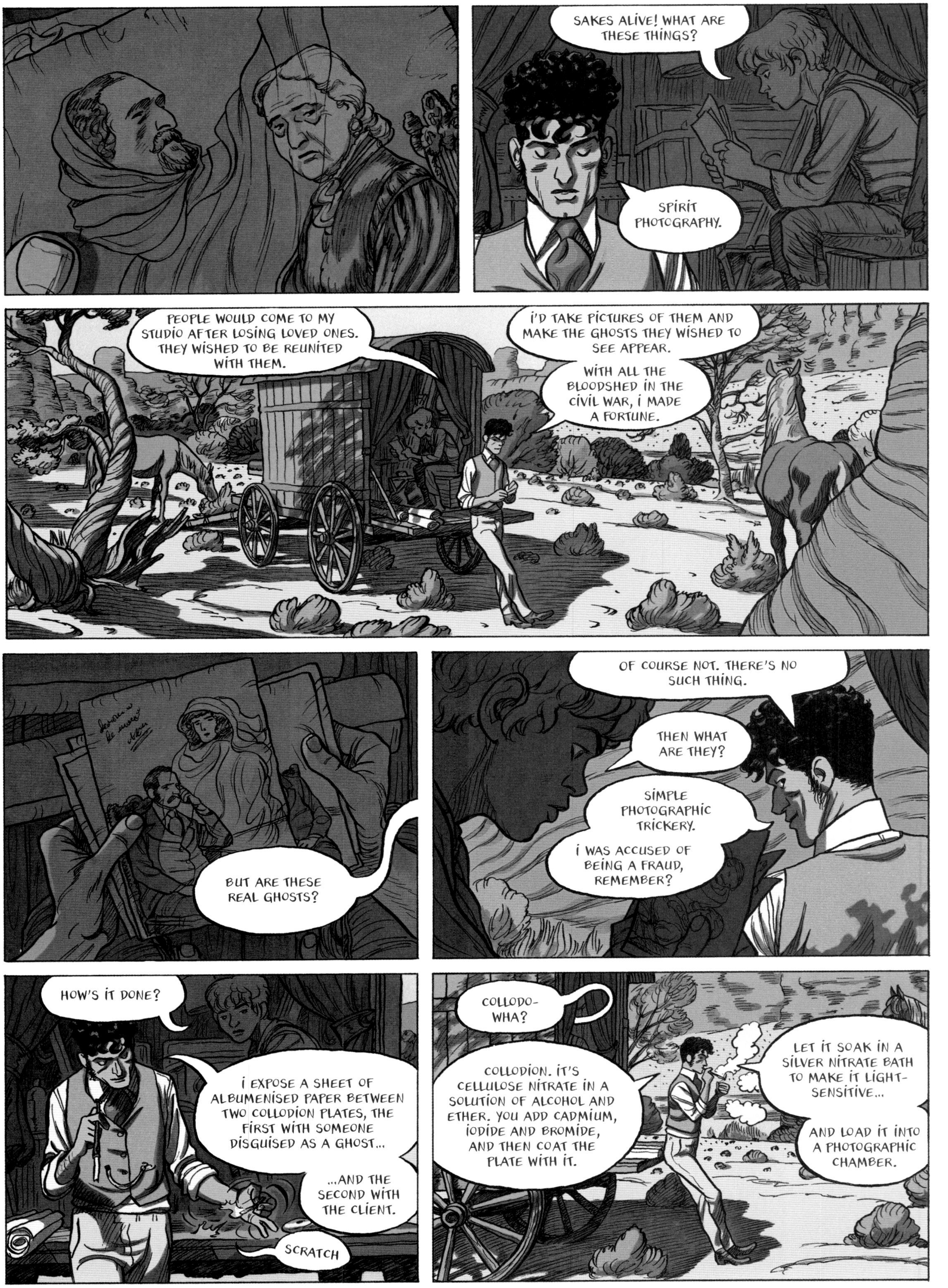

SAKES ALIVE! WHAT ARE THESE THINGS?
SPIRIT PHOTOGRAPHY.
PEOPLE WOULD COME TO MY STUDIO AFTER LOSING LOVED ONES. THEY WISHED TO BE REUNITED WITH THEM.
I'D TAKE PICTURES OF THEM AND MAKE THE GHOSTS THEY WISHED TO SEE APPEAR.
WITH ALL THE BLOODSHED IN THE CIVIL WAR, I MADE A FORTUNE.
BUT ARE THESE REAL GHOSTS?
OF COURSE NOT. THERE'S NO SUCH THING.
THEN WHAT ARE THEY?
SIMPLE PHOTOGRAPHIC TRICKERY.
I WAS ACCUSED OF BEING A FRAUD, REMEMBER?
HOW'S IT DONE?
I EXPOSE A SHEET OF ALBUMENISED PAPER BETWEEN TWO COLLODION PLATES, THE FIRST WITH SOMEONE DISGUISED AS A GHOST...
...AND THE SECOND WITH THE CLIENT.
SCRATCH
COLLODO-WHA?
COLLODION. IT'S CELLULOSE NITRATE IN A SOLUTION OF ALCOHOL AND ETHER. YOU ADD CADMIUM, IODIDE AND BROMIDE, AND THEN COAT THE PLATE WITH IT.
LET IT SOAK IN A SILVER NITRATE BATH TO MAKE IT LIGHT-SENSITIVE...
AND LOAD IT INTO A PHOTOGRAPHIC CHAMBER.

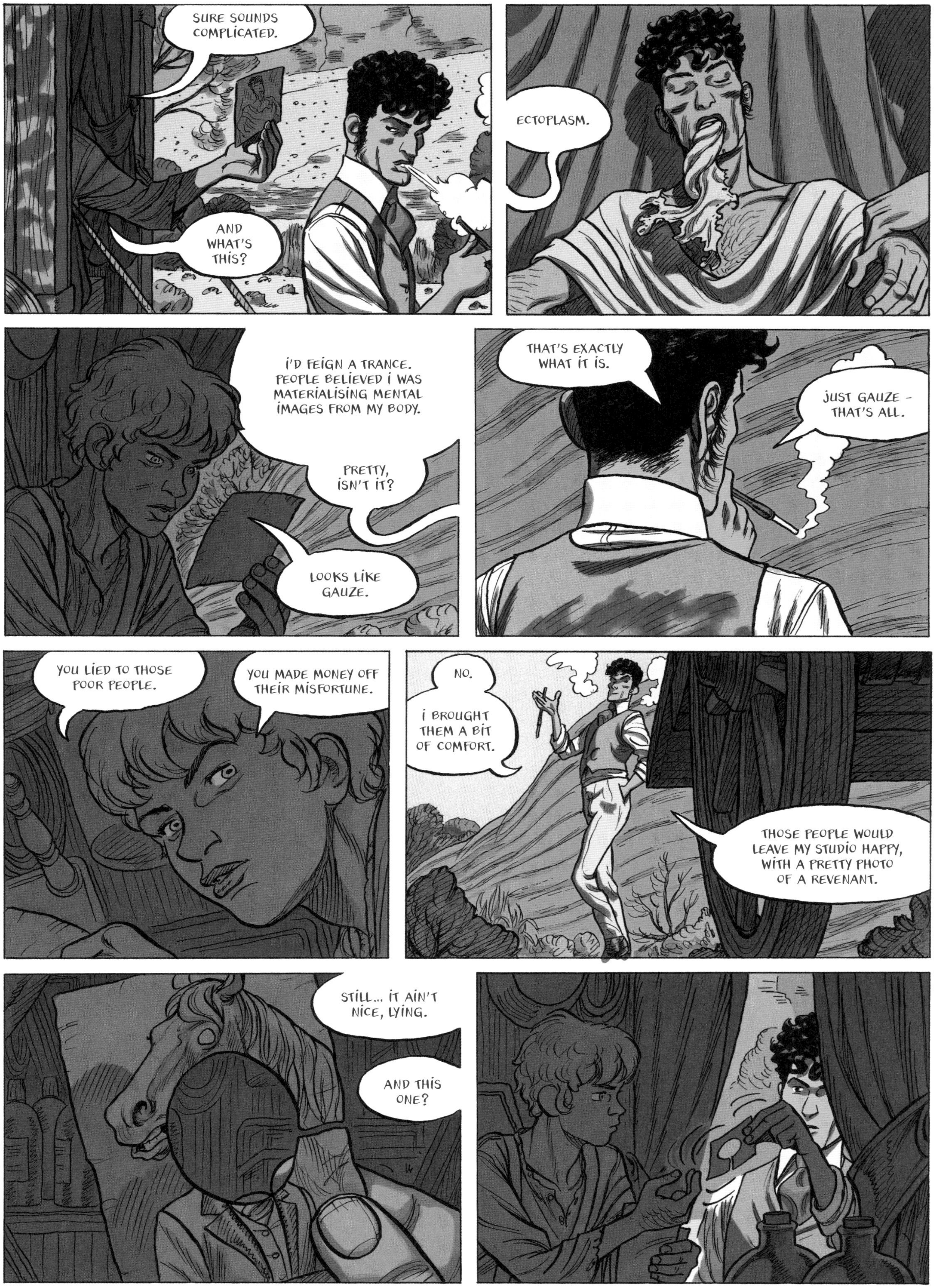
SURE SOUNDS COMPLICATED.
AND WHAT'S THIS?
ECTOPLASM.
I'D FEIGN A TRANCE. PEOPLE BELIEVED I WAS MATERIALISING MENTAL IMAGES FROM MY BODY.
PRETTY, ISN'T IT?
LOOKS LIKE GAUZE.
THAT'S EXACTLY WHAT IT IS.
JUST GAUZE - THAT'S ALL.
YOU LIED TO THOSE POOR PEOPLE.
YOU MADE MONEY OFF THEIR MISFORTUNE.
NO.
I BROUGHT THEM A BIT OF COMFORT.
THOSE PEOPLE WOULD LEAVE MY STUDIO HAPPY, WITH A PRETTY PHOTO OF A REVENANT.
STILL... IT AIN'T NICE, LYING.
AND THIS ONE?

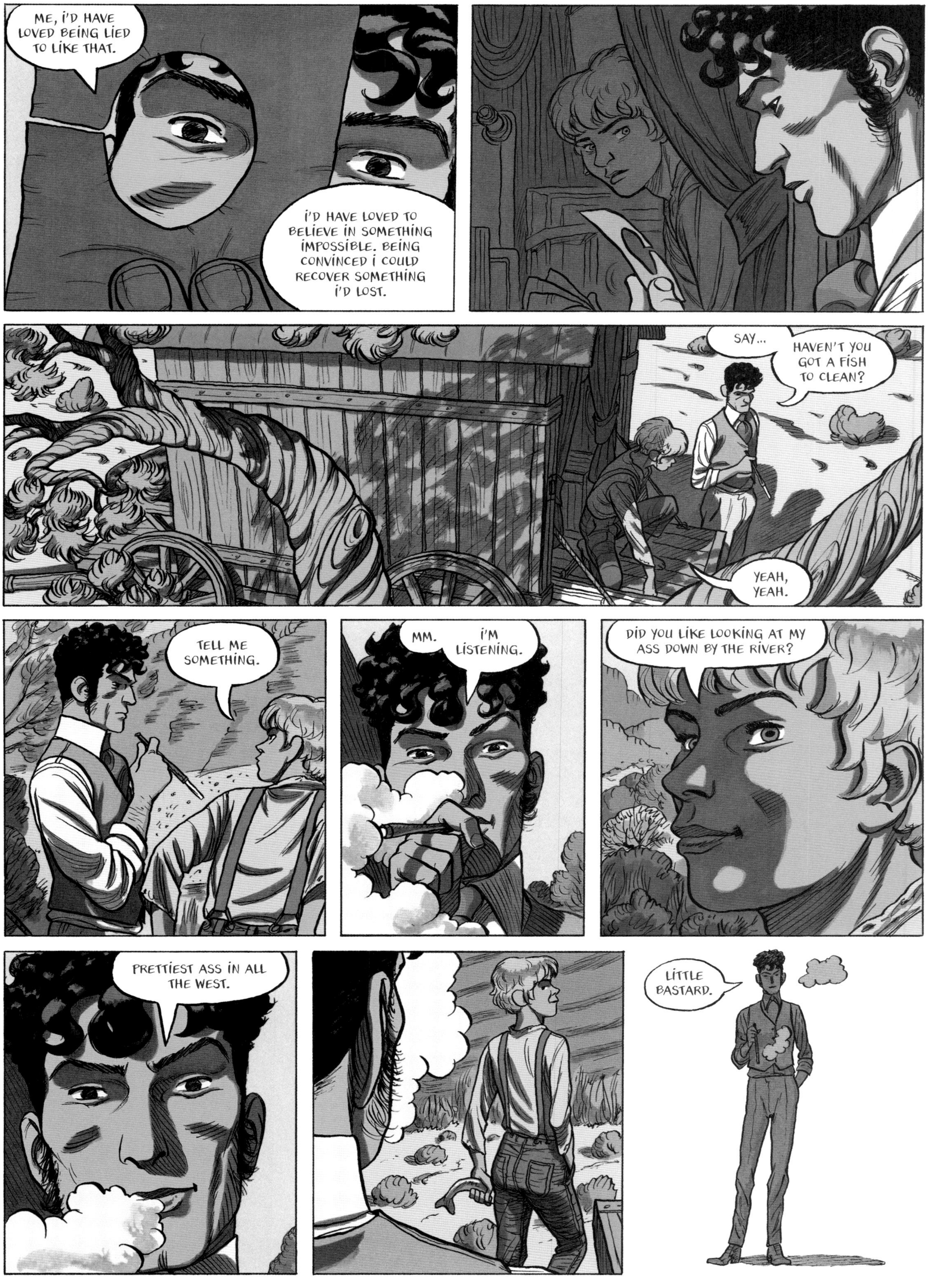

ME, I'D HAVE LOVED BEING LIED TO LIKE THAT.
I'D HAVE LOVED TO BELIEVE IN SOMETHING IMPOSSIBLE. BEING CONVINCED I COULD RECOVER SOMETHING I'D LOST.
SAY...
HAVEN'T YOU GOT A FISH TO CLEAN?
YEAH, YEAH.
TELL ME SOMETHING.
MM.
I'M LISTENING.
DID YOU LIKE LOOKING AT MY ASS DOWN BY THE RIVER?
PRETTIEST ASS IN ALL THE WEST.
LITTLE BASTARD.

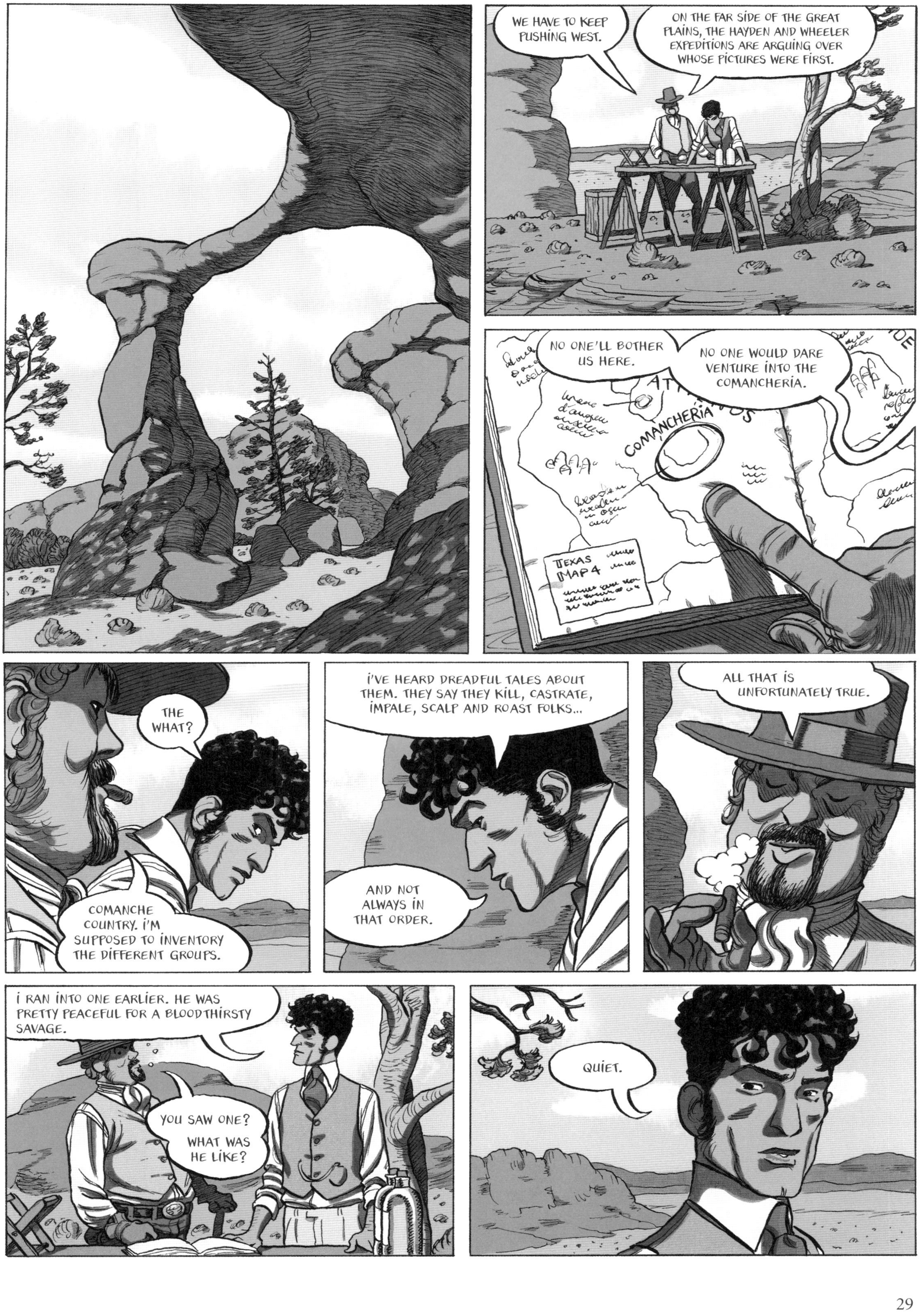

WE HAVE TO KEEP PUSHING WEST.
ON THE FAR SIDE OF THE GREAT PLAINS, THE HAYDEN AND WHEELER EXPEDITIONS ARE ARGUING OVER WHOSE PICTURES WERE FIRST.
NO ONE'LL BOTHER US HERE.
NO ONE WOULD DARE VENTURE INTO THE COMANCHERIA.
COMANCHERIA
TEXAS MAP 4
THE WHAT?
COMANCHE COUNTRY. I'M SUPPOSED TO INVENTORY THE DIFFERENT GROUPS.
I'VE HEARD DREADFUL TALES ABOUT THEM. THEY SAY THEY KILL, CASTRATE, IMPALE, SCALP AND ROAST FOLKS...
AND NOT ALWAYS IN THAT ORDER.
ALL THAT IS UNFORTUNATELY TRUE.
I RAN INTO ONE EARLIER. HE WAS PRETTY PEACEFUL FOR A BLOODTHIRSTY SAVAGE.
YOU SAW ONE? WHAT WAS HE LIKE?
QUIET.

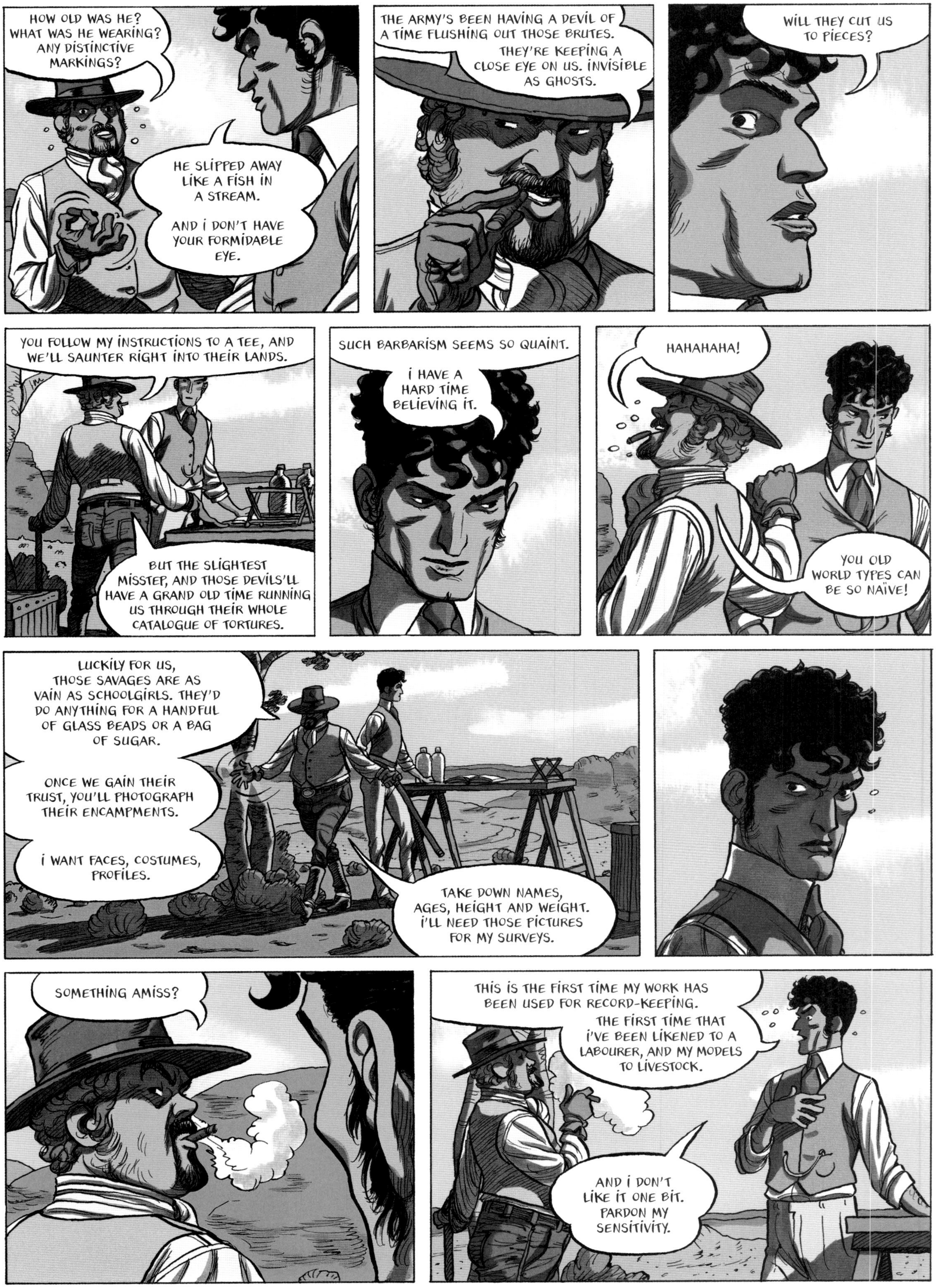
HOW OLD WAS HE? WHAT WAS HE WEARING? ANY DISTINCTIVE MARKINGS?
HE SLIPPED AWAY LIKE A FISH IN A STREAM.
AND I DON'T HAVE YOUR FORMIDABLE EYE.
THE ARMY'S BEEN HAVING A DEVIL OF A TIME FLUSHING OUT THOSE BRUTES.
THEY'RE KEEPING A CLOSE EYE ON US. INVISIBLE AS GHOSTS.
WILL THEY CUT US TO PIECES?
YOU FOLLOW MY INSTRUCTIONS TO A TEE, AND WE'LL SAUNTER RIGHT INTO THEIR LANDS.
BUT THE SLIGHTEST MISSTEP, AND THOSE DEVILS'LL HAVE A GRAND OLD TIME RUNNING US THROUGH THEIR WHOLE CATALOGUE OF TORTURES.
SUCH BARBARISM SEEMS SO QUAINT.
I HAVE A HARD TIME BELIEVING IT.
HAHAHAHA!
YOU OLD WORLD TYPES CAN BE SO NAÏVE!
LUCKILY FOR US, THOSE SAVAGES ARE AS VAIN AS SCHOOLGIRLS. THEY'D DO ANYTHING FOR A HANDFUL OF GLASS BEADS OR A BAG OF SUGAR.
ONCE WE GAIN THEIR TRUST, YOU'LL PHOTOGRAPH THEIR ENCAMPMENTS.
I WANT FACES, COSTUMES, PROFILES.
TAKE DOWN NAMES, AGES, HEIGHT AND WEIGHT. I'LL NEED THOSE PICTURES FOR MY SURVEYS.
SOMETHING AMISS?
THIS IS THE FIRST TIME MY WORK HAS BEEN USED FOR RECORD-KEEPING.
THE FIRST TIME THAT I'VE BEEN LIKENED TO A LABOURER, AND MY MODELS TO LIVESTOCK.
AND I DON'T LIKE IT ONE BIT. PARDON MY SENSITIVITY.

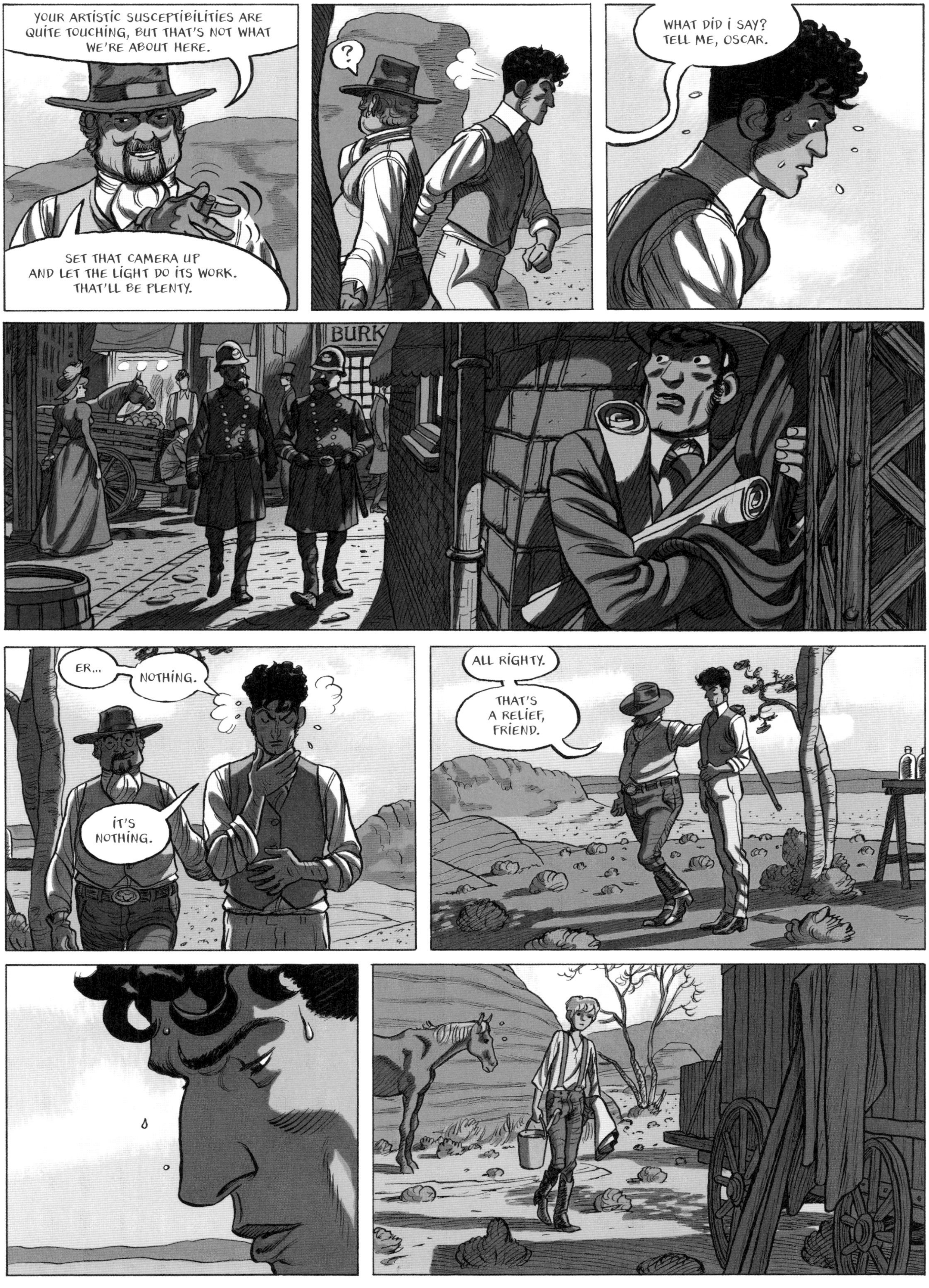
YOUR ARTISTIC SUSCEPTIBILITIES ARE QUITE TOUCHING, BUT THAT'S NOT WHAT WE'RE ABOUT HERE.
SET THAT CAMERA UP AND LET THE LIGHT DO ITS WORK. THAT'LL BE PLENTY.
?
WHAT DID I SAY? TELL ME, OSCAR.
BURK
ER...
NOTHING.
IT'S NOTHING.
ALL RIGHTY.
THAT'S A RELIEF, FRIEND.

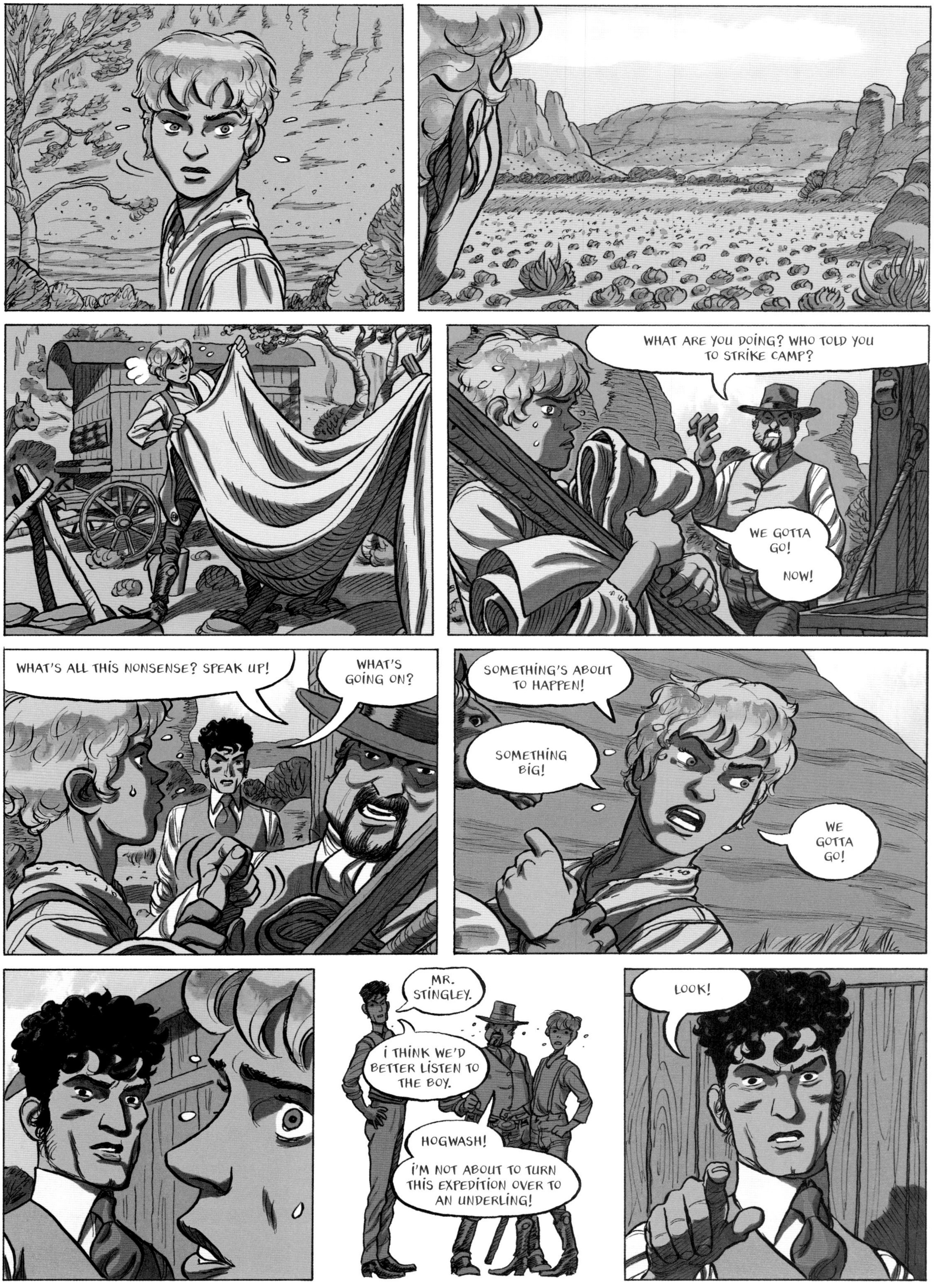
WHAT ARE YOU DOING? WHO TOLD YOU TO STRIKE CAMP?
WE GOTTA GO!
NOW!
WHAT'S ALL THIS NONSENSE? SPEAK UP!
WHAT'S GOING ON?
SOMETHING'S ABOUT TO HAPPEN!
SOMETHING BIG!
WE GOTTA GO!
MR. STINGLEY.
I THINK WE'D BETTER LISTEN TO THE BOY.
HOGWASH!
I'M NOT ABOUT TO TURN THIS EXPEDITION OVER TO AN UNDERLING!
LOOK!

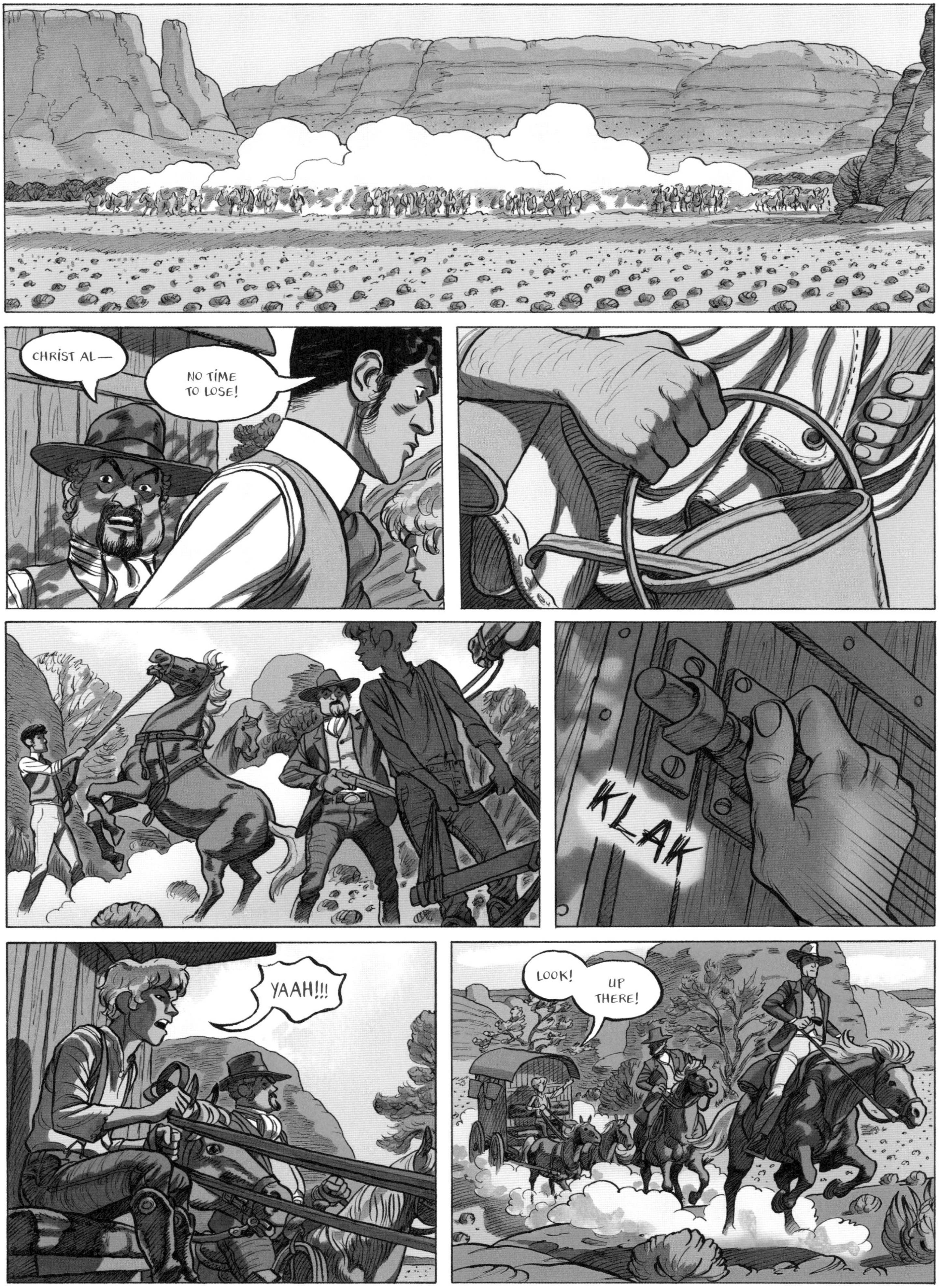
CHRIST AL—
NO TIME TO LOSE!
KLAK
YAAH!!!
LOOK!
UP THERE!

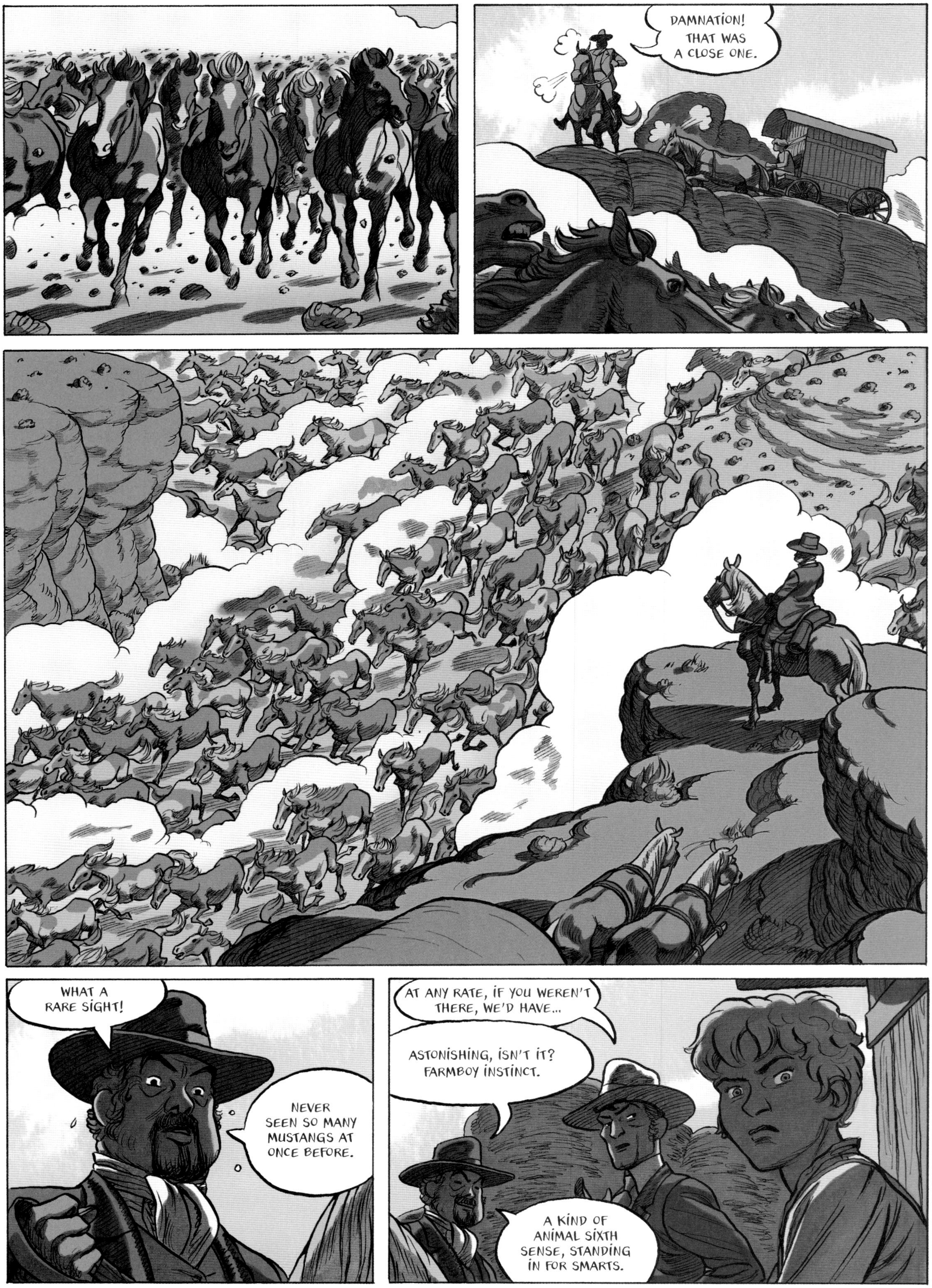
DAMNATION! THAT WAS A CLOSE ONE.
WHAT A RARE SIGHT!
NEVER SEEN SO MANY MUSTANGS AT ONCE BEFORE.
AT ANY RATE, IF YOU WEREN'T THERE, WE'D HAVE...
ASTONISHING, ISN'T IT? FARMBOY INSTINCT.
A KIND OF ANIMAL SIXTH SENSE, STANDING IN FOR SMARTS.

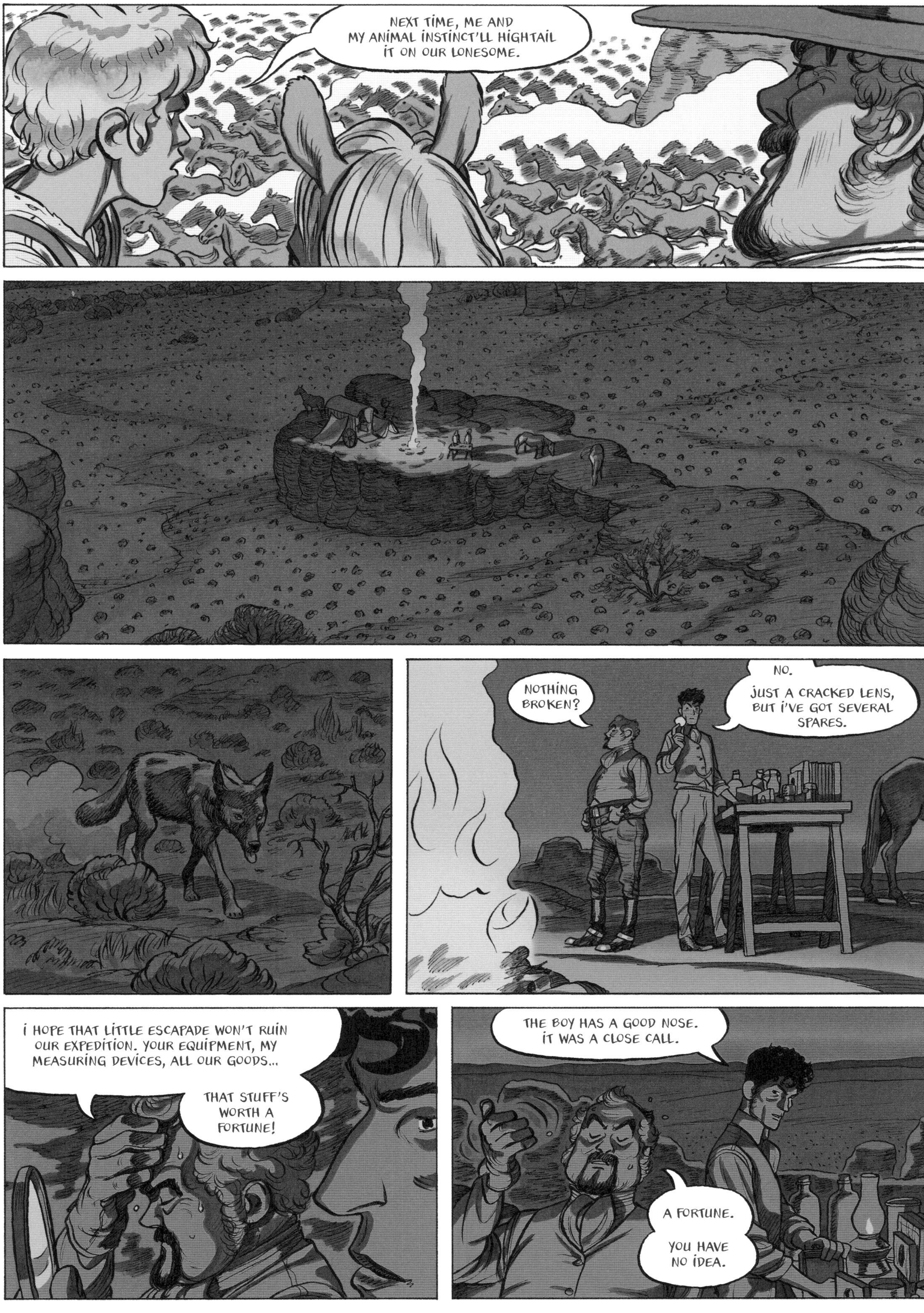
NEXT TIME, ME AND MY ANIMAL INSTINCT'LL HIGHTAIL IT ON OUR LONESOME.
NOTHING BROKEN?
NO.
JUST A CRACKED LENS, BUT I'VE GOT SEVERAL SPARES.
I HOPE THAT LITTLE ESCAPADE WON'T RUIN OUR EXPEDITION. YOUR EQUIPMENT, MY MEASURING DEVICES, ALL OUR GOODS...
THAT STUFF'S WORTH A FORTUNE!
THE BOY HAS A GOOD NOSE. IT WAS A CLOSE CALL.
A FORTUNE.
YOU HAVE NO IDEA.

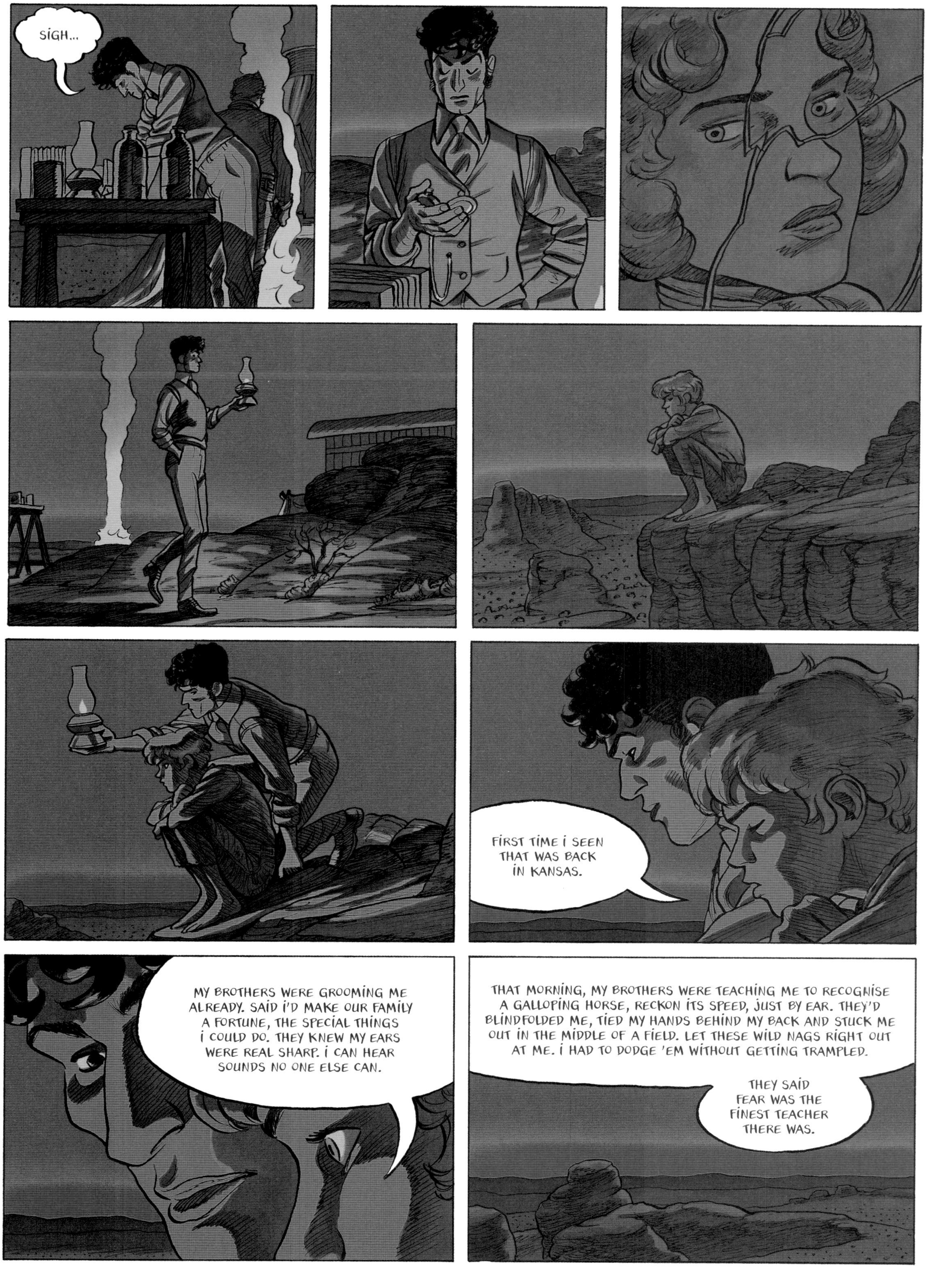
SIGH...
FIRST TIME I SEEN THAT WAS BACK IN KANSAS.
MY BROTHERS WERE GROOMING ME ALREADY. SAID I'D MAKE OUR FAMILY A FORTUNE, THE SPECIAL THINGS I COULD DO. THEY KNEW MY EARS WERE REAL SHARP. I CAN HEAR SOUNDS NO ONE ELSE CAN.
THAT MORNING, MY BROTHERS WERE TEACHING ME TO RECOGNISE A GALLOPING HORSE, RECKON ITS SPEED, JUST BY EAR. THEY'D BLINDFOLDED ME, TIED MY HANDS BEHIND MY BACK AND STUCK ME OUT IN THE MIDDLE OF A FIELD. LET THESE WILD NAGS RIGHT OUT AT ME. I HAD TO DODGE 'EM WITHOUT GETTING TRAMPLED.
THEY SAID FEAR WAS THE FINEST TEACHER THERE WAS.

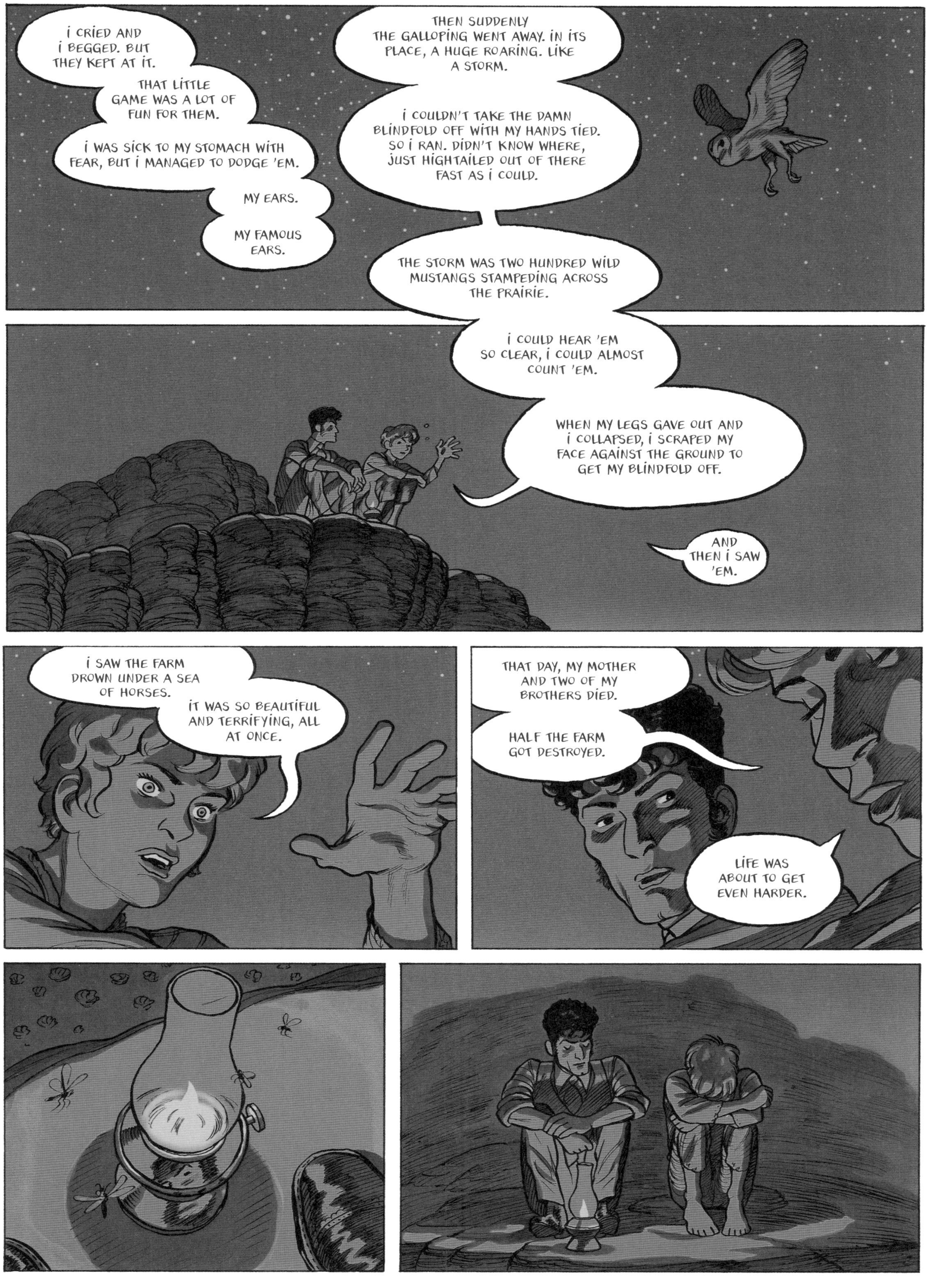
I CRIED AND I BEGGED. BUT THEY KEPT AT IT.
THAT LITTLE GAME WAS A LOT OF FUN FOR THEM.
I WAS SICK TO MY STOMACH WITH FEAR, BUT I MANAGED TO DODGE 'EM.
MY EARS.
MY FAMOUS EARS.
THEN SUDDENLY THE GALLOPING WENT AWAY. IN ITS PLACE, A HUGE ROARING. LIKE A STORM.
I COULDN'T TAKE THE DAMN BLINDFOLD OFF WITH MY HANDS TIED. SO I RAN. DIDN'T KNOW WHERE, JUST HIGHTAILED OUT OF THERE FAST AS I COULD.
THE STORM WAS TWO HUNDRED WILD MUSTANGS STAMPEDING ACROSS THE PRAIRIE.
I COULD HEAR 'EM SO CLEAR, I COULD ALMOST COUNT 'EM.
WHEN MY LEGS GAVE OUT AND I COLLAPSED, I SCRAPED MY FACE AGAINST THE GROUND TO GET MY BLINDFOLD OFF.
AND THEN I SAW 'EM.
I SAW THE FARM DROWN UNDER A SEA OF HORSES.
IT WAS SO BEAUTIFUL AND TERRIFYING, ALL AT ONCE.
THAT DAY, MY MOTHER AND TWO OF MY BROTHERS DIED.
HALF THE FARM GOT DESTROYED.
LIFE WAS ABOUT TO GET EVEN HARDER.

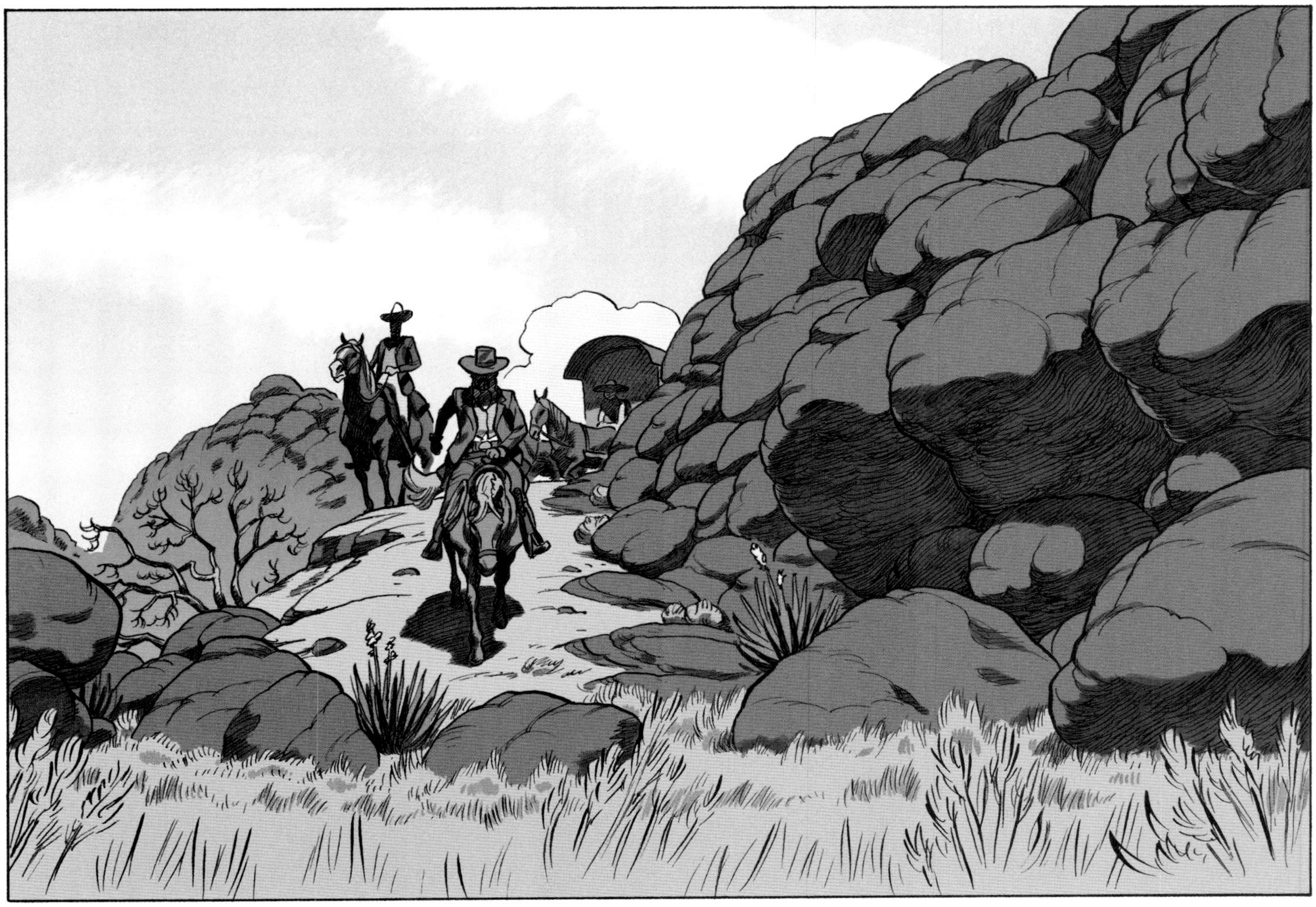

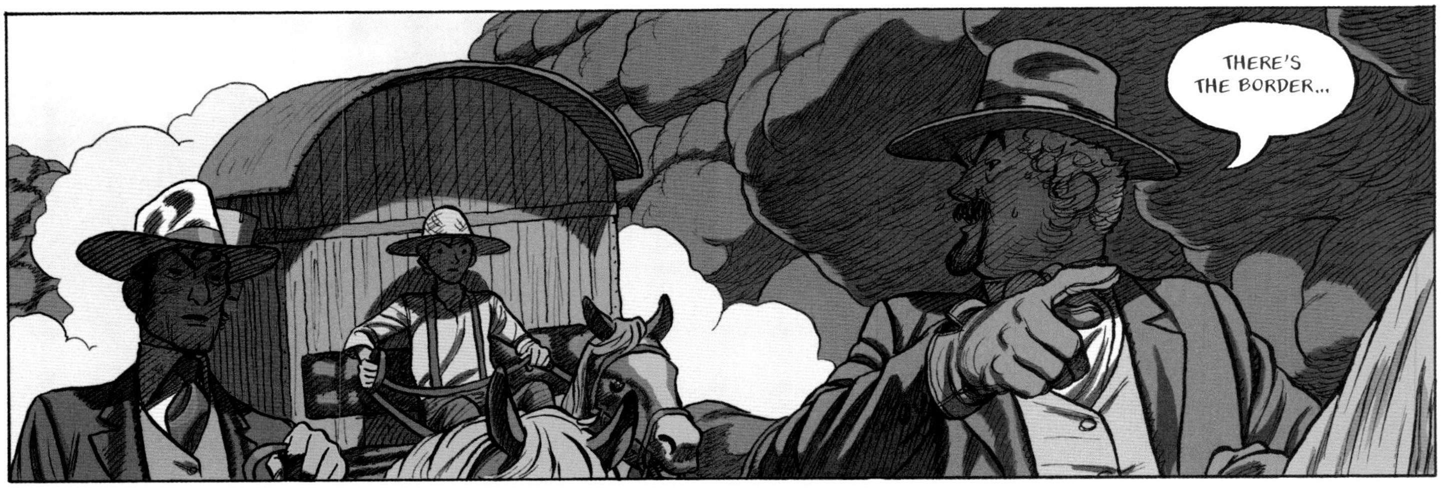
THERE'S THE BORDER...

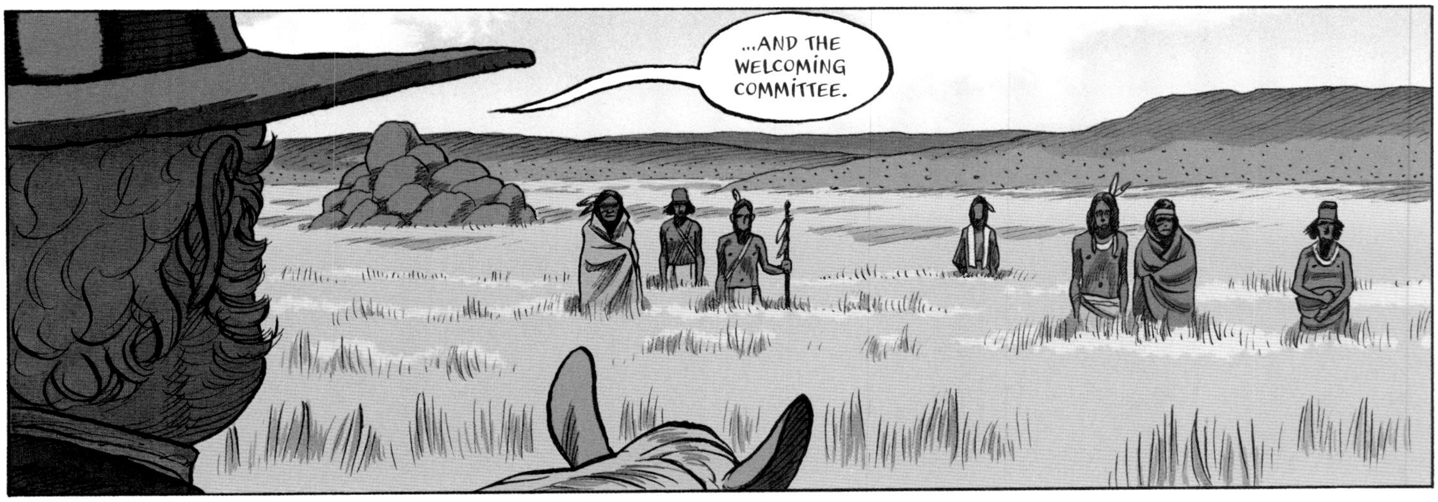
...AND THE WELCOMING COMMITTEE.

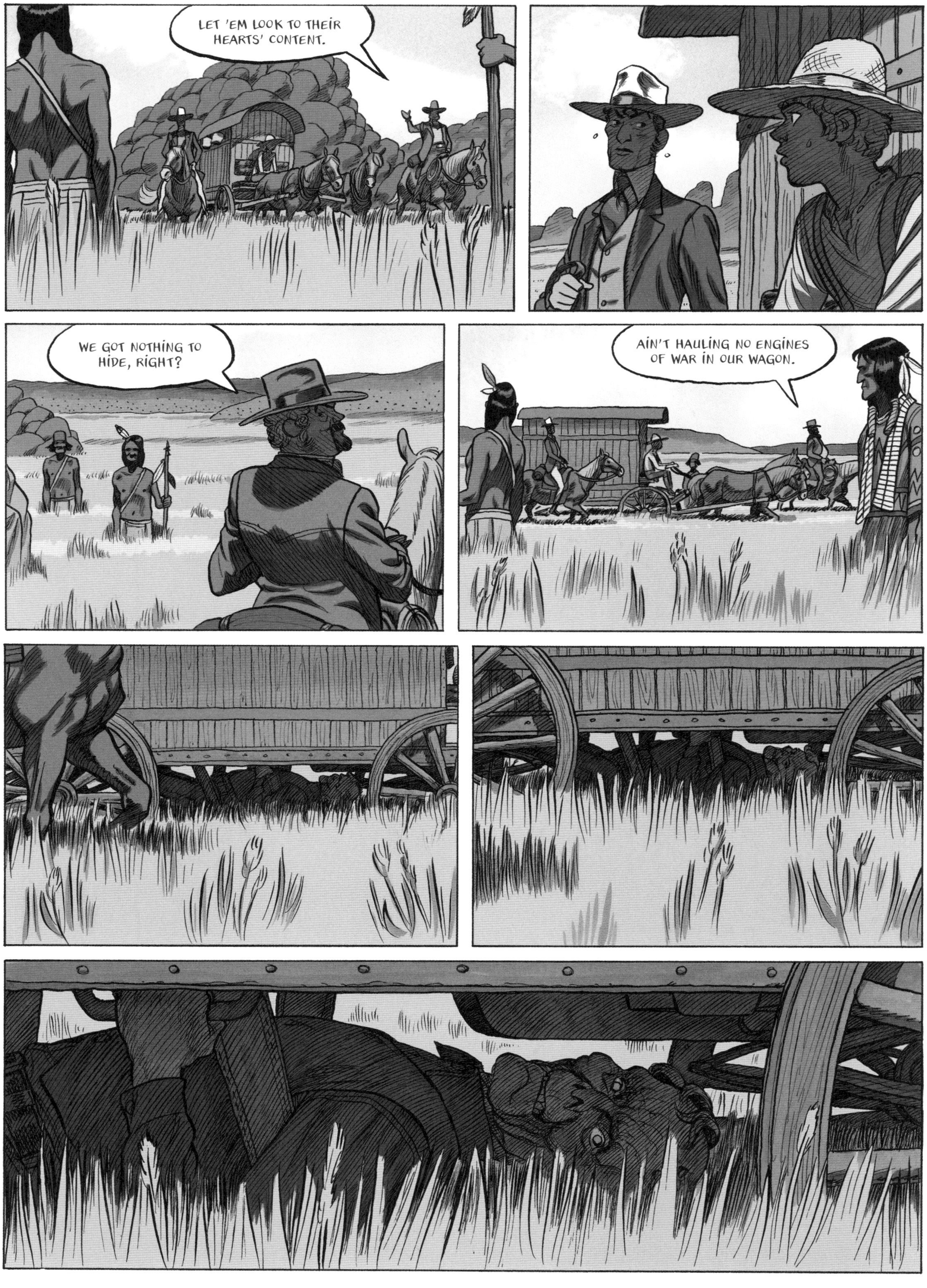
LET 'EM LOOK TO THEIR HEARTS' CONTENT.
WE GOT NOTHING TO HIDE, RIGHT?
AIN'T HAULING NO ENGINES OF WAR IN OUR WAGON.

COMANCHERIA

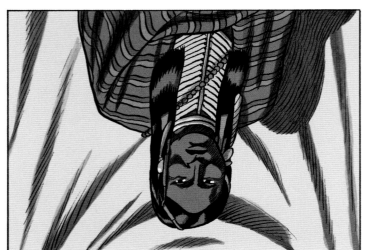

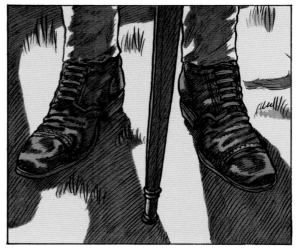

I WANT HIM STANDING IN THE PHOTO.

WANT TO SEE THE DETAILS ON HIS DRESS.

SLIK

HE'S OLD. HE CAN'T HOLD THE POSE. THE IMAGE WILL BE BLURRY.

A PROFESSIONAL LIKE YOU CAN'T BE SHORT ON TRICKS OF THE TRADE. YOU FIGURE IT OUT.

HMM...

WELL, I'LL LET YOU GET TO WORK.

SURE.

IT'S OK. YOU CAN GO NOW.

?

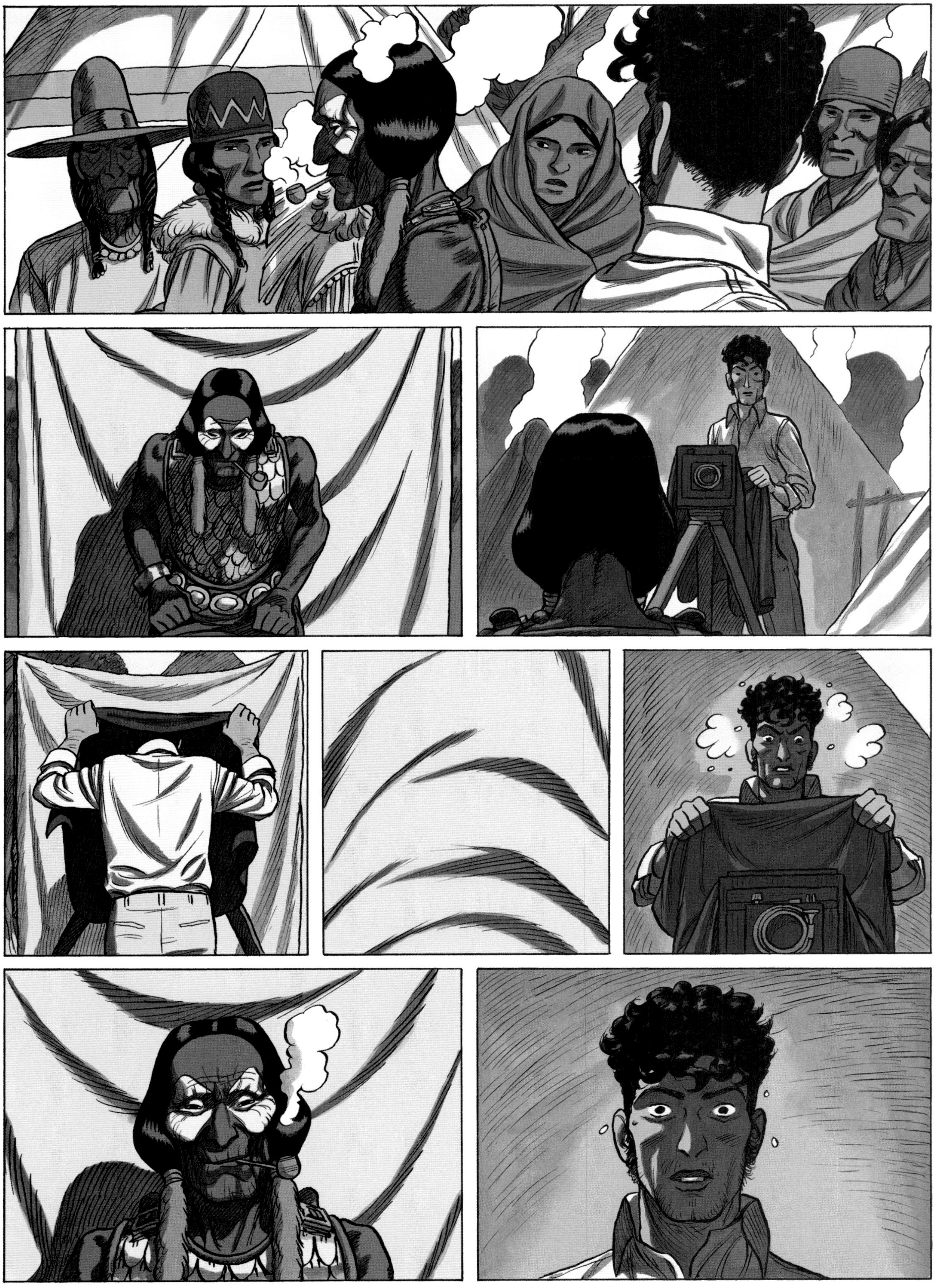

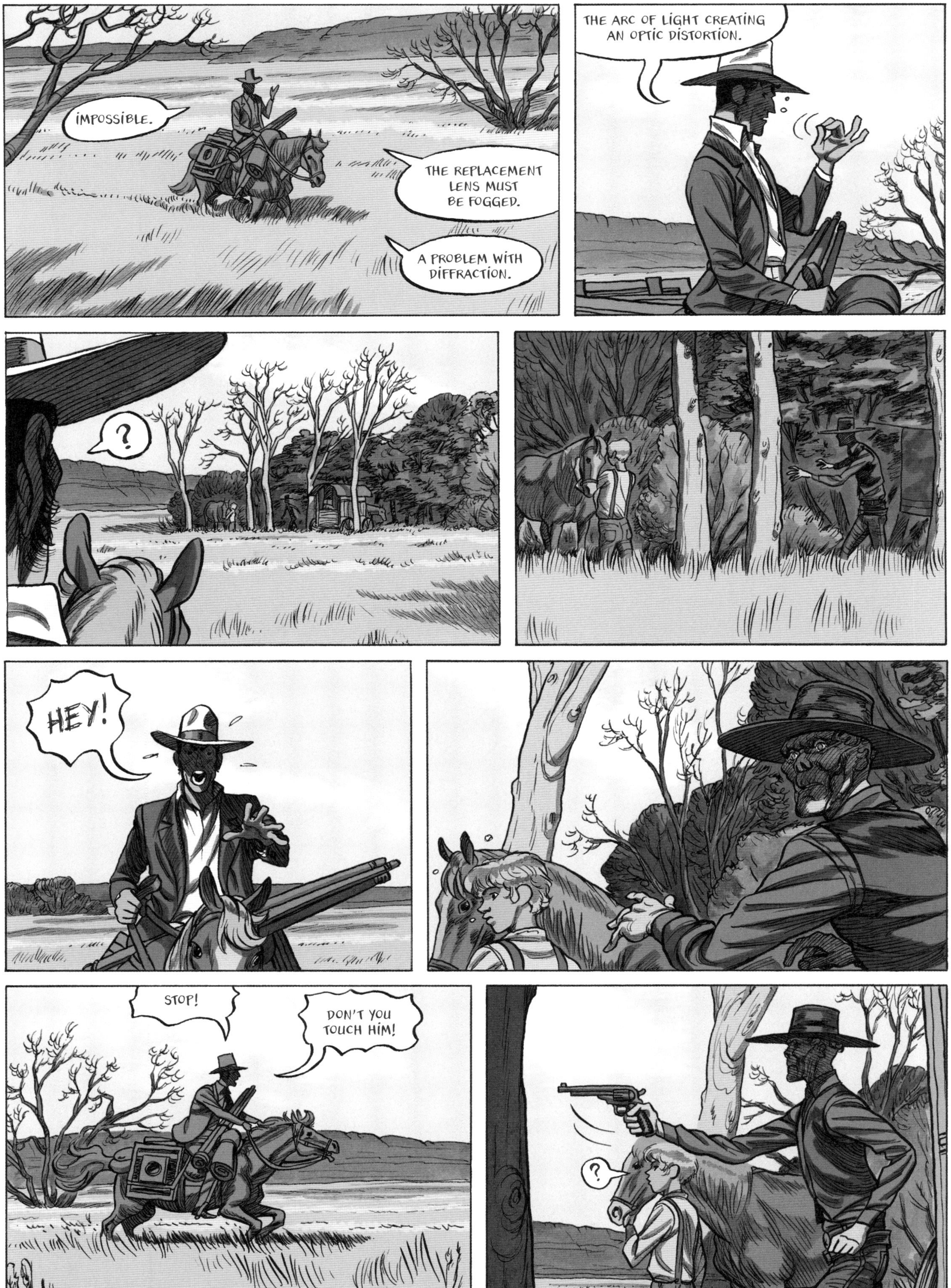
IMPOSSIBLE.
THE REPLACEMENT LENS MUST BE FOGGED.
A PROBLEM WITH DIFFRACTION.
THE ARC OF LIGHT CREATING AN OPTIC DISTORTION.
?
HEY!
STOP!
DON'T YOU TOUCH HIM!
?

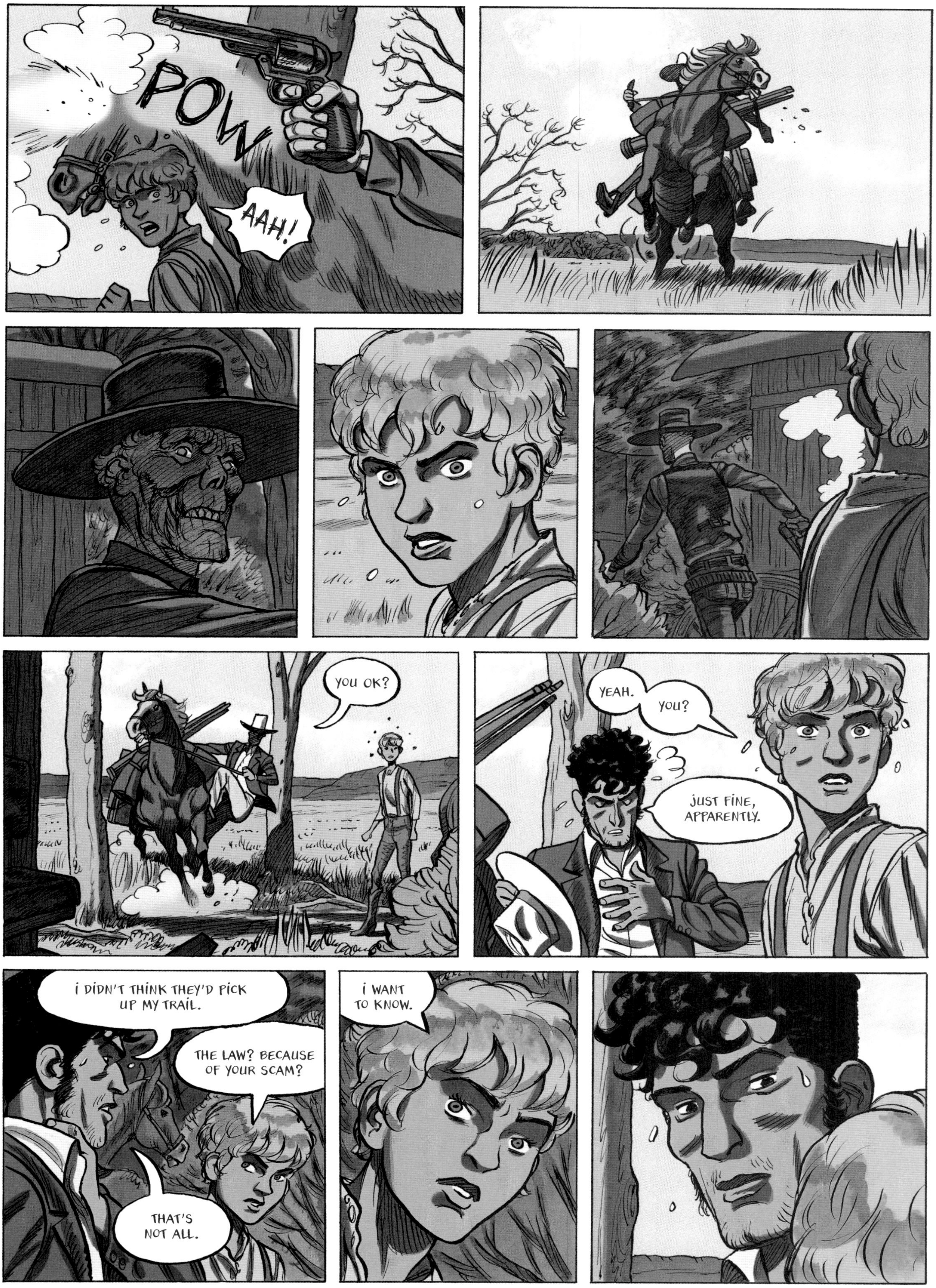
POW
AAH!
YOU OK?
YEAH.
YOU?
JUST FINE, APPARENTLY.
I DIDN'T THINK THEY'D PICK UP MY TRAIL.
THE LAW? BECAUSE OF YOUR SCAM?
THAT'S NOT ALL.
I WANT TO KNOW.

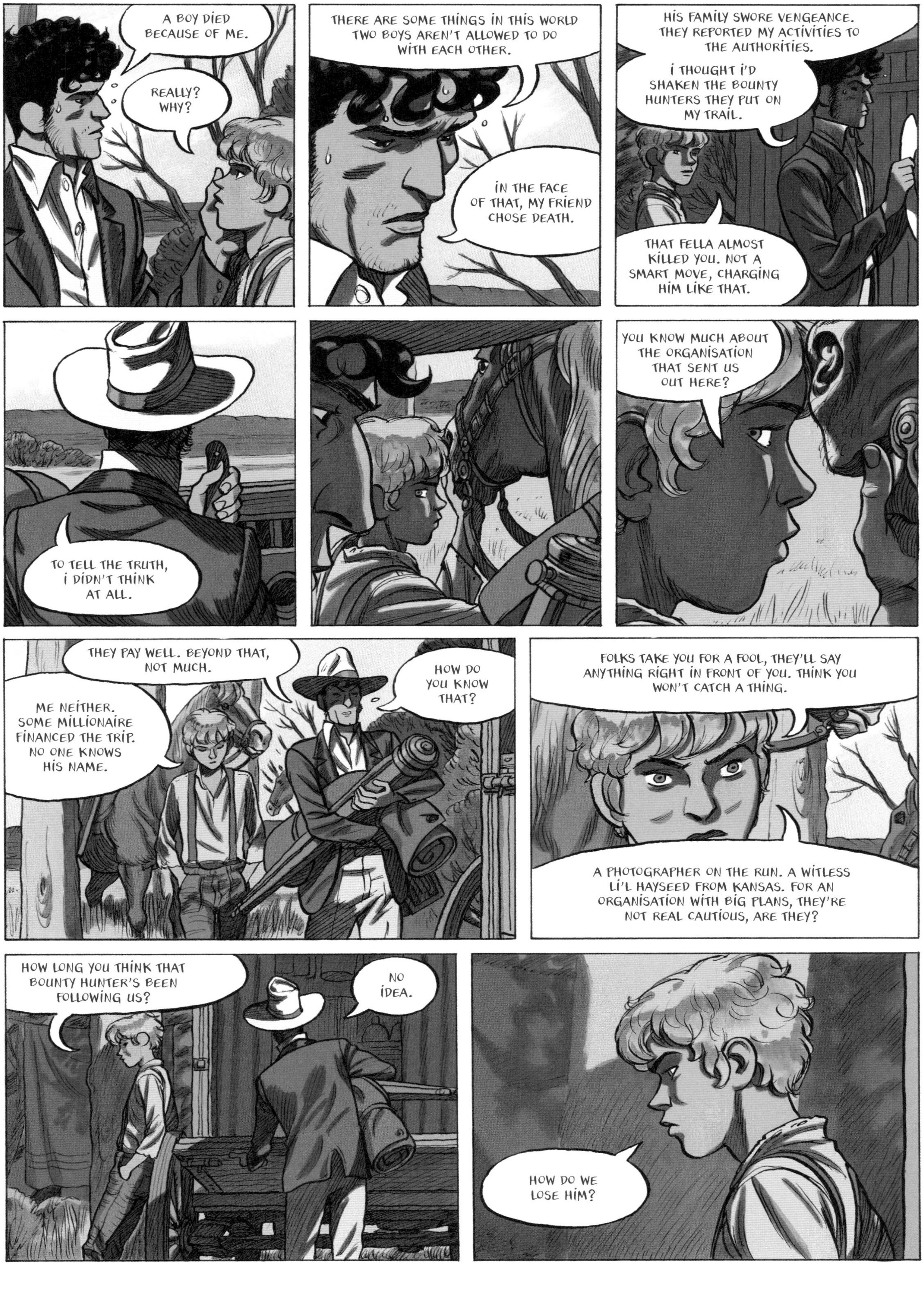
A BOY DIED BECAUSE OF ME.
REALLY? WHY?
THERE ARE SOME THINGS IN THIS WORLD TWO BOYS AREN'T ALLOWED TO DO WITH EACH OTHER.
IN THE FACE OF THAT, MY FRIEND CHOSE DEATH.
HIS FAMILY SWORE VENGEANCE. THEY REPORTED MY ACTIVITIES TO THE AUTHORITIES.
I THOUGHT I'D SHAKEN THE BOUNTY HUNTERS THEY PUT ON MY TRAIL.
THAT FELLA ALMOST KILLED YOU. NOT A SMART MOVE, CHARGING HIM LIKE THAT.
TO TELL THE TRUTH, I DIDN'T THINK AT ALL.
YOU KNOW MUCH ABOUT THE ORGANISATION THAT SENT US OUT HERE?
THEY PAY WELL. BEYOND THAT, NOT MUCH.
ME NEITHER. SOME MILLIONAIRE FINANCED THE TRIP. NO ONE KNOWS HIS NAME.
HOW DO YOU KNOW THAT?
FOLKS TAKE YOU FOR A FOOL, THEY'LL SAY ANYTHING RIGHT IN FRONT OF YOU. THINK YOU WON'T CATCH A THING.
A PHOTOGRAPHER ON THE RUN. A WITLESS LI'L HAYSEED FROM KANSAS. FOR AN ORGANISATION WITH BIG PLANS, THEY'RE NOT REAL CAUTIOUS, ARE THEY?
HOW LONG YOU THINK THAT BOUNTY HUNTER'S BEEN FOLLOWING US?
NO IDEA.
HOW DO WE LOSE HIM?

VILLAGE N° 1

orses	245
ults	36

36 adult males
14 male children
50 exploitable subjects

9
11
12
13
14

40 ADULT FEMALES.

15 FEMALE CHILDREN.

HMM...

EQUALS 55 SUBJECTS TO BE ELIMINATED.

SKRITCH SKRITCH

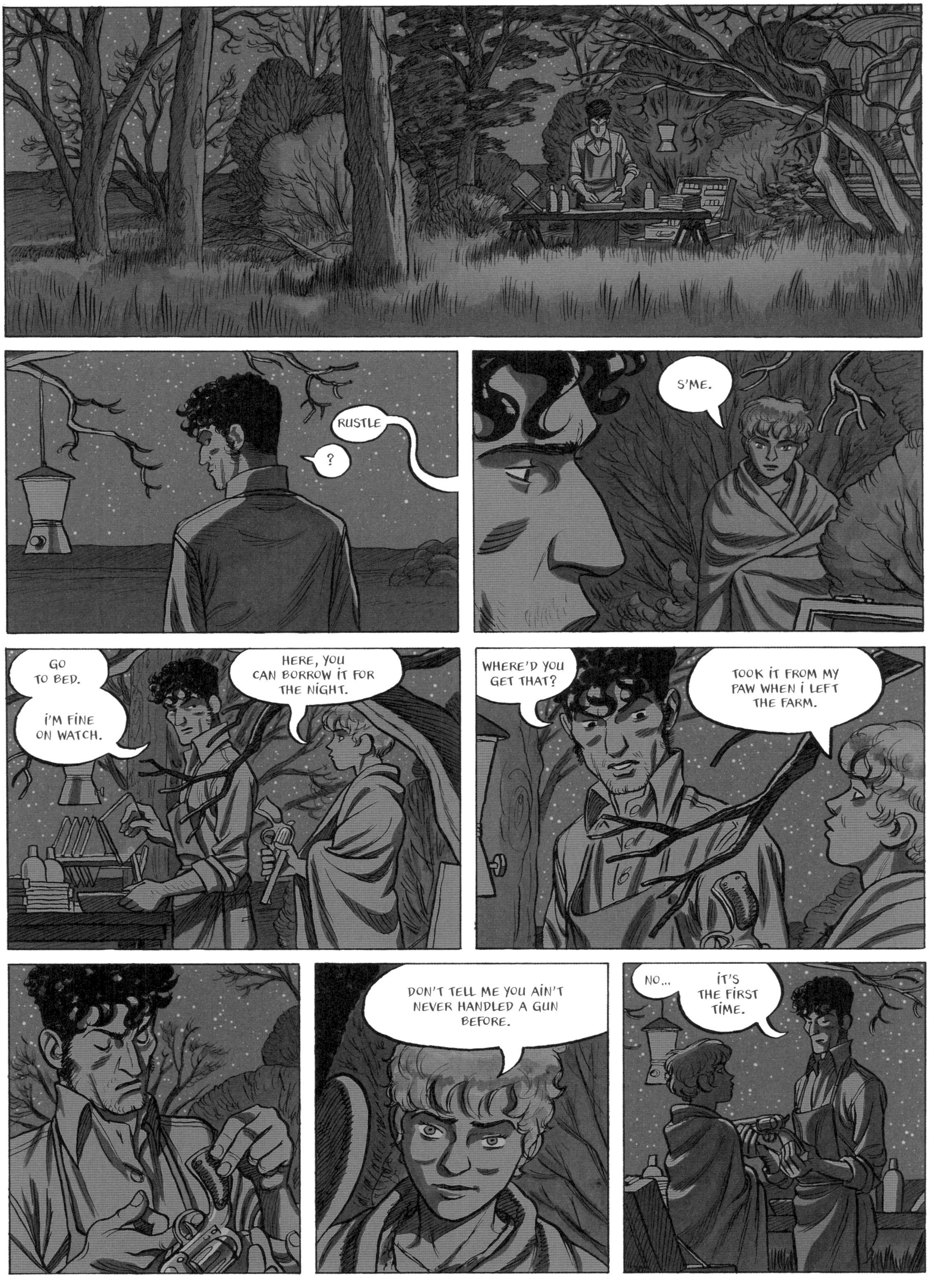
RUSTLE
?
S'ME.
GO TO BED.
I'M FINE ON WATCH.
HERE, YOU CAN BORROW IT FOR THE NIGHT.
WHERE'D YOU GET THAT?
TOOK IT FROM MY PAW WHEN I LEFT THE FARM.
DON'T TELL ME YOU AIN'T NEVER HANDLED A GUN BEFORE.
NO...
IT'S THE FIRST TIME.

HOLD THE BUTT IN YOUR PALM LIKE SO, AND SLIP YOUR FINGER OVER THE TRIGGER.

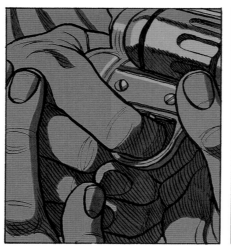

CAREFUL... THING COULD GO OFF ON ITS OWN.

?

GOOD LORD...

IT CAN'T BE!

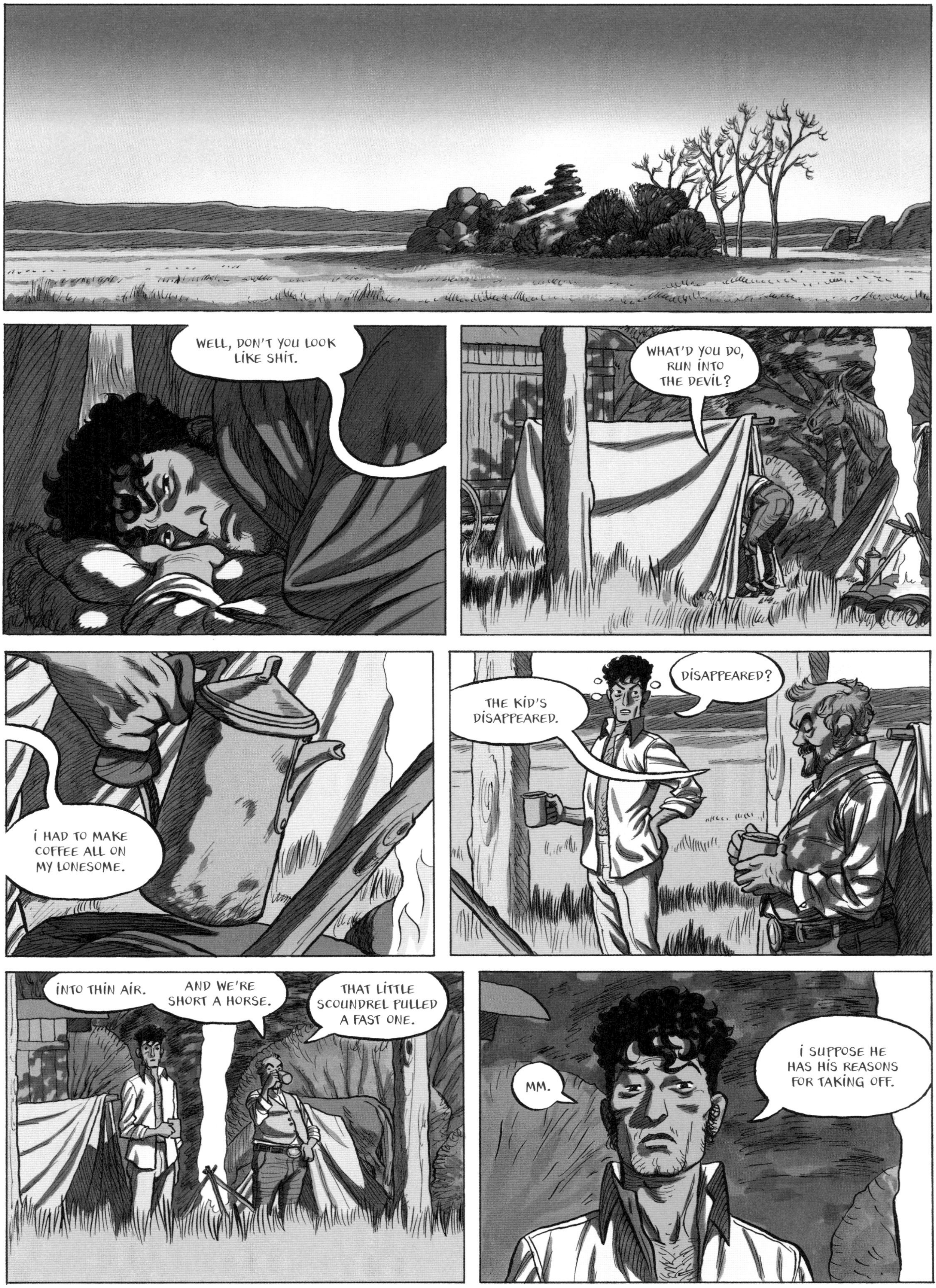
WELL, DON'T YOU LOOK LIKE SHIT.
WHAT'D YOU DO, RUN INTO THE DEVIL?
I HAD TO MAKE COFFEE ALL ON MY LONESOME.
THE KID'S DISAPPEARED.
DISAPPEARED?
INTO THIN AIR.
AND WE'RE SHORT A HORSE.
THAT LITTLE SCOUNDREL PULLED A FAST ONE.
MM.
I SUPPOSE HE HAS HIS REASONS FOR TAKING OFF.

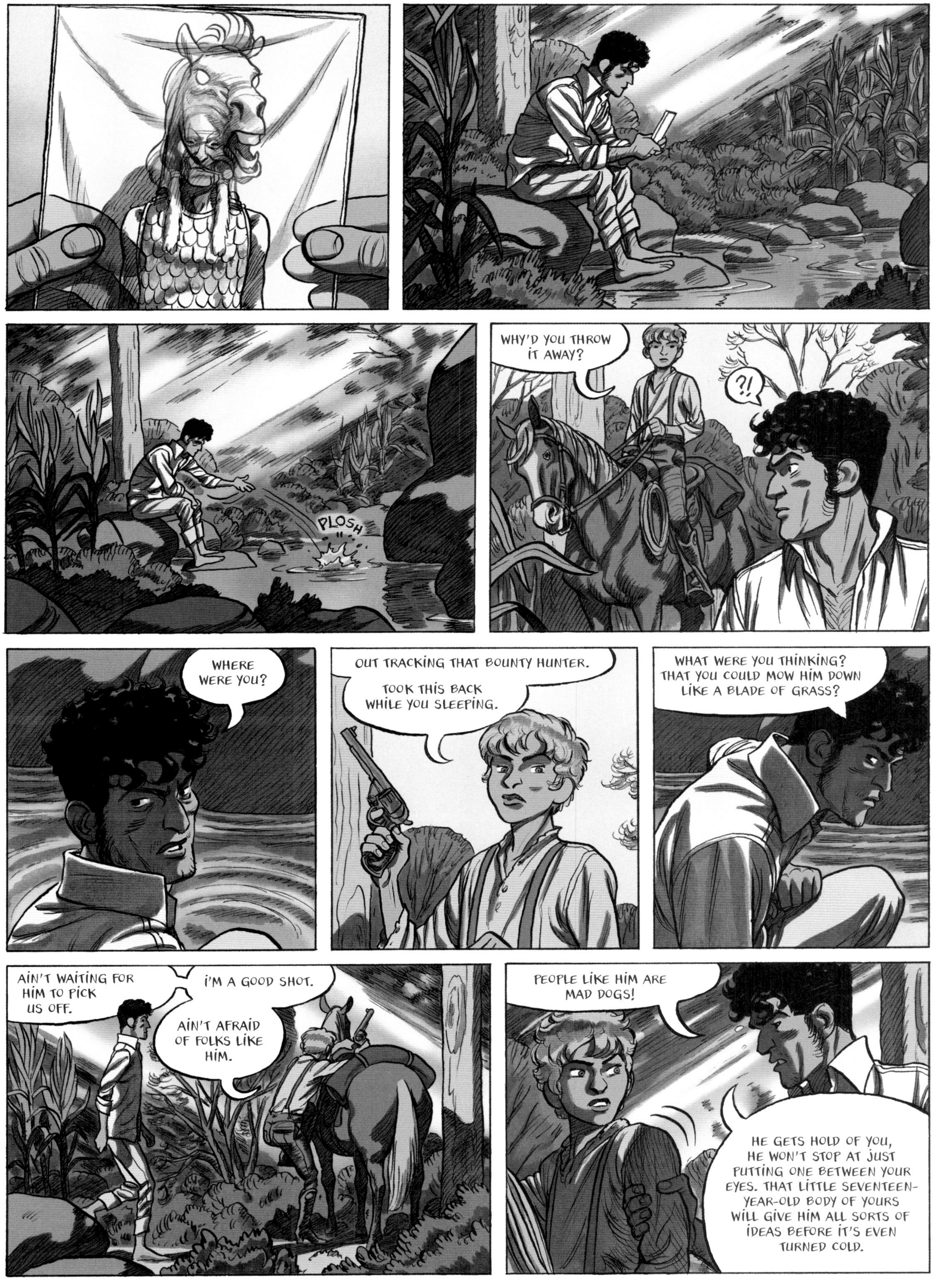
PLOSH
WHY'D YOU THROW IT AWAY?
?!
WHERE WERE YOU?
OUT TRACKING THAT BOUNTY HUNTER.
TOOK THIS BACK WHILE YOU SLEEPING.
WHAT WERE YOU THINKING? THAT YOU COULD MOW HIM DOWN LIKE A BLADE OF GRASS?
AIN'T WAITING FOR HIM TO PICK US OFF.
I'M A GOOD SHOT.
AIN'T AFRAID OF FOLKS LIKE HIM.
PEOPLE LIKE HIM ARE MAD DOGS!
HE GETS HOLD OF YOU, HE WON'T STOP AT JUST PUTTING ONE BETWEEN YOUR EYES. THAT LITTLE SEVENTEEN-YEAR-OLD BODY OF YOURS WILL GIVE HIM ALL SORTS OF IDEAS BEFORE IT'S EVEN TURNED COLD.

I GREW UP WITH A PACK OF MAD DOGS. I KNOW WHAT GOES THROUGH THEIR HEADS.

I KNOW HOW THEY ARE, AND I KNOW WHAT I GOTTA DO.

YOU'RE JUST A CHILD!

I WON'T LET YOU GO BACK THERE. I WON'T LET YOU GET YOURSELF KILLED!

NO ONE TELLS ME WHAT TO DO!

SLAP

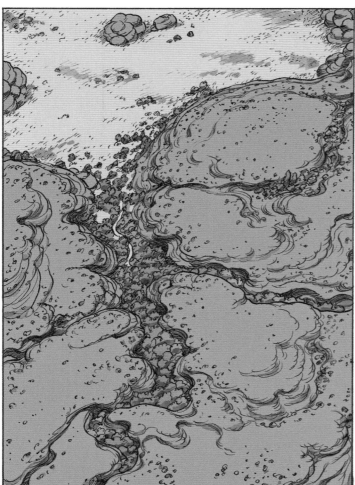

WHAT THIS PLACE NEEDS IS SOME VERTICALITY. I SEE FACTORIES, TOWERS AND CITIES RIGHT HERE.

I PREFER DESERTED LANDSCAPES.

PAGAN PEOPLES GIVE GREAT CREDENCE TO VISIONS. THEY SAY THE WORLD WE LIVE IN MIGHT JUST BE A VAST DREAM IN SOMEONE'S HEAD.

FUNNY, ISN'T IT?

MR. STINGLEY, I'M SURPRISED A MAN LIKE YOU COULD FALL FOR SUCH TALL TALES.

SO WHOSE DREAM ARE WE IN RIGHT NOW?

PROBABLY SOME LUNATIC'S.

A MADMAN WHOSE SENSE OF HUMOUR I SURELY DON'T SHARE.

IT'S NOT AS DUMB AS ALL THAT. IF EVERYTHING GOES WELL, WHAT I SEE IN MY HEAD COULD BECOME REAL IN THE NEAR FUTURE.

YOU'VE BEEN IN A REAL MOOD THIS MORNING.

PRAIRIE MADNESS GETTING TO YOU?

WHAT ARE YOU TALKING ABOUT?

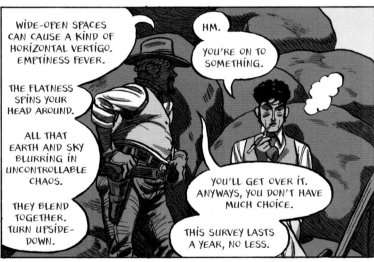

WIDE-OPEN SPACES CAN CAUSE A KIND OF HORIZONTAL VERTIGO. EMPTINESS FEVER.

THE FLATNESS SPINS YOUR HEAD AROUND.

ALL THAT EARTH AND SKY BLURRING IN UNCONTROLLABLE CHAOS.

THEY BLEND TOGETHER. TURN UPSIDE-DOWN.

HM.

YOU'RE ON TO SOMETHING.

YOU'LL GET OVER IT. ANYWAYS, YOU DON'T HAVE MUCH CHOICE.

THIS SURVEY LASTS A YEAR, NO LESS.

HOW MANY TIMES HAVE YOU BEEN OUT IN THESE PARTS?

A FAIR NUMBER.

FOR THE ORGANISATION?

YOU COULD SAY THAT.

MRS. STINGLEY MUSTN'T SEE YOUR FACE MUCH.

THERE IS NO MRS. STINGLEY. THERE'S NO FEMININE PRESENCE IN MY PLACE BACK IN KANSAS.

IT'S PERFECT, LIKE THIS.

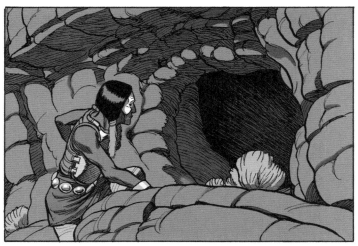

KLING KLONG

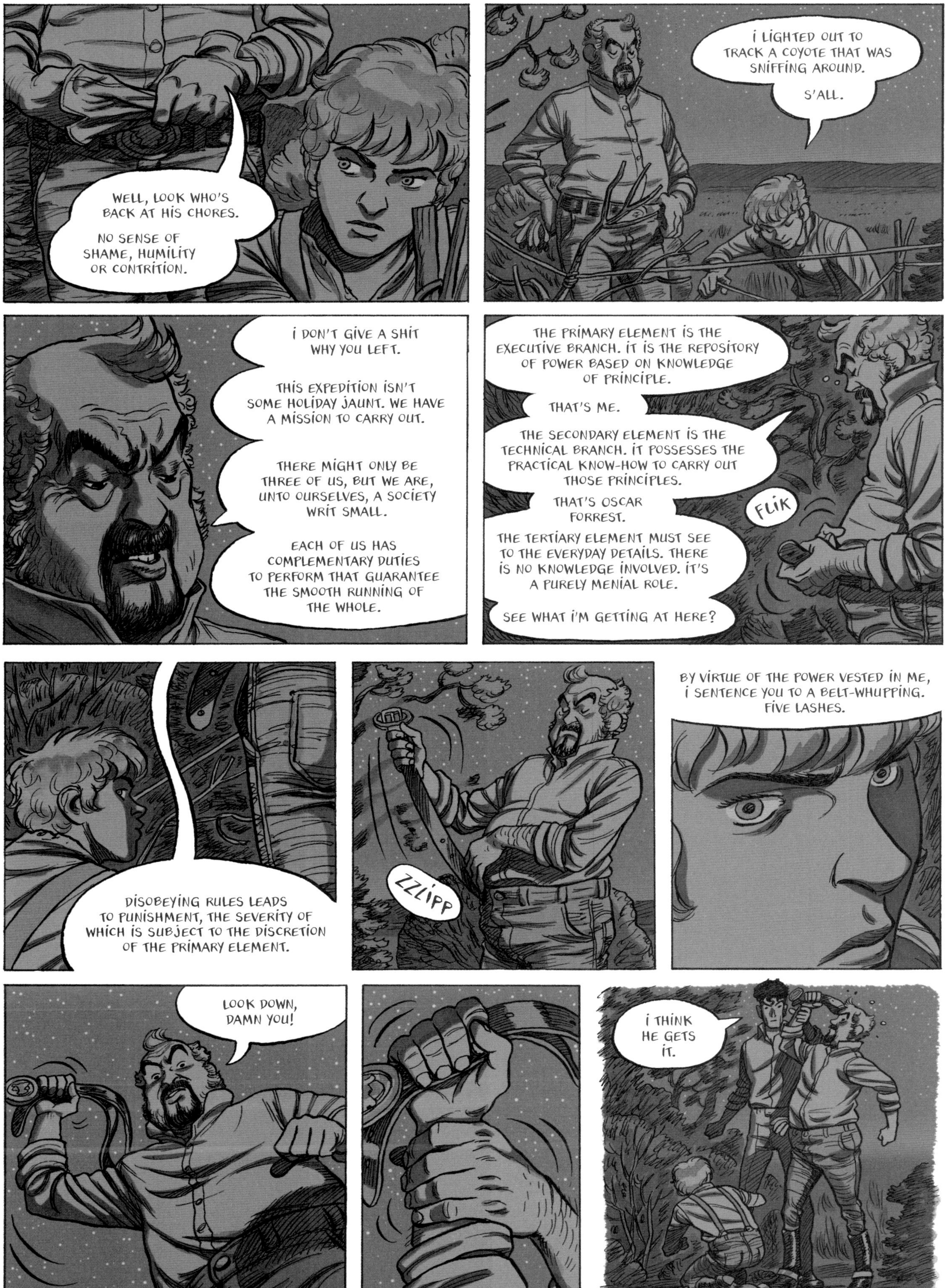
WELL, LOOK WHO'S BACK AT HIS CHORES.
NO SENSE OF SHAME, HUMILITY OR CONTRITION.
I LIGHTED OUT TO TRACK A COYOTE THAT WAS SNIFFING AROUND.
S'ALL.
I DON'T GIVE A SHIT WHY YOU LEFT.
THIS EXPEDITION ISN'T SOME HOLIDAY JAUNT. WE HAVE A MISSION TO CARRY OUT.
THERE MIGHT ONLY BE THREE OF US, BUT WE ARE, UNTO OURSELVES, A SOCIETY WRIT SMALL.
EACH OF US HAS COMPLEMENTARY DUTIES TO PERFORM THAT GUARANTEE THE SMOOTH RUNNING OF THE WHOLE.
THE PRIMARY ELEMENT IS THE EXECUTIVE BRANCH. IT IS THE REPOSITORY OF POWER BASED ON KNOWLEDGE OF PRINCIPLE.
THAT'S ME.
THE SECONDARY ELEMENT IS THE TECHNICAL BRANCH. IT POSSESSES THE PRACTICAL KNOW-HOW TO CARRY OUT THOSE PRINCIPLES.
THAT'S OSCAR FORREST.
THE TERTIARY ELEMENT MUST SEE TO THE EVERYDAY DETAILS. THERE IS NO KNOWLEDGE INVOLVED. IT'S A PURELY MENIAL ROLE.
SEE WHAT I'M GETTING AT HERE?
FLIK
DISOBEYING RULES LEADS TO PUNISHMENT, THE SEVERITY OF WHICH IS SUBJECT TO THE DISCRETION OF THE PRIMARY ELEMENT.
ZZLIPP
BY VIRTUE OF THE POWER VESTED IN ME, I SENTENCE YOU TO A BELT-WHUPPING. FIVE LASHES.
LOOK DOWN, DAMN YOU!
I THINK HE GETS IT.

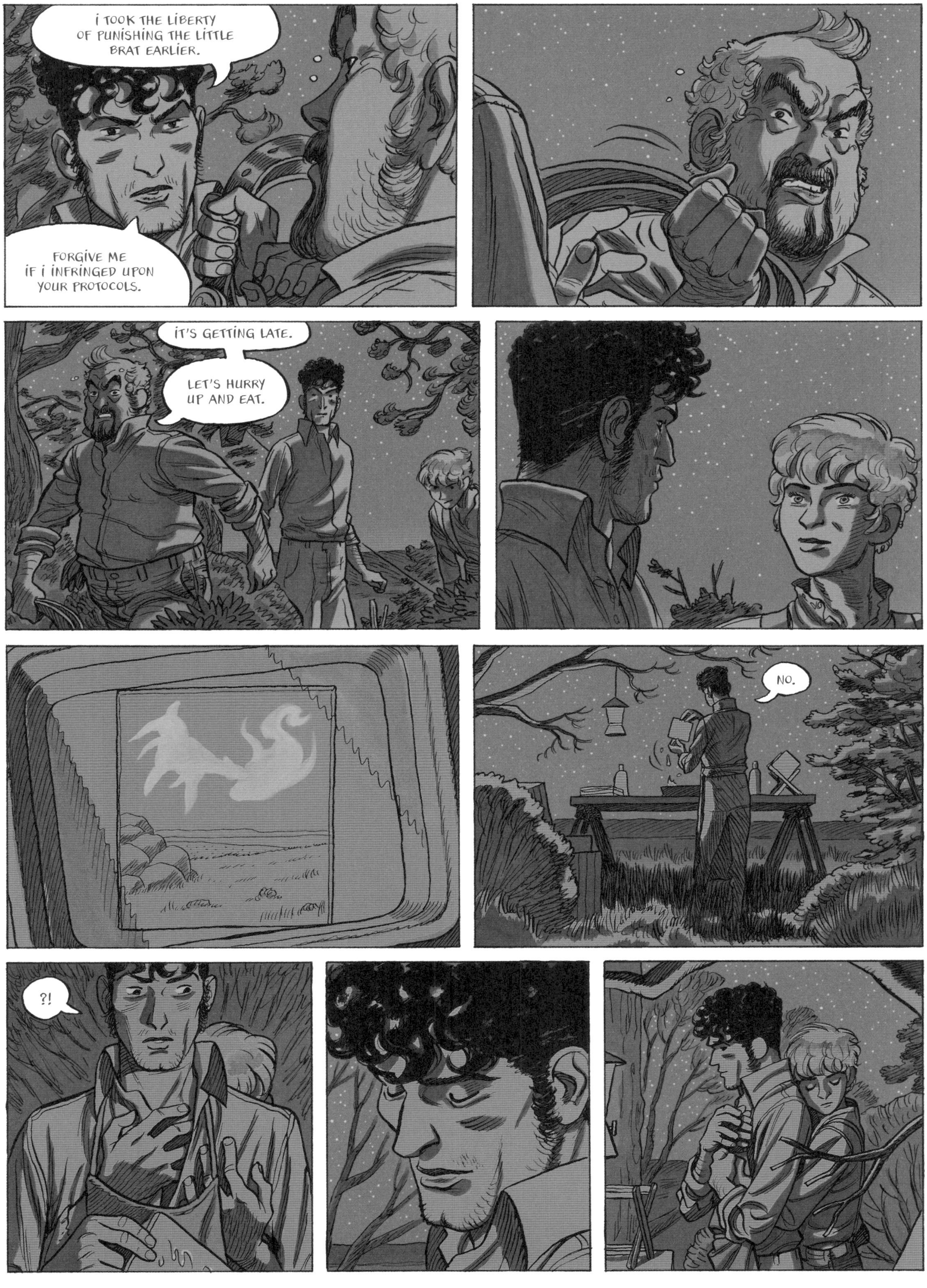
I TOOK THE LIBERTY OF PUNISHING THE LITTLE BRAT EARLIER.
FORGIVE ME IF I INFRINGED UPON YOUR PROTOCOLS.
IT'S GETTING LATE.
LET'S HURRY UP AND EAT.
NO.
?!

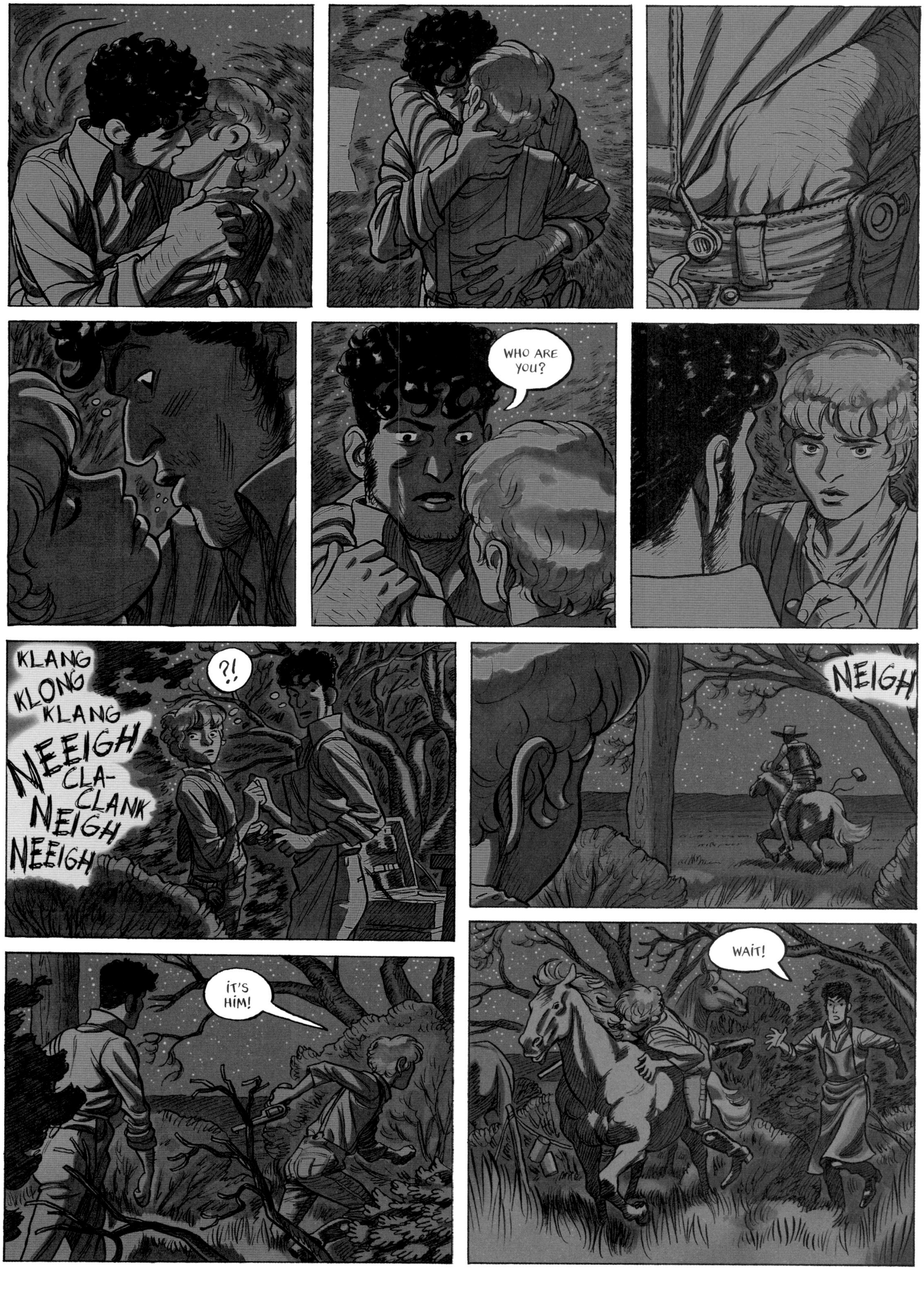
WHO ARE YOU?
KLANG
KLONG
KLANG
NEEIGH
CLA-CLANK
NEIGH
NEEIGH
?!
NEIGH
IT'S HIM!
WAIT!

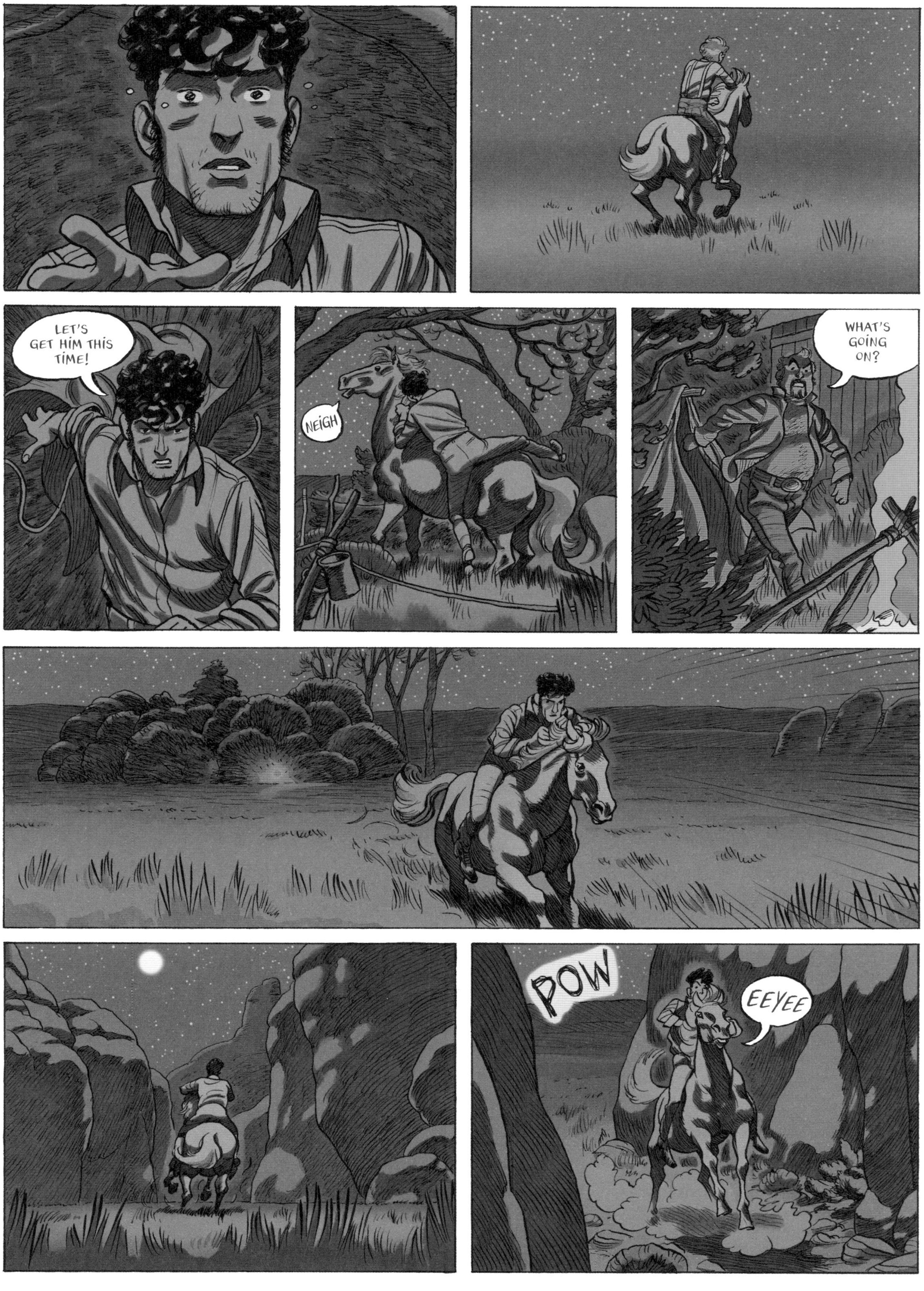
LET'S GET HIM THIS TIME!
NEIGH
WHAT'S GOING ON?
POW
EEYEE

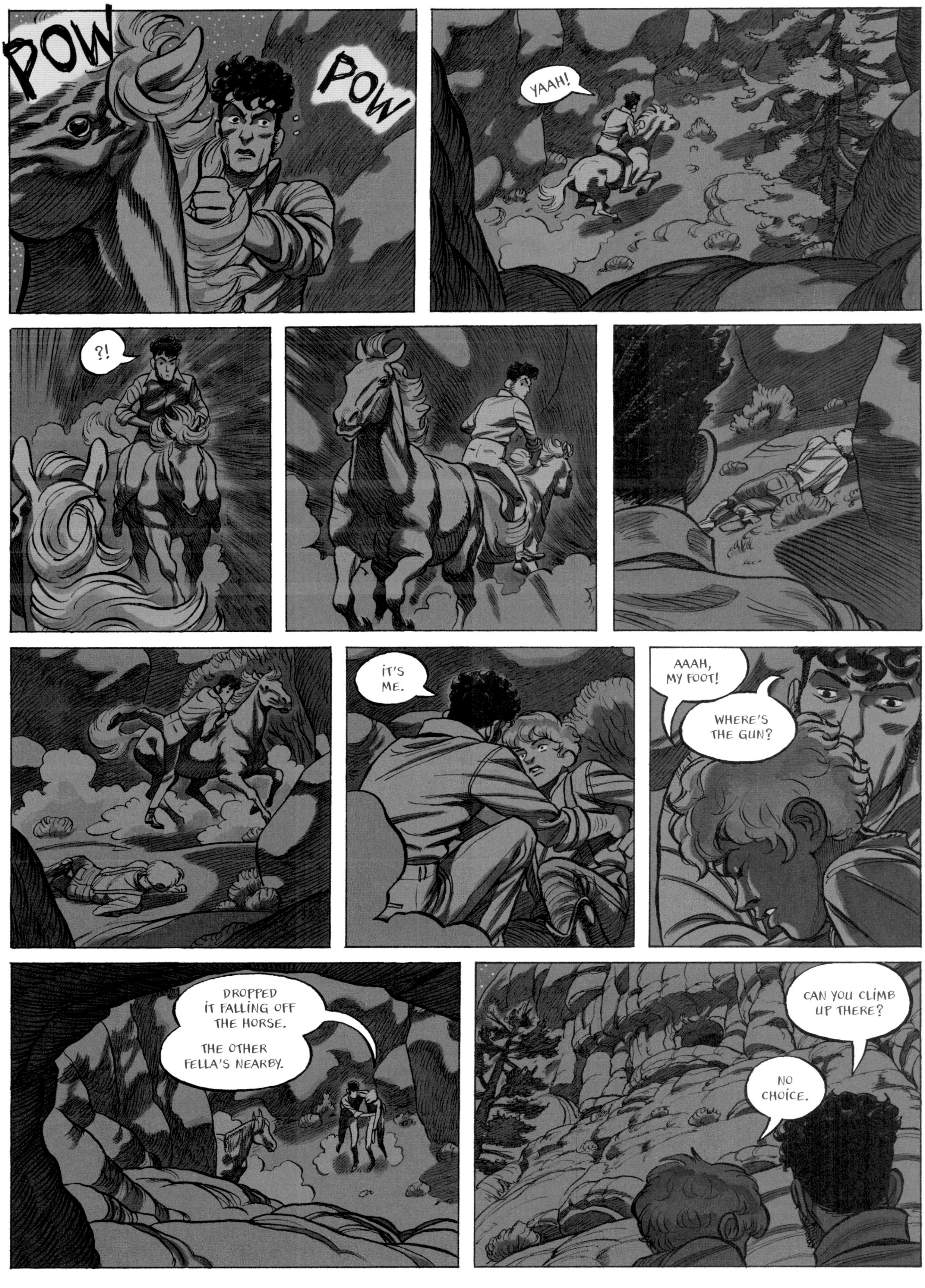
POW
POW
YAAH!
?!
IT'S ME.
AAAH, MY FOOT!
WHERE'S THE GUN?
DROPPED IT FALLING OFF THE HORSE.
THE OTHER FELLA'S NEARBY.
CAN YOU CLIMB UP THERE?
NO CHOICE.

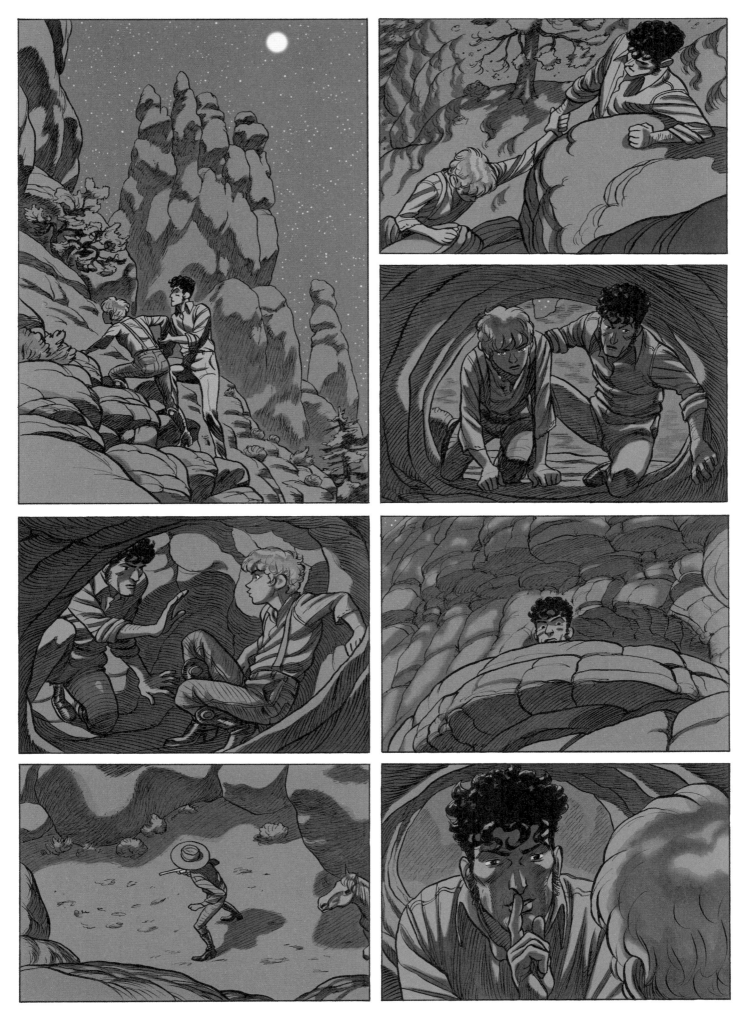

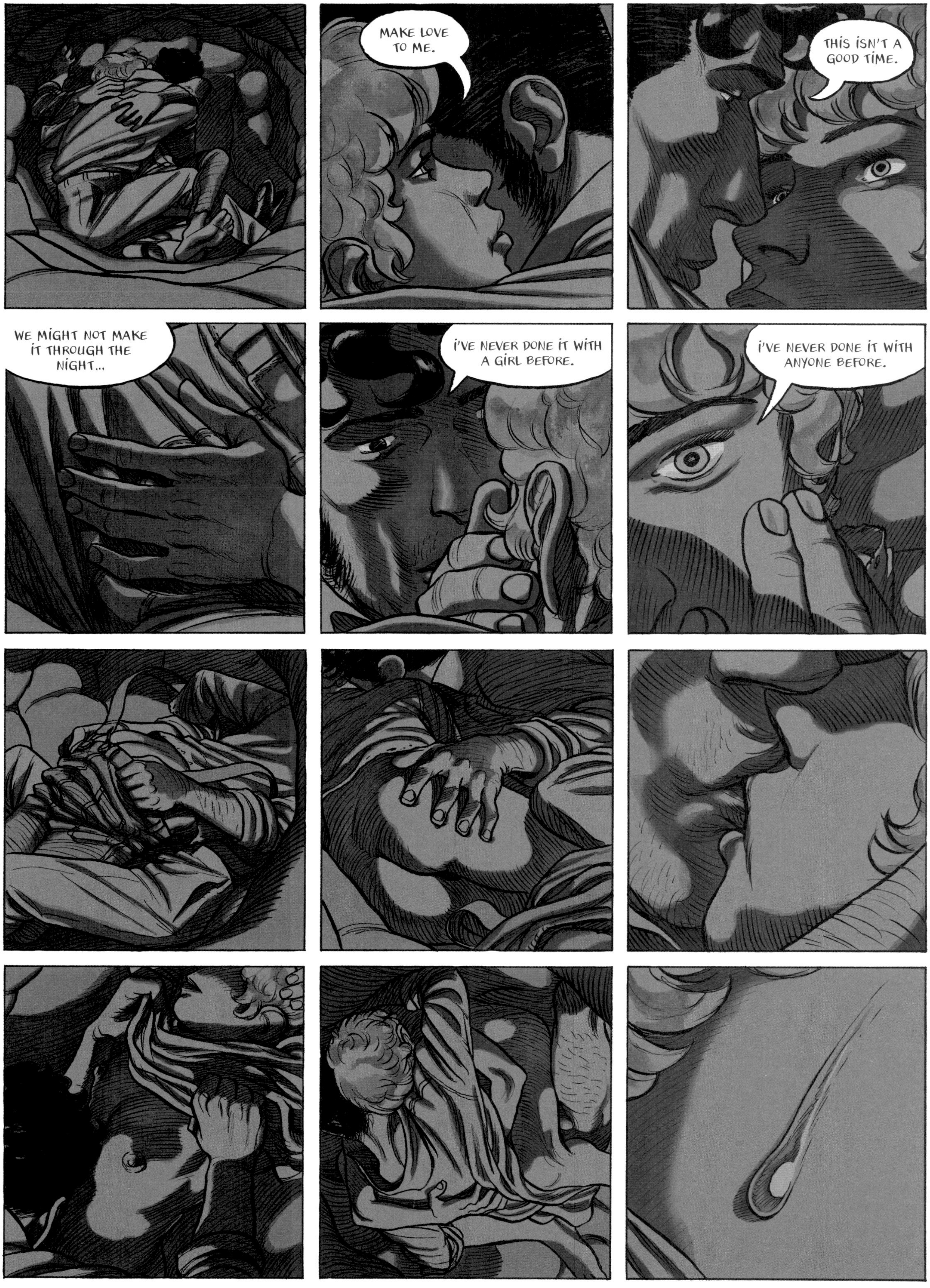
MAKE LOVE TO ME.
THIS ISN'T A GOOD TIME.
WE MIGHT NOT MAKE IT THROUGH THE NIGHT...
I'VE NEVER DONE IT WITH A GIRL BEFORE.
I'VE NEVER DONE IT WITH ANYONE BEFORE.

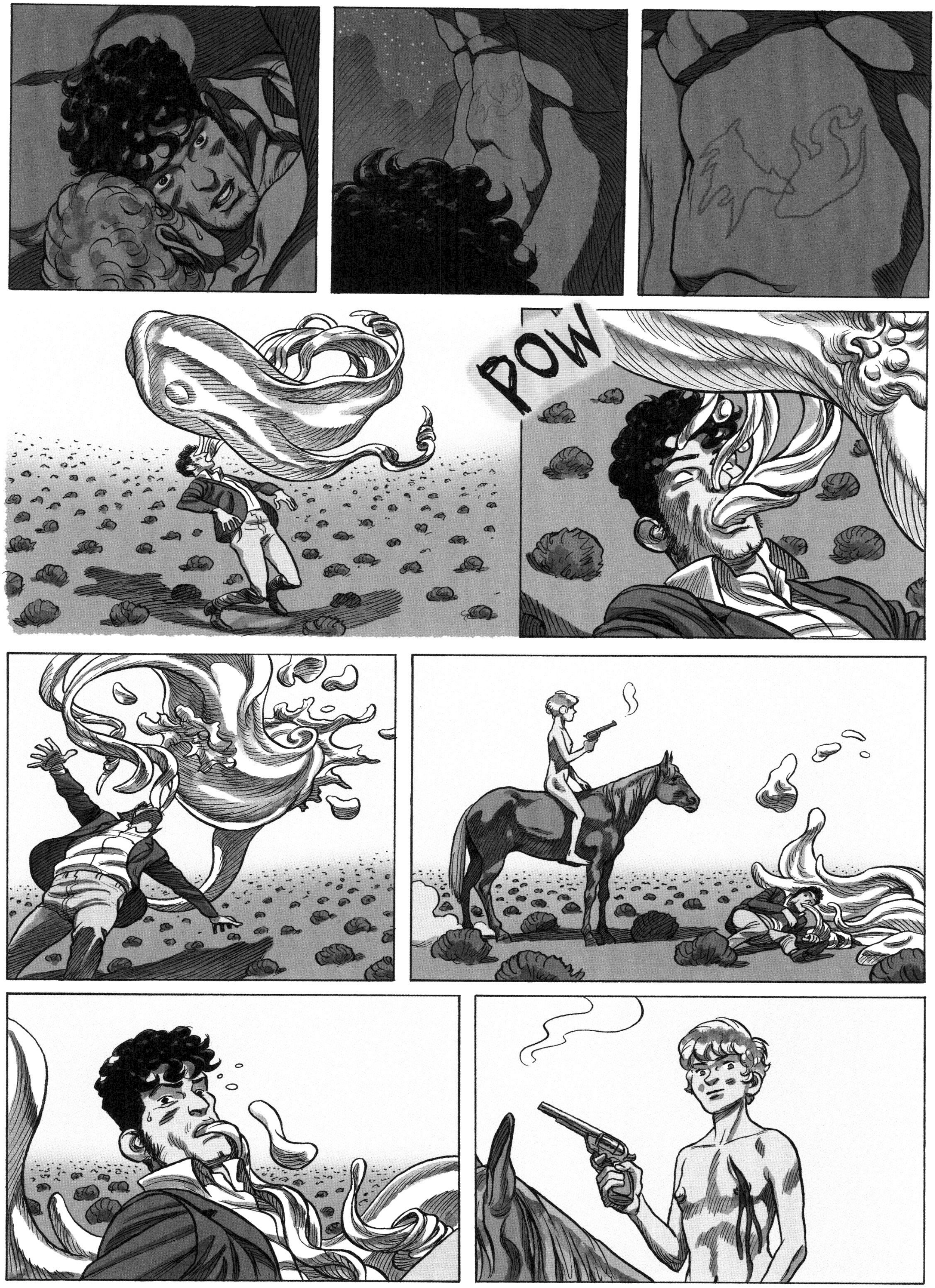
POW

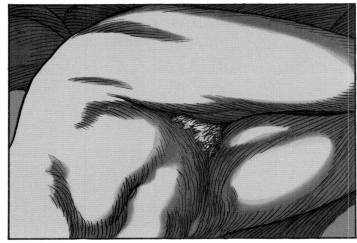

MORE THAN EVER.

ARE WE STILL ALIVE?

MY NAME ISN'T MILTON.

IT'S WEATHER.

IT SUITS YOU.

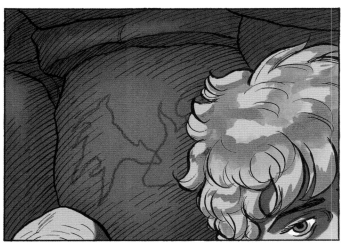

YOU'RE TREMBLING.

AND GETTING HARD.

I'M LOOKING AT YOU, AND GETTING HARD.

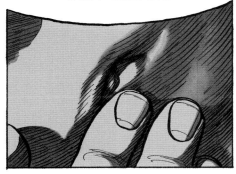

WHAT'S HAPPENING TO ME? GIRLS AREN'T USUALLY MY THING. IT'S... UNCHARTED TERRITORY. A BRAND NEW GEOGRAPHY I'VE NEVER BOTHERED WITH. I DON'T WANT TO ENVISION IT.

YOU'RE NOT LIKE ANYONE ELSE I KNOW.

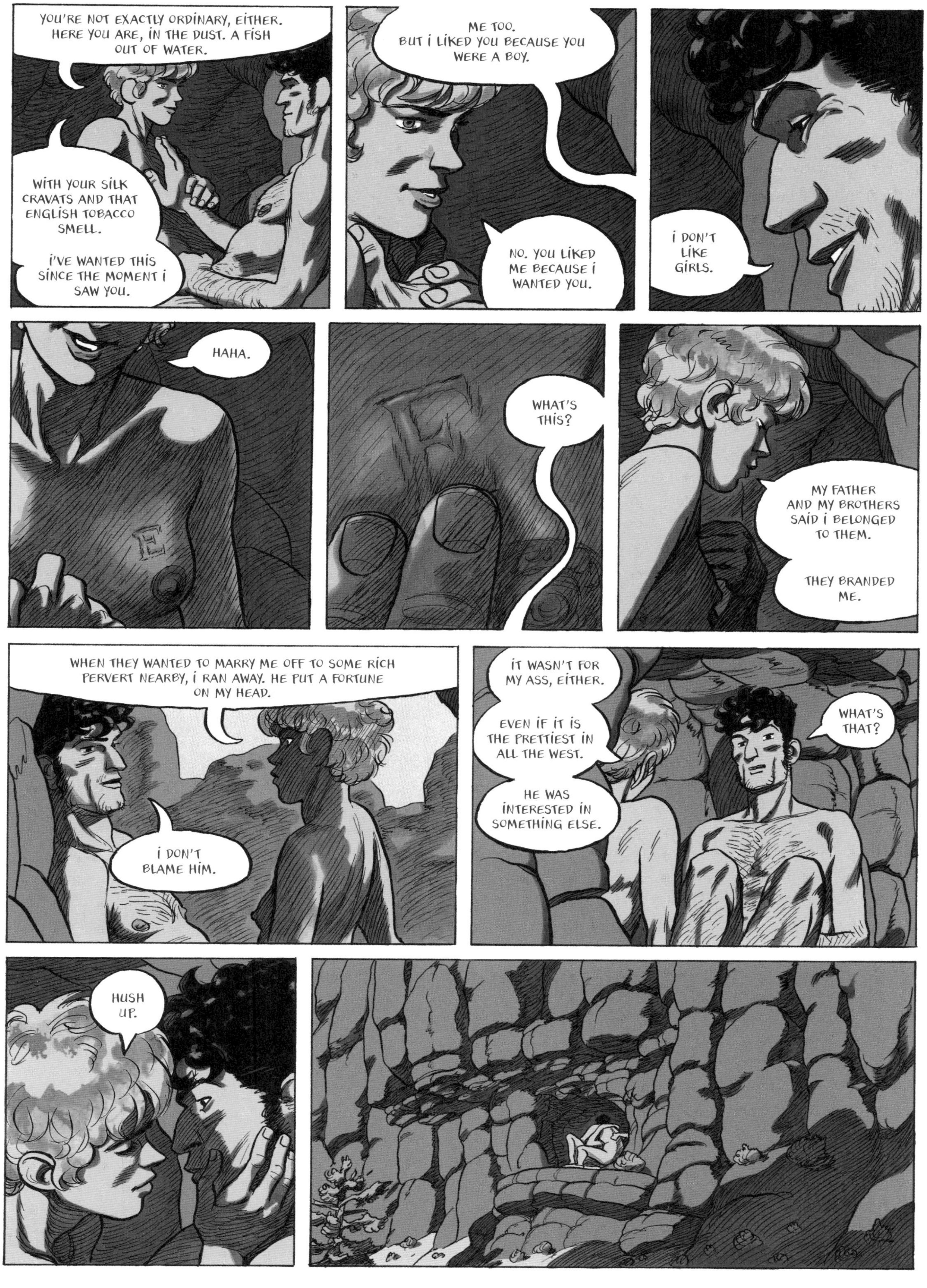
YOU'RE NOT EXACTLY ORDINARY, EITHER. HERE YOU ARE, IN THE DUST. A FISH OUT OF WATER.
WITH YOUR SILK CRAVATS AND THAT ENGLISH TOBACCO SMELL.
I'VE WANTED THIS SINCE THE MOMENT I SAW YOU.
ME TOO. BUT I LIKED YOU BECAUSE YOU WERE A BOY.
NO. YOU LIKED ME BECAUSE I WANTED YOU.
I DON'T LIKE GIRLS.
HAHA.
WHAT'S THIS?
MY FATHER AND MY BROTHERS SAID I BELONGED TO THEM.
THEY BRANDED ME.
WHEN THEY WANTED TO MARRY ME OFF TO SOME RICH PERVERT NEARBY, I RAN AWAY. HE PUT A FORTUNE ON MY HEAD.
I DON'T BLAME HIM.
IT WASN'T FOR MY ASS, EITHER.
EVEN IF IT IS THE PRETTIEST IN ALL THE WEST.
HE WAS INTERESTED IN SOMETHING ELSE.
WHAT'S THAT?
HUSH UP.

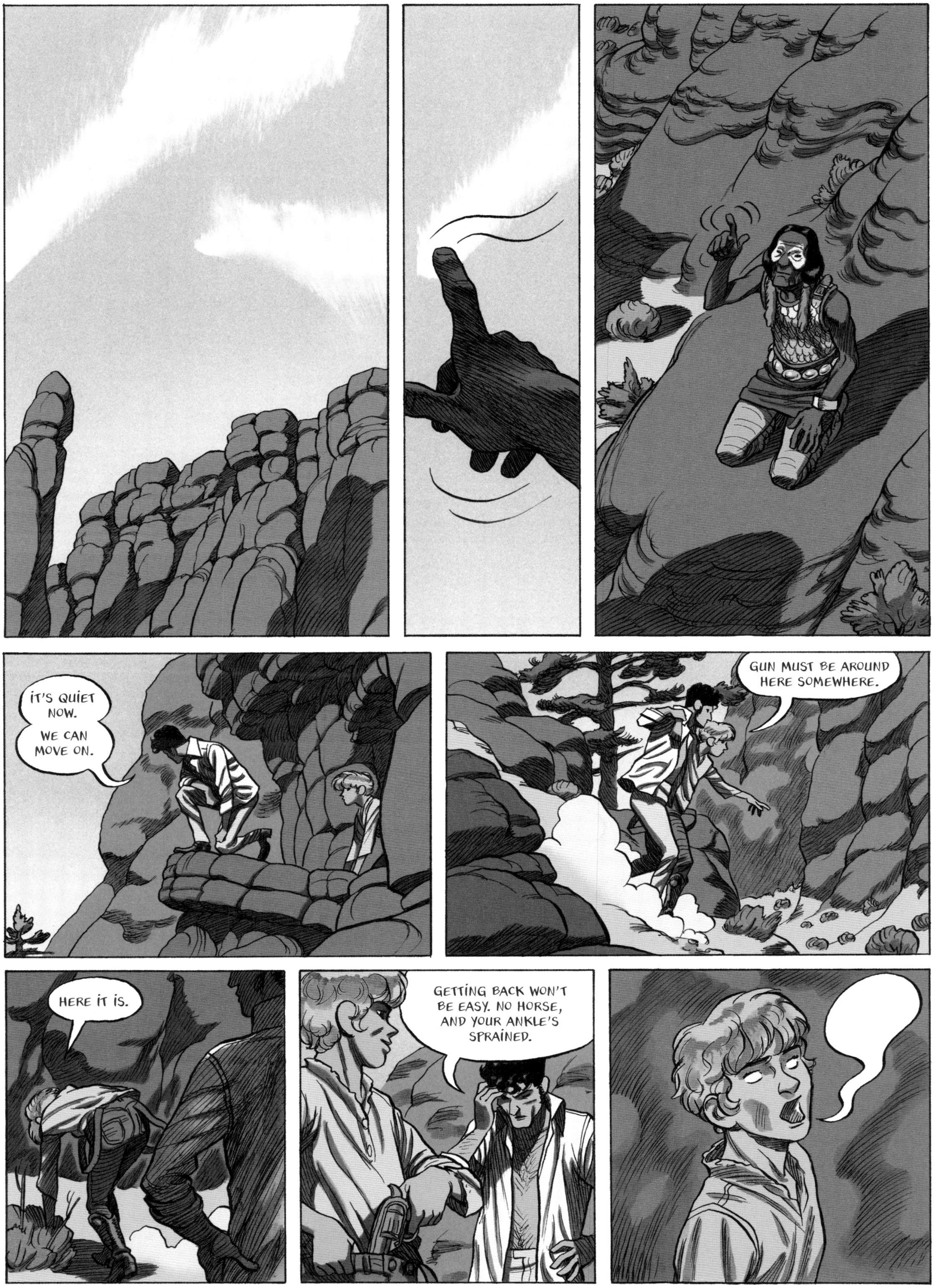
IT'S QUIET NOW.
WE CAN MOVE ON.
GUN MUST BE AROUND HERE SOMEWHERE.
HERE IT IS.
GETTING BACK WON'T BE EASY. NO HORSE, AND YOUR ANKLE'S SPRAINED.

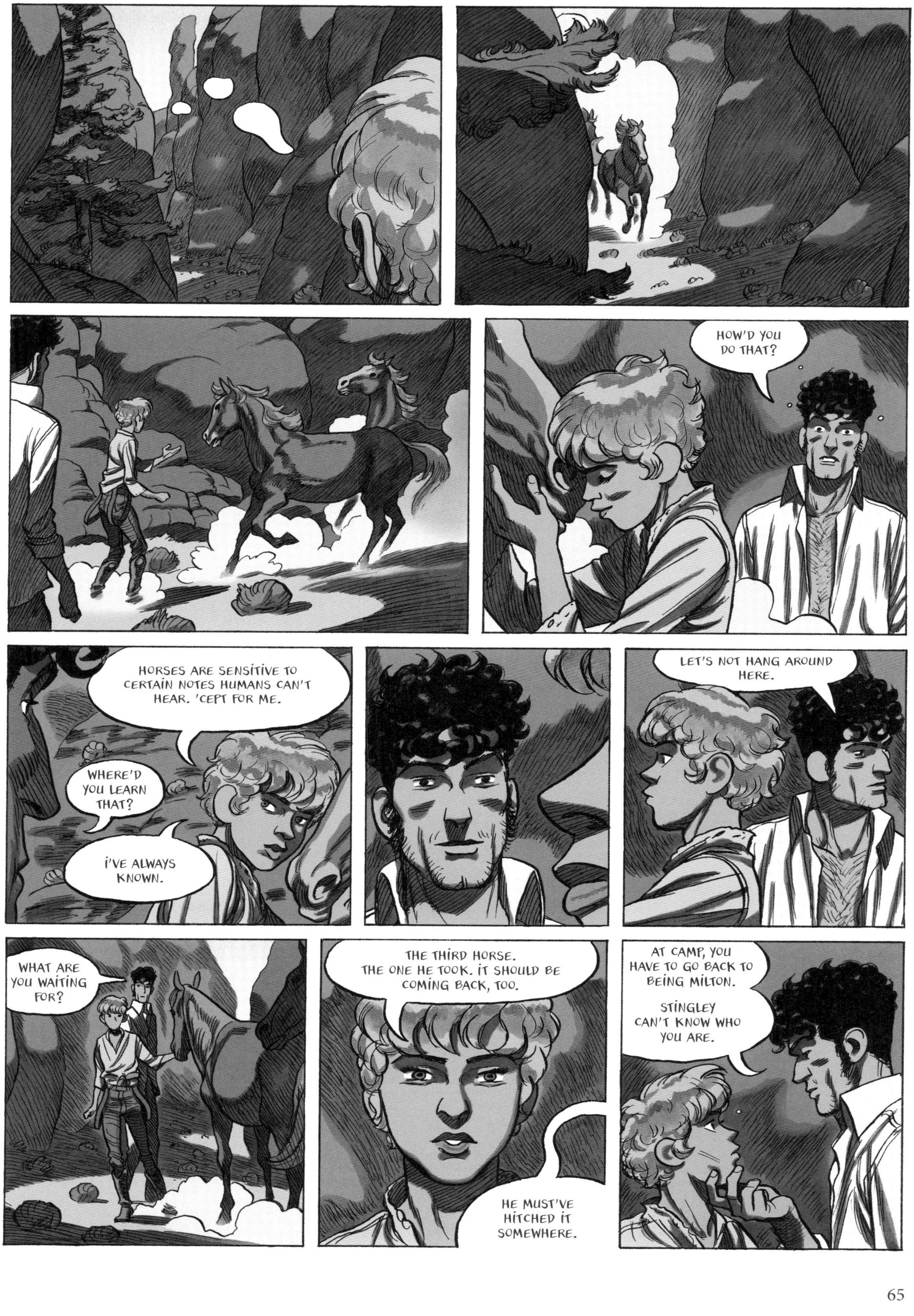
HOW'D YOU DO THAT?
HORSES ARE SENSITIVE TO CERTAIN NOTES HUMANS CAN'T HEAR. 'CEPT FOR ME.
WHERE'D YOU LEARN THAT?
I'VE ALWAYS KNOWN.
LET'S NOT HANG AROUND HERE.
WHAT ARE YOU WAITING FOR?
THE THIRD HORSE. THE ONE HE TOOK. IT SHOULD BE COMING BACK, TOO.
HE MUST'VE HITCHED IT SOMEWHERE.
AT CAMP, YOU HAVE TO GO BACK TO BEING MILTON.
STINGLEY CAN'T KNOW WHO YOU ARE.

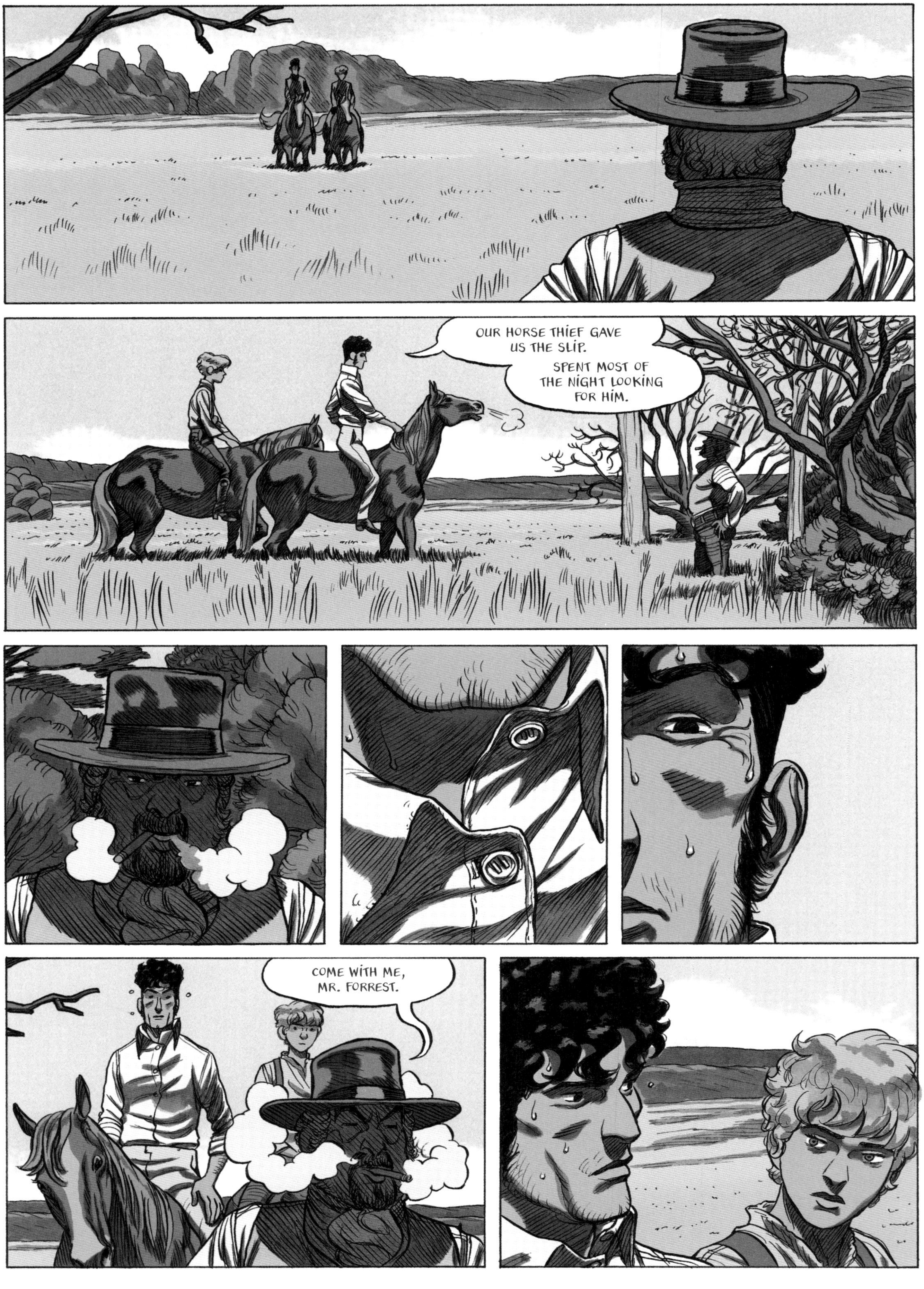
OUR HORSE THIEF GAVE US THE SLIP.
SPENT MOST OF THE NIGHT LOOKING FOR HIM.
COME WITH ME, MR. FORREST.

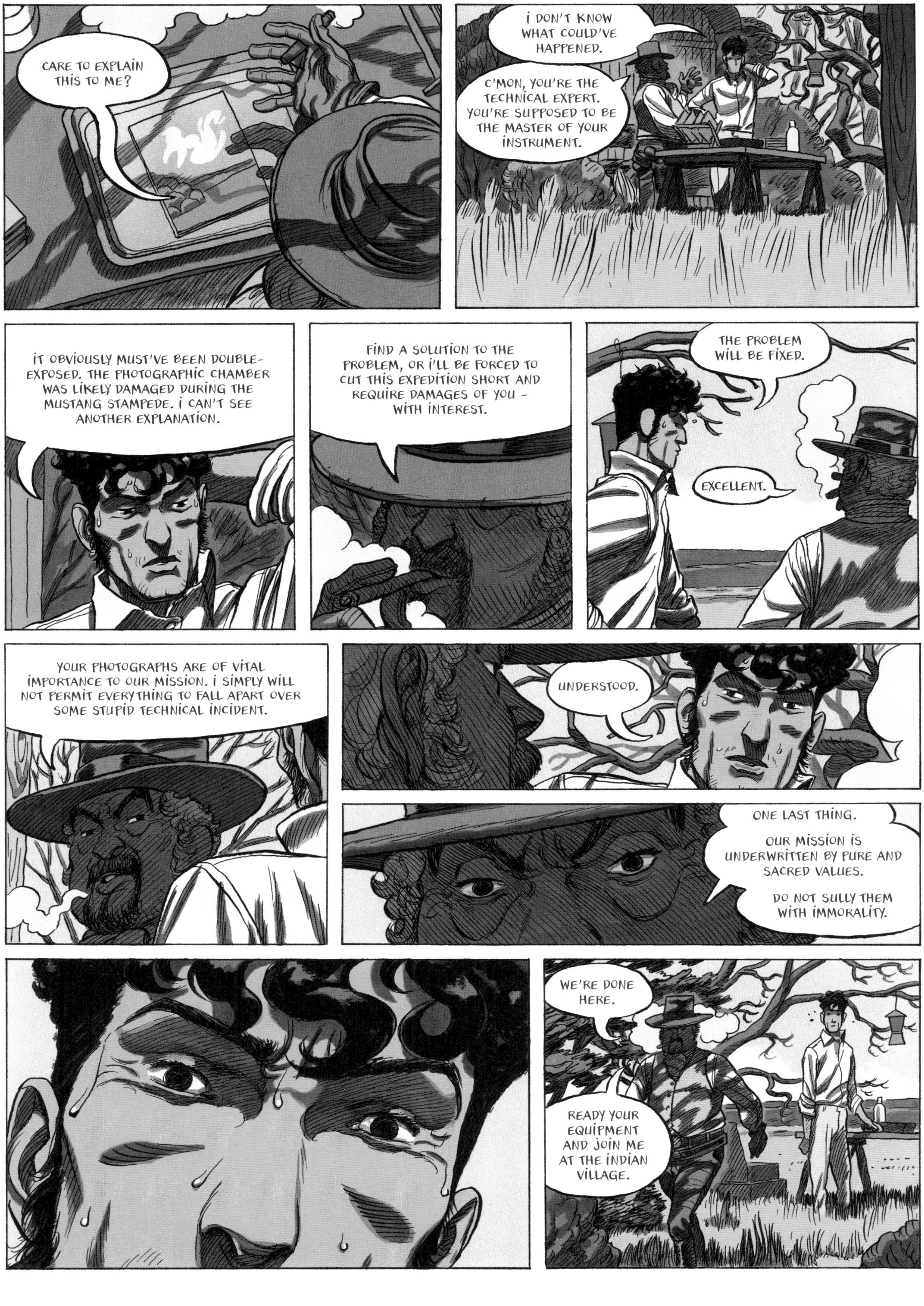
CARE TO EXPLAIN THIS TO ME?
I DON'T KNOW WHAT COULD'VE HAPPENED.
C'MON, YOU'RE THE TECHNICAL EXPERT. YOU'RE SUPPOSED TO BE THE MASTER OF YOUR INSTRUMENT.
IT OBVIOUSLY MUST'VE BEEN DOUBLE-EXPOSED. THE PHOTOGRAPHIC CHAMBER WAS LIKELY DAMAGED DURING THE MUSTANG STAMPEDE. I CAN'T SEE ANOTHER EXPLANATION.
FIND A SOLUTION TO THE PROBLEM, OR I'LL BE FORCED TO CUT THIS EXPEDITION SHORT AND REQUIRE DAMAGES OF YOU – WITH INTEREST.
THE PROBLEM WILL BE FIXED.
EXCELLENT.
YOUR PHOTOGRAPHS ARE OF VITAL IMPORTANCE TO OUR MISSION. I SIMPLY WILL NOT PERMIT EVERYTHING TO FALL APART OVER SOME STUPID TECHNICAL INCIDENT.
UNDERSTOOD.
ONE LAST THING.
OUR MISSION IS UNDERWRITTEN BY PURE AND SACRED VALUES.
DO NOT SULLY THEM WITH IMMORALITY.
WE'RE DONE HERE.
READY YOUR EQUIPMENT AND JOIN ME AT THE INDIAN VILLAGE.

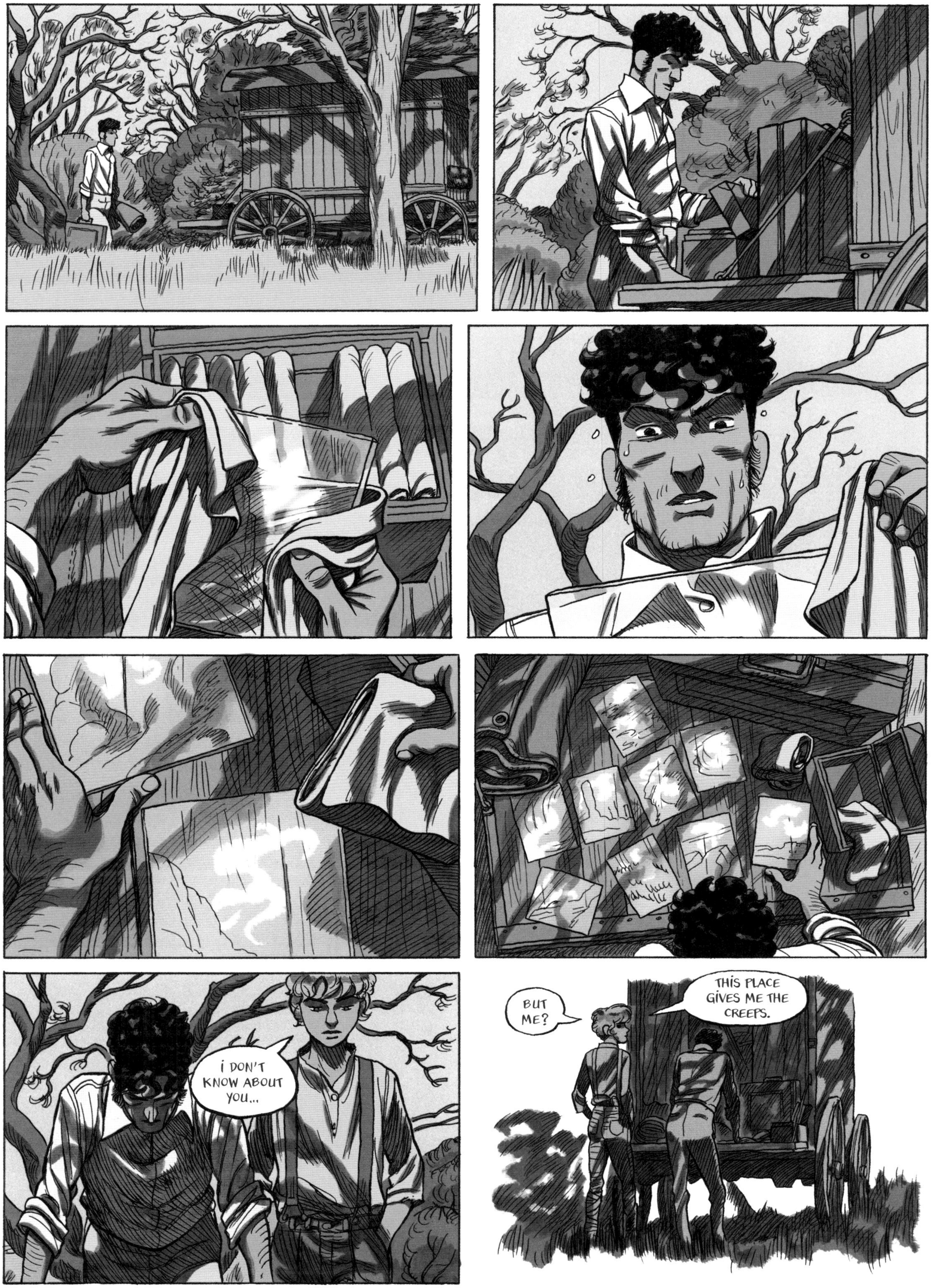
I DON'T KNOW ABOUT YOU...
BUT ME?
THIS PLACE GIVES ME THE CREEPS.

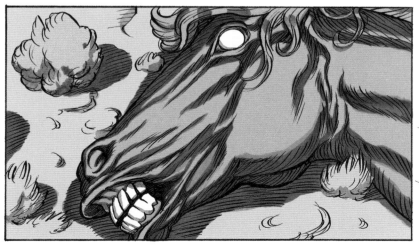

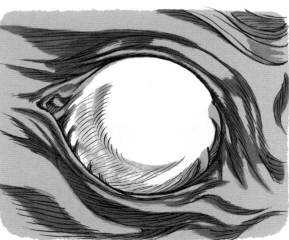

A PERFECT WORLD

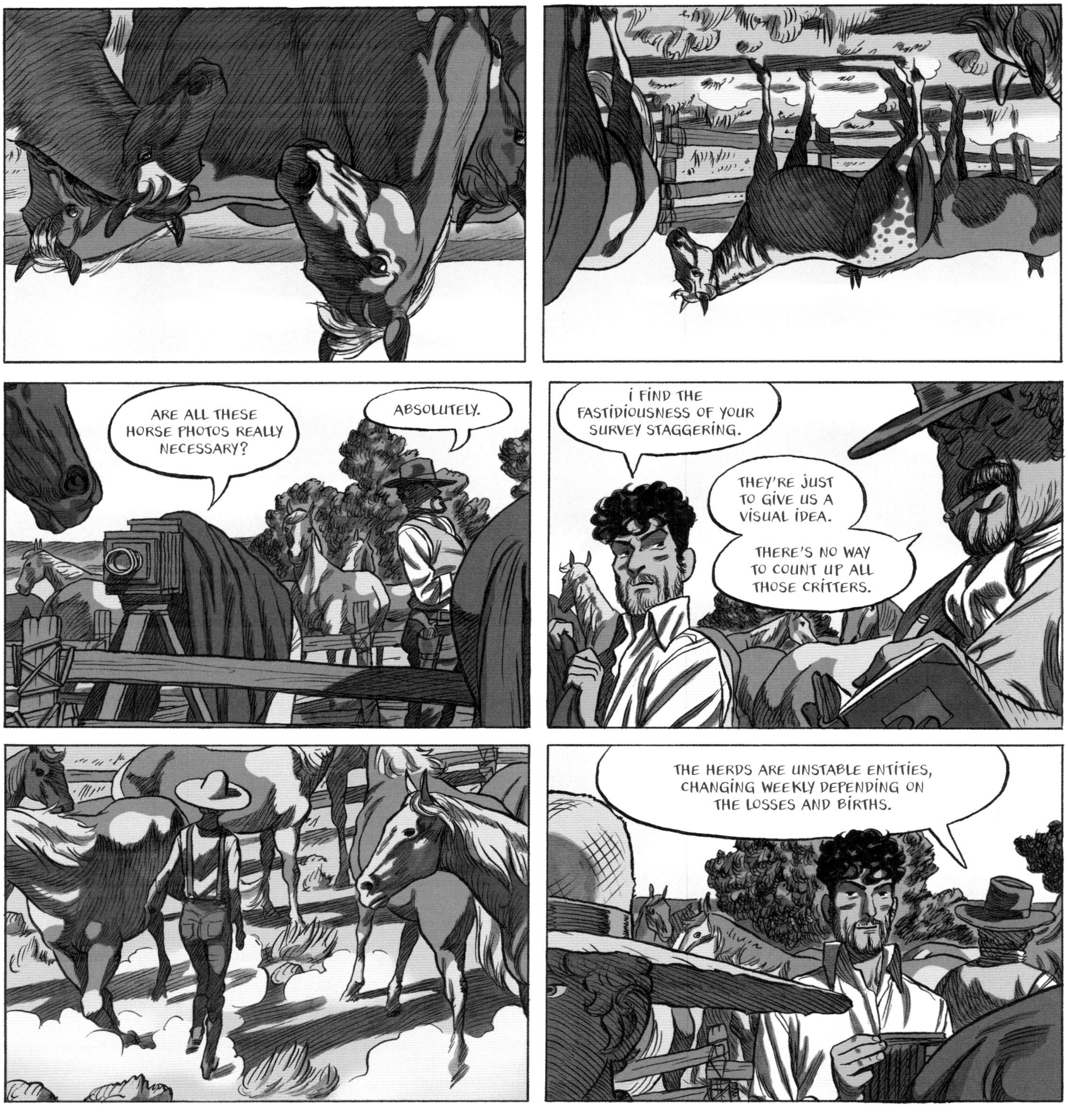
ARE ALL THESE HORSE PHOTOS REALLY NECESSARY?
ABSOLUTELY.
I FIND THE FASTIDIOUSNESS OF YOUR SURVEY STAGGERING.
THEY'RE JUST TO GIVE US A VISUAL IDEA.
THERE'S NO WAY TO COUNT UP ALL THOSE CRITTERS.
THE HERDS ARE UNSTABLE ENTITIES, CHANGING WEEKLY DEPENDING ON THE LOSSES AND BIRTHS.

HORSES ARE THE COMANCHES' RICHES.

THEY'RE WHAT GIVE THE TRIBE POWER. WITHOUT THEIR MOUNTS, THOSE FIERCE WARRIORS WOULD GO RIGHT BACK TO THE PITIFUL STATE THEY WERE IN BEFORE.

BEFORE WHAT?

BEFORE THE SPANIARDS CAME. THEY INTRODUCED HORSES TO THIS CONTINENT. THANKS TO HORSES, THEY CONQUERED AND ENSLAVED THE NATIVES IN THE BLINK OF AN EYE.

SO HOW'D THE COMANCHES GET HOLD OF HORSES?

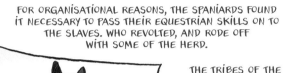

FOR ORGANISATIONAL REASONS, THE SPANIARDS FOUND IT NECESSARY TO PASS THEIR EQUESTRIAN SKILLS ON TO THE SLAVES. WHO REVOLTED, AND RODE OFF WITH SOME OF THE HERD.

THE TRIBES OF THE WEST LEARNED TO TAME THEM, AND THE COMANCHES BECAME THE MOST FORMIDABLE RIDERS.

WHAT A RIDICULOUS STORY. THE SPANIARDS LAND WITH AN ENGINE OF WAR – THE HORSE – AND IT TURNS AGAINST THEM.

LAUGHABLE.

RIGHT YOU ARE.

THERE ARE RADICAL METHODS FOR PREVENTING REVOLTS AND OTHER SETBACKS.

SUCH AS?

POPULATION CONTROL.

REPRODUCTION'S THE MAIN PROBLEM, Y'KNOW.

THERE IS A RADICAL AND DELIGHTFUL WAY OF AVOIDING SUCH SETBACKS.

71

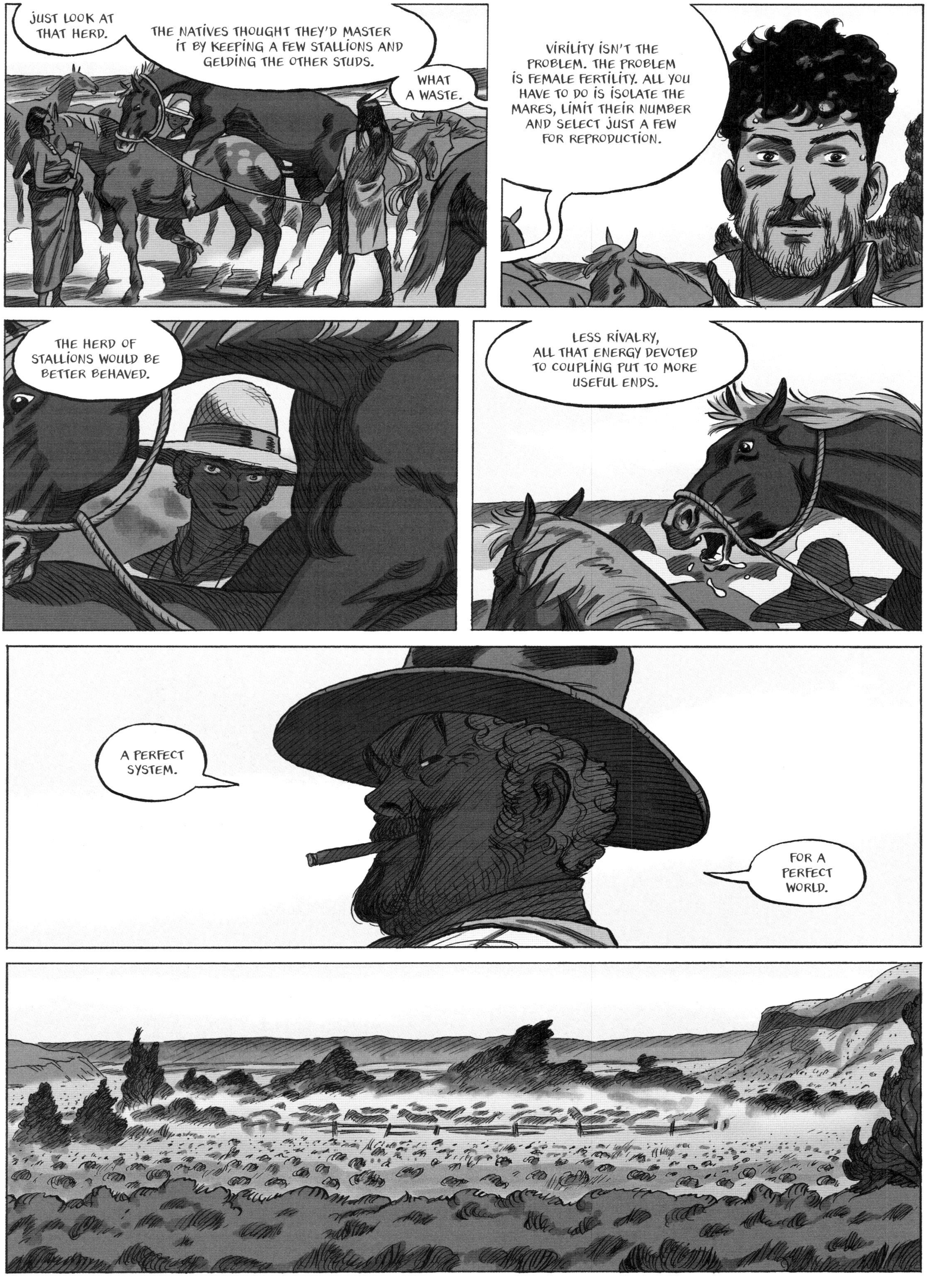
JUST LOOK AT THAT HERD.
THE NATIVES THOUGHT THEY'D MASTER IT BY KEEPING A FEW STALLIONS AND GELDING THE OTHER STUDS.
WHAT A WASTE.
VIRILITY ISN'T THE PROBLEM. THE PROBLEM IS FEMALE FERTILITY. ALL YOU HAVE TO DO IS ISOLATE THE MARES, LIMIT THEIR NUMBER AND SELECT JUST A FEW FOR REPRODUCTION.
THE HERD OF STALLIONS WOULD BE BETTER BEHAVED.
LESS RIVALRY, ALL THAT ENERGY DEVOTED TO COUPLING PUT TO MORE USEFUL ENDS.
A PERFECT SYSTEM.
FOR A PERFECT WORLD.

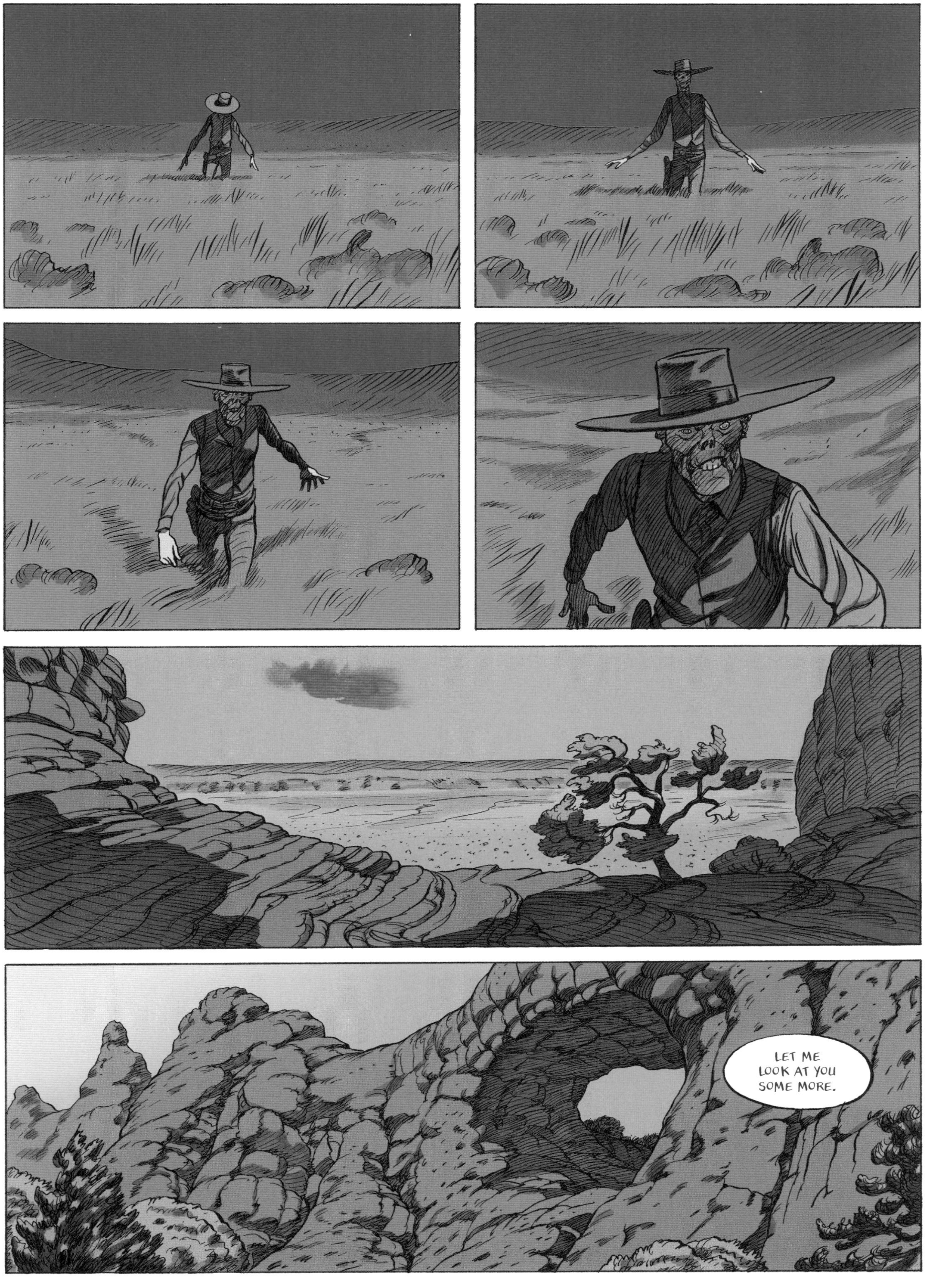
LET ME
LOOK AT YOU
SOME MORE.

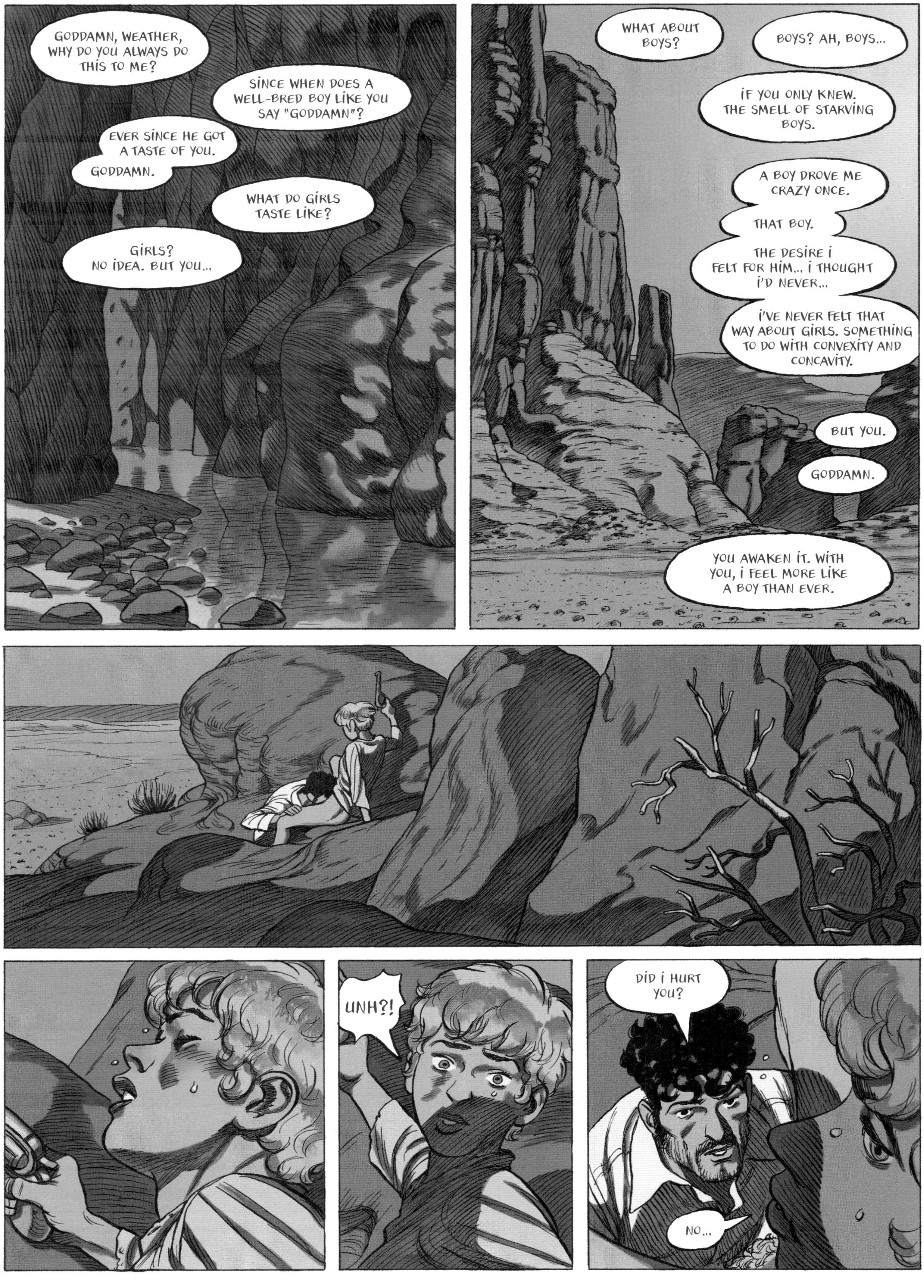
GODDAMN, WEATHER, WHY DO YOU ALWAYS DO THIS TO ME?
SINCE WHEN DOES A WELL-BRED BOY LIKE YOU SAY "GODDAMN"?
EVER SINCE HE GOT A TASTE OF YOU.
GODDAMN.
WHAT DO GIRLS TASTE LIKE?
GIRLS? NO IDEA. BUT YOU...
WHAT ABOUT BOYS?
BOYS? AH, BOYS...
IF YOU ONLY KNEW. THE SMELL OF STARVING BOYS.
A BOY DROVE ME CRAZY ONCE.
THAT BOY.
THE DESIRE I FELT FOR HIM... I THOUGHT I'D NEVER...
I'VE NEVER FELT THAT WAY ABOUT GIRLS. SOMETHING TO DO WITH CONVEXITY AND CONCAVITY.
BUT YOU.
GODDAMN.
YOU AWAKEN IT. WITH YOU, I FEEL MORE LIKE A BOY THAN EVER.
UNH?!
DID I HURT YOU?
NO...

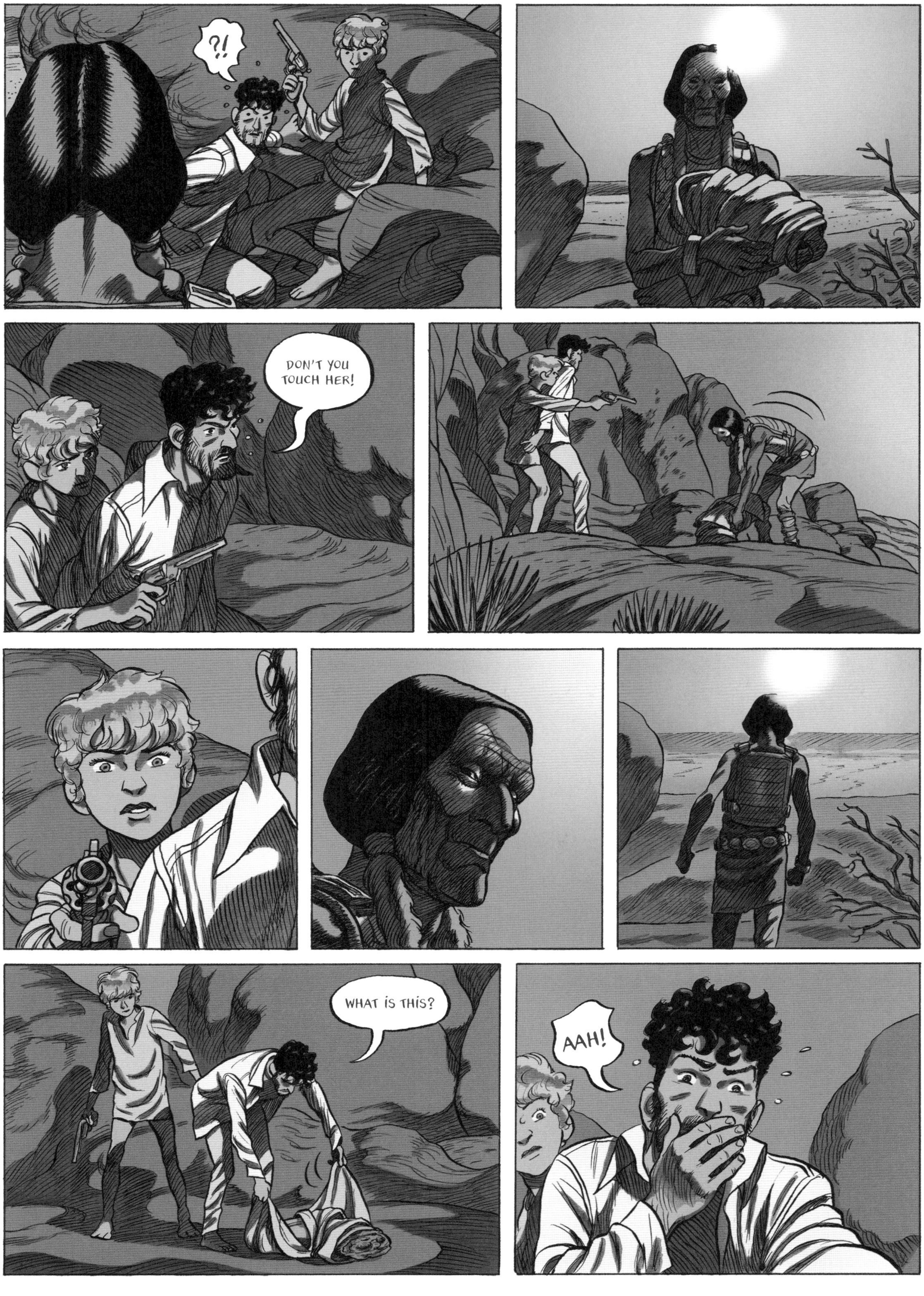
?!
DON'T YOU TOUCH HER!
WHAT IS THIS?
AAH!

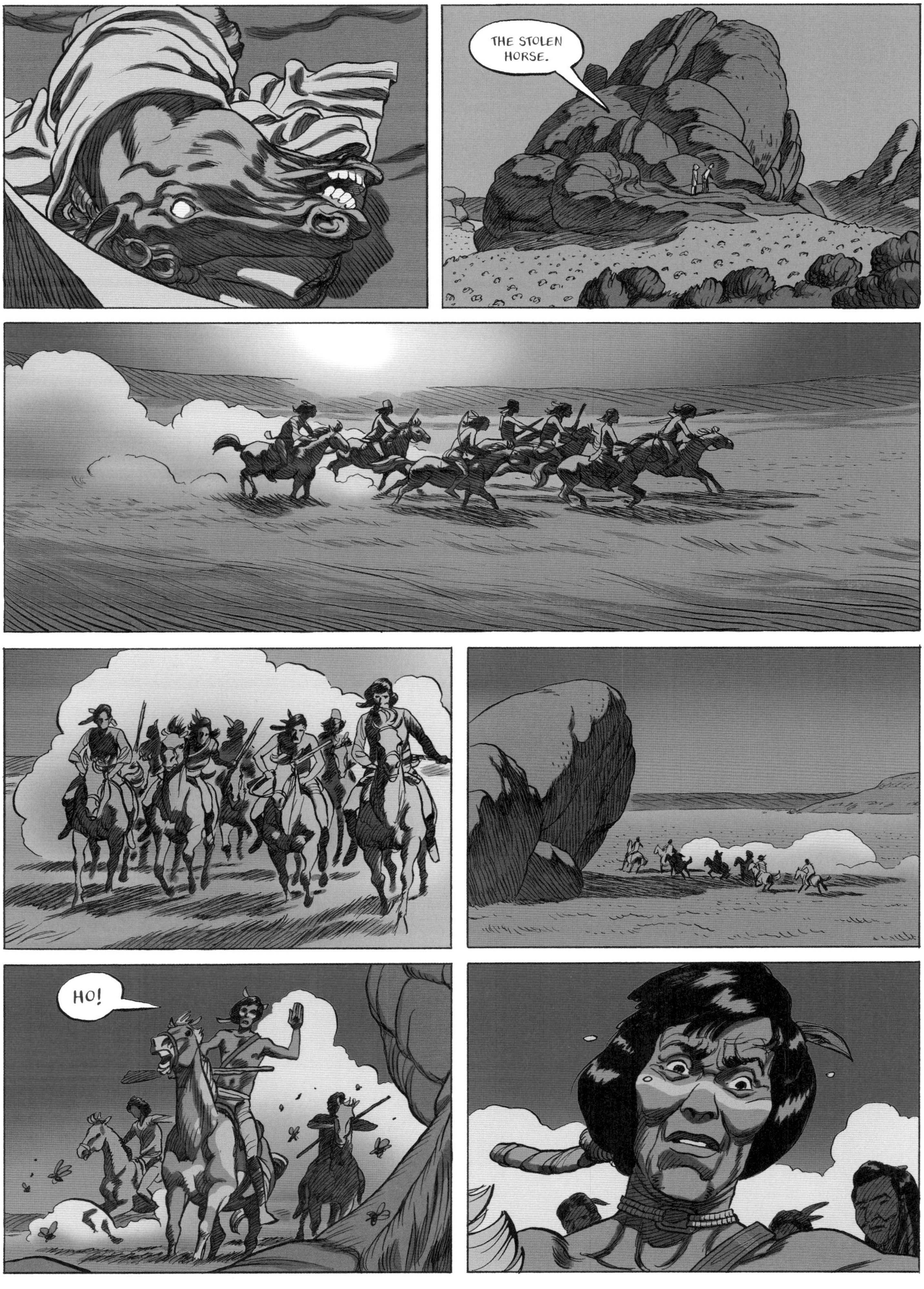
THE STOLEN HORSE.
HO!

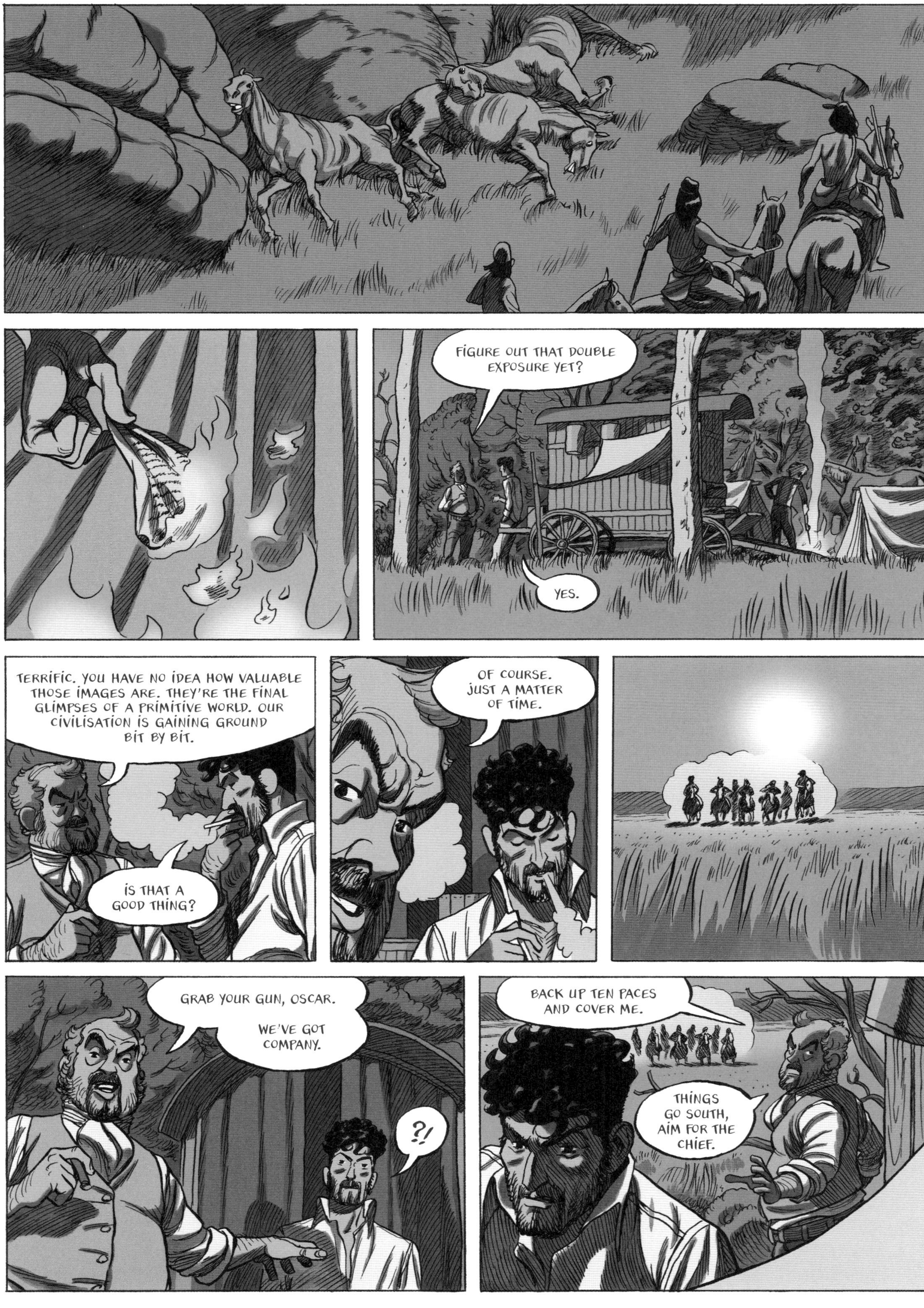
FIGURE OUT THAT DOUBLE EXPOSURE YET?
YES.
TERRIFIC. YOU HAVE NO IDEA HOW VALUABLE THOSE IMAGES ARE. THEY'RE THE FINAL GLIMPSES OF A PRIMITIVE WORLD. OUR CIVILISATION IS GAINING GROUND BIT BY BIT.
IS THAT A GOOD THING?
OF COURSE. JUST A MATTER OF TIME.
GRAB YOUR GUN, OSCAR.
WE'VE GOT COMPANY.
?!
BACK UP TEN PACES AND COVER ME.
THINGS GO SOUTH, AIM FOR THE CHIEF.

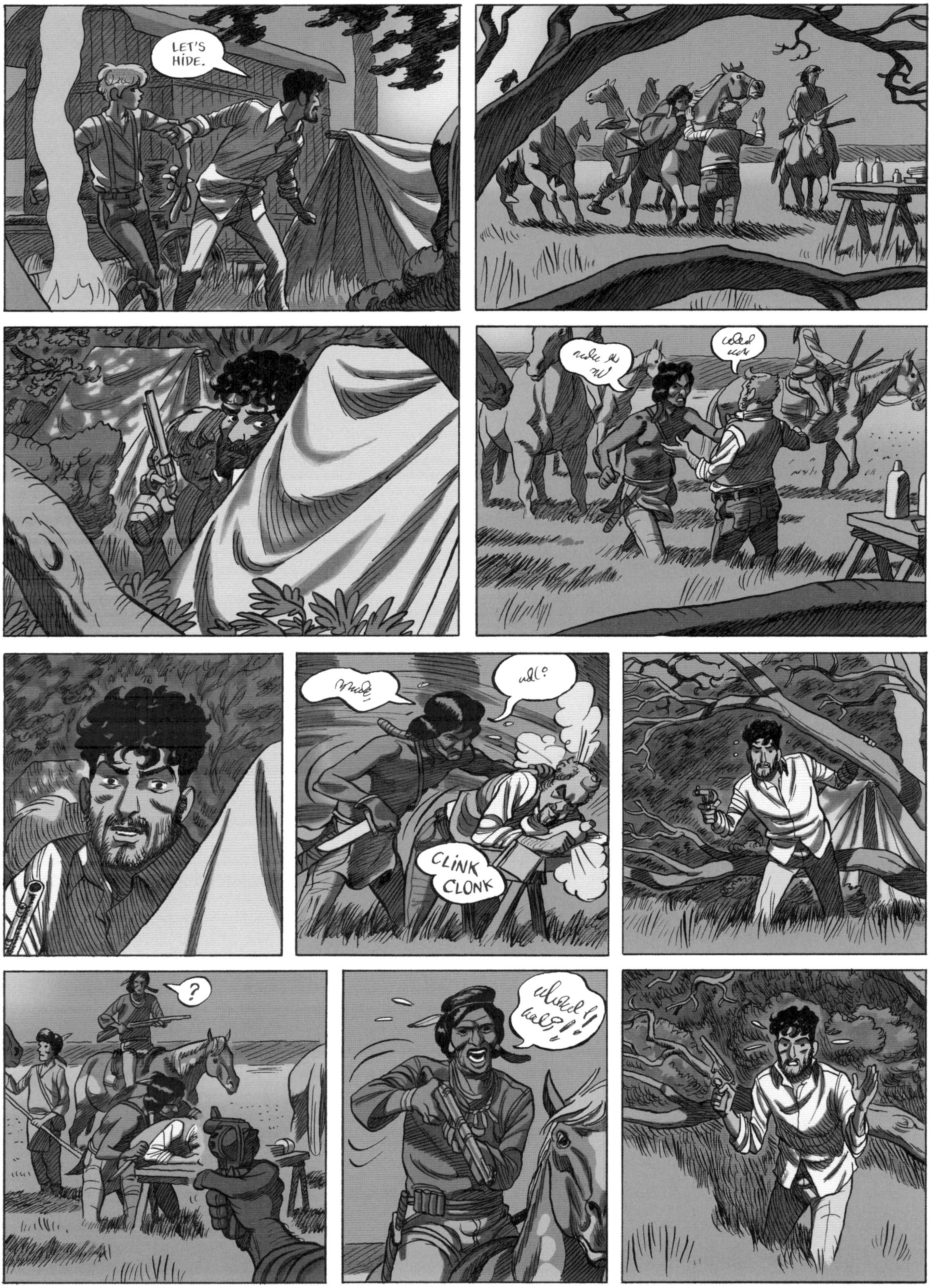
LET'S HIDE.
CLINK
CLONK
?

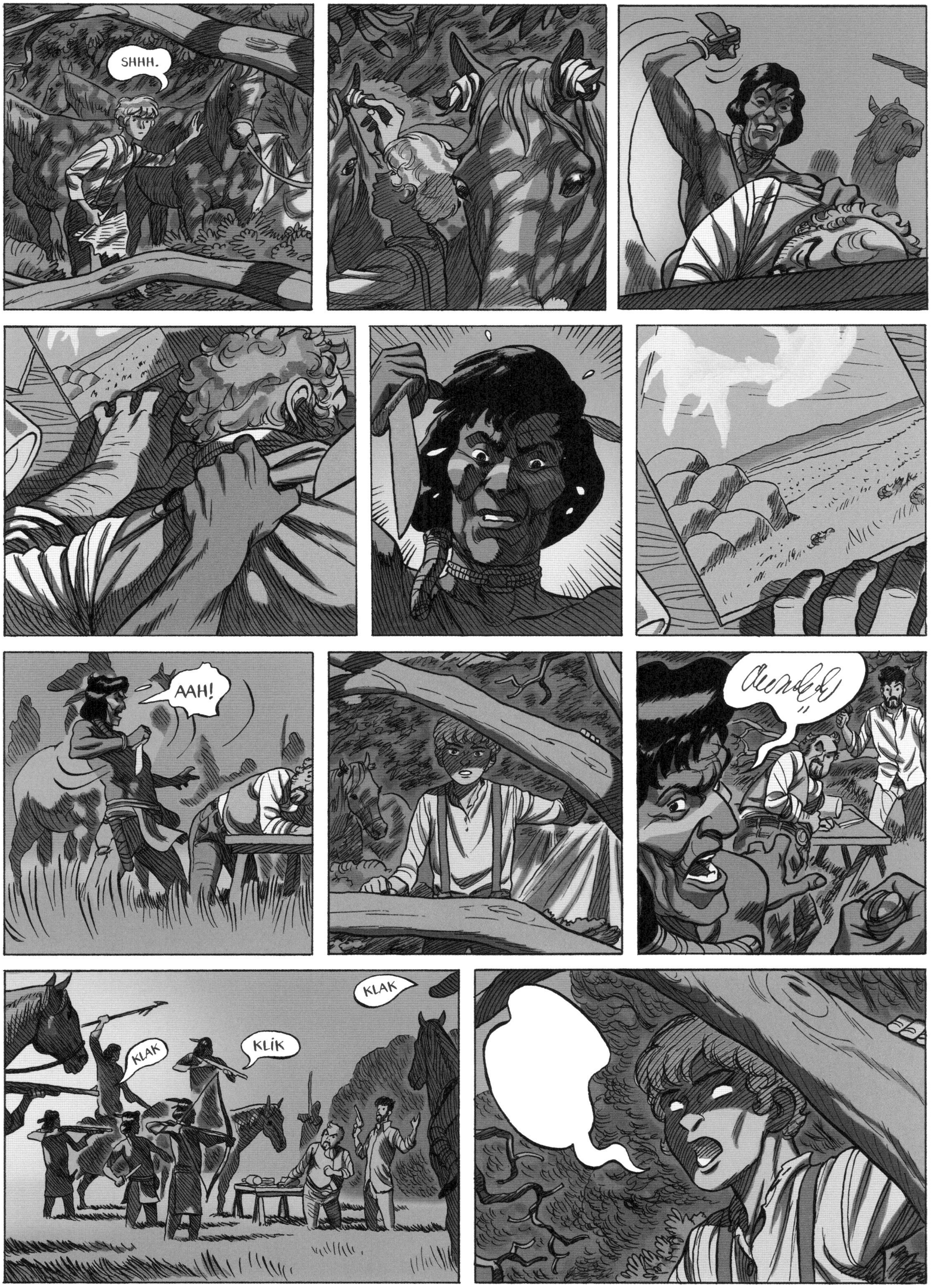
SHHH.
AAH!
KLAK
KLIK
KLAK

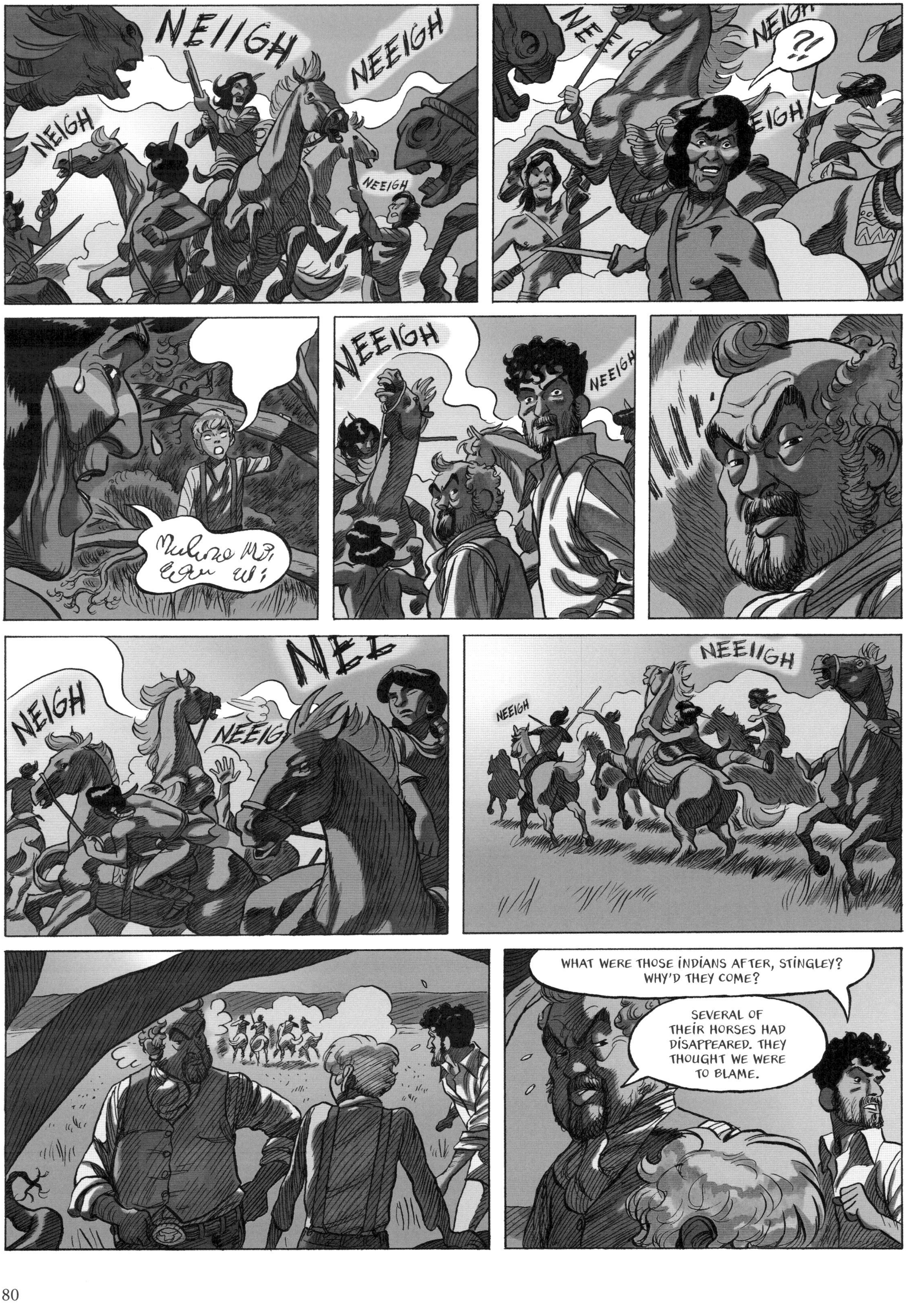
NEIIGH
NEEIGH
NEIGH
NEEIGH
?!
NEEIGH
NEEIGH
NEIGH
NEEIIGH
NEEIGH
WHAT WERE THOSE INDIANS AFTER, STINGLEY? WHY'D THEY COME?
SEVERAL OF THEIR HORSES HAD DISAPPEARED. THEY THOUGHT WE WERE TO BLAME.

THAT'S STUPID. WHERE WOULD WE EVEN HIDE THEIR NAGS?

THEY WEREN'T ACCUSING US OF THEFT, BUT OF WITCHCRAFT.

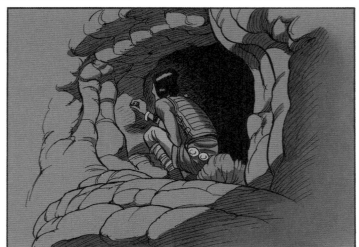

THEY FOUND THE HORSES, BUT THEY WERE COMPLETELY DRAINED OF BLOOD.

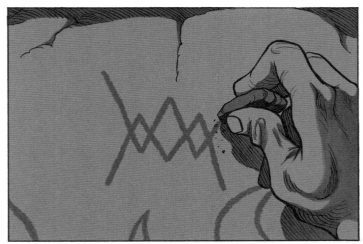

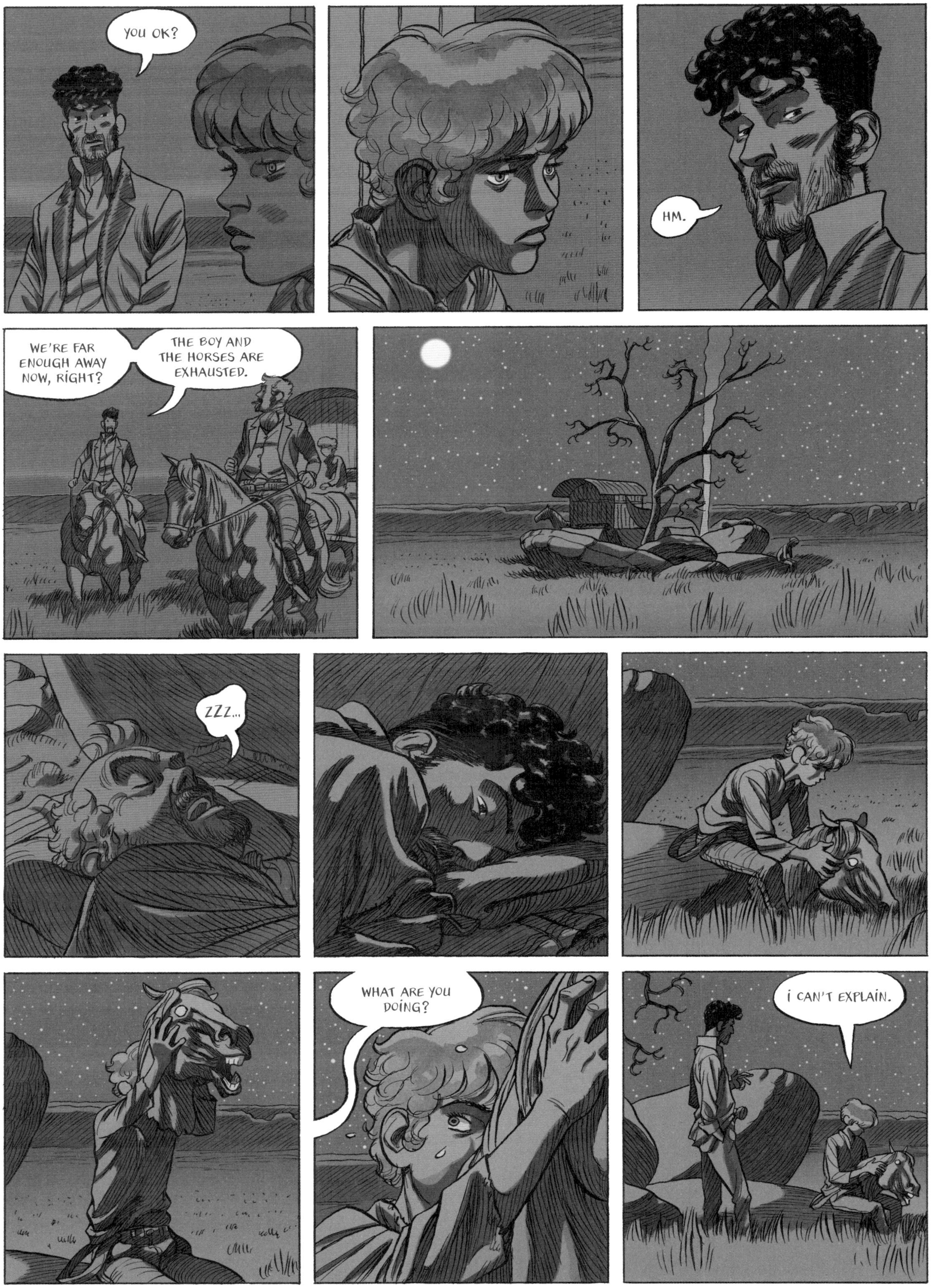
YOU OK?
HM.
WE'RE FAR ENOUGH AWAY NOW, RIGHT?
THE BOY AND THE HORSES ARE EXHAUSTED.
ZZZ...
WHAT ARE YOU DOING?
I CAN'T EXPLAIN.

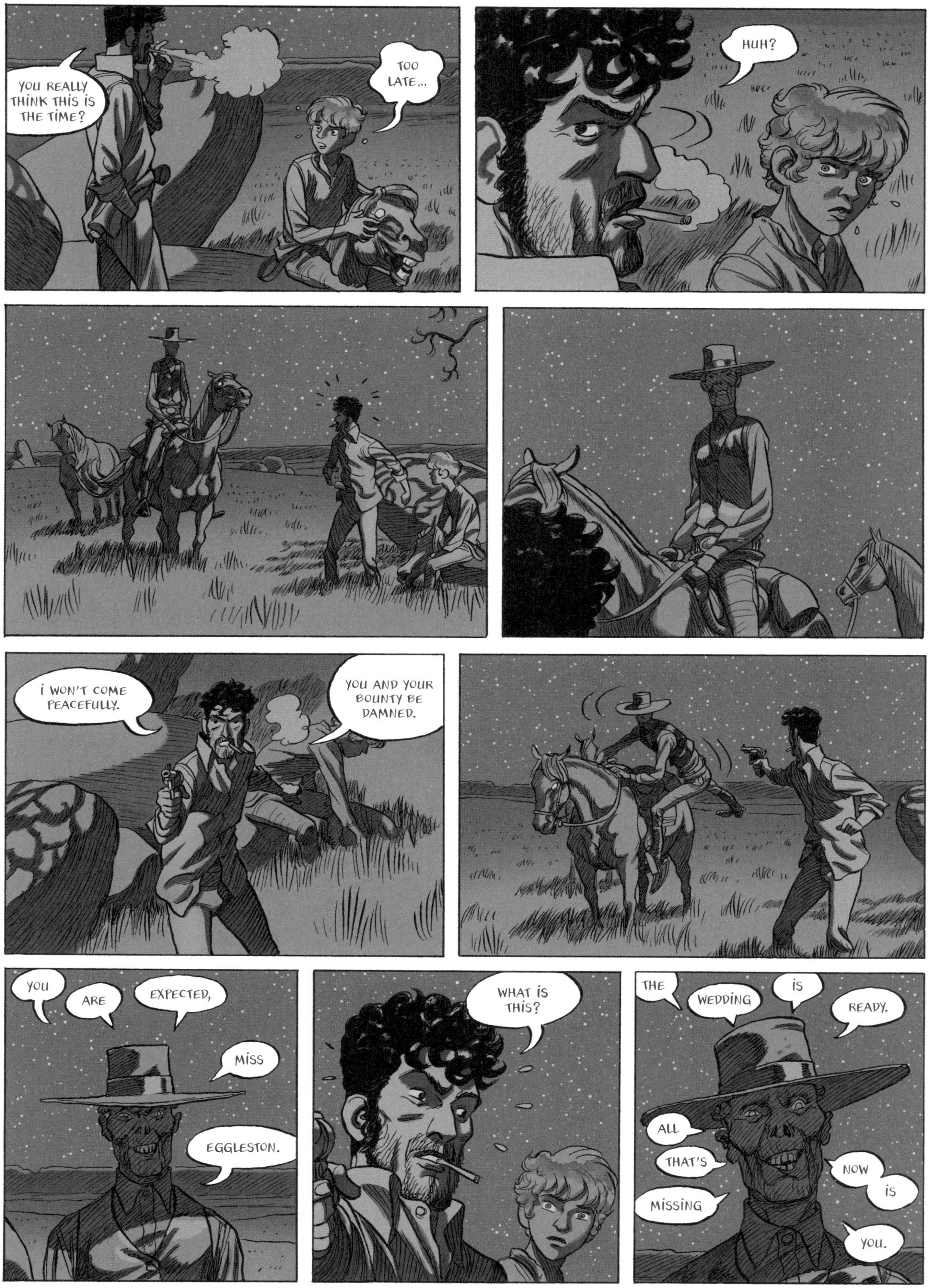
YOU REALLY THINK THIS IS THE TIME?
TOO LATE...
HUH?
I WON'T COME PEACEFULLY.
YOU AND YOUR BOUNTY BE DAMNED.
YOU
ARE
EXPECTED,
MISS
EGGLESTON.
WHAT IS THIS?
THE
WEDDING
IS
READY.
ALL
THAT'S
MISSING
NOW
IS
YOU.

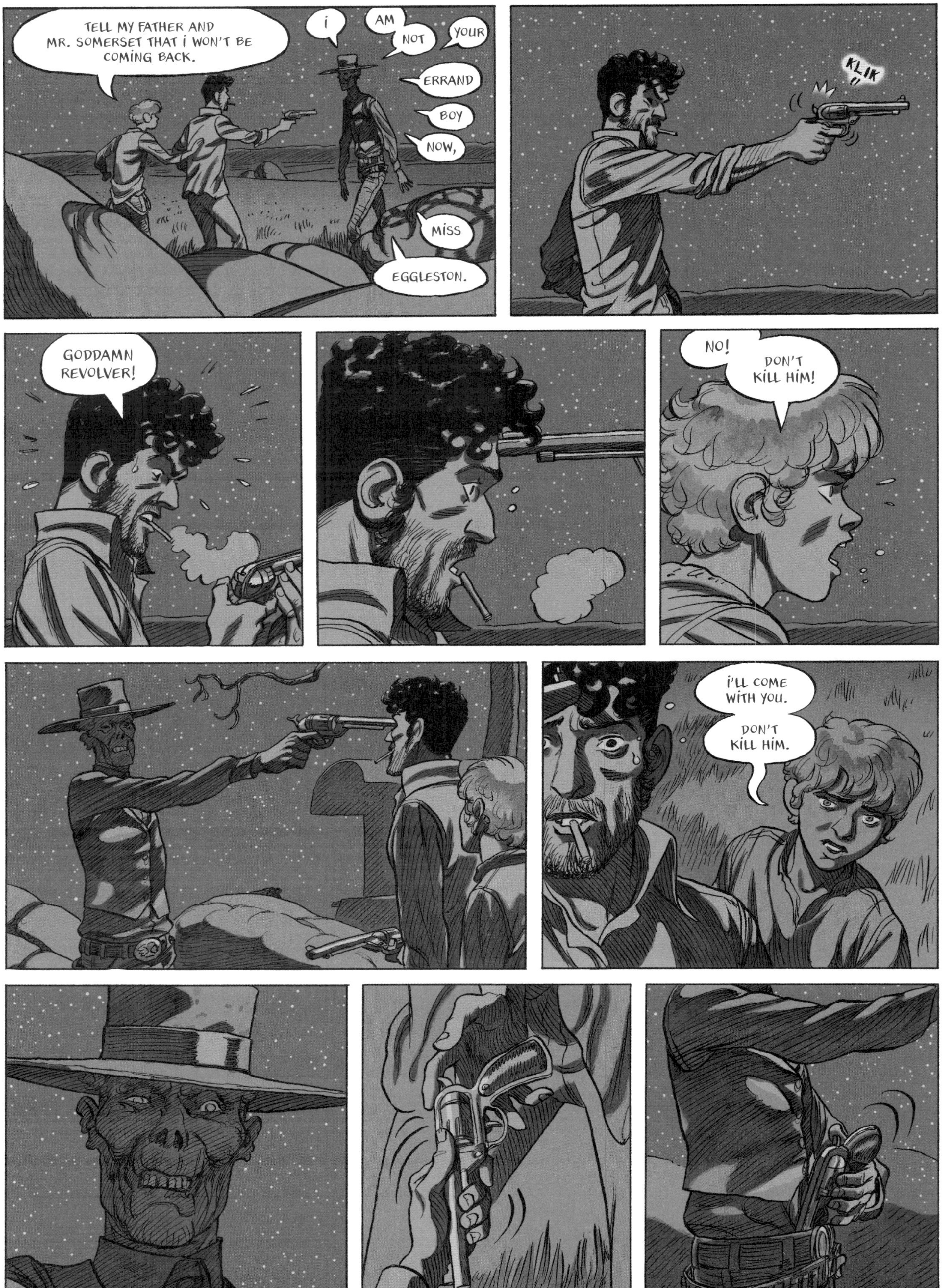
TELL MY FATHER AND MR. SOMERSET THAT i WON'T BE COMING BACK.
i
AM
NOT
YOUR
ERRAND
BOY
NOW,
MISS
EGGLESTON.
KLIK
GODDAMN REVOLVER!
NO!
DON'T KiLL HiM!
i'LL COME WiTH YOU.
DON'T KiLL HiM.

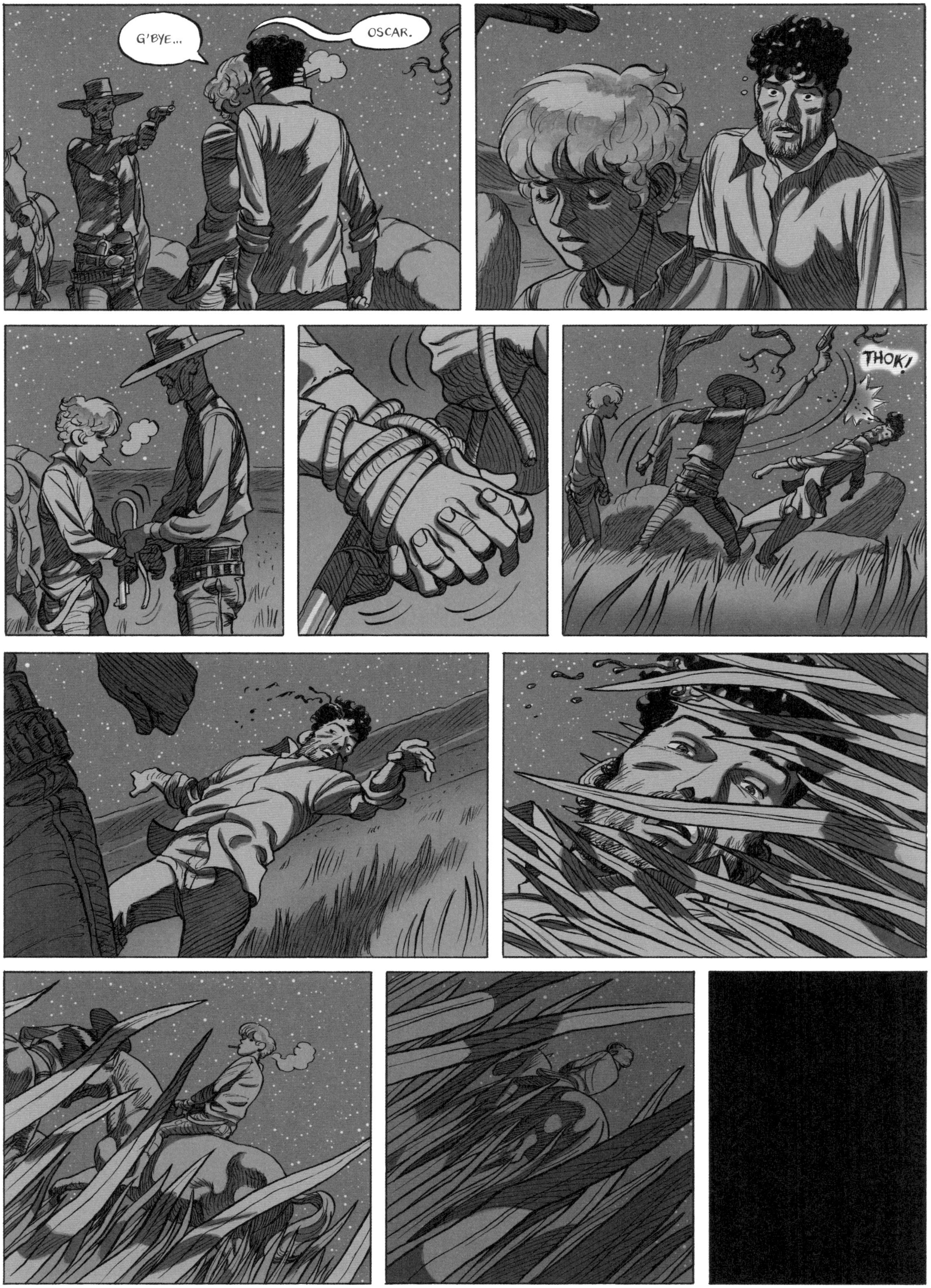
G'BYE...
OSCAR.
THOK!

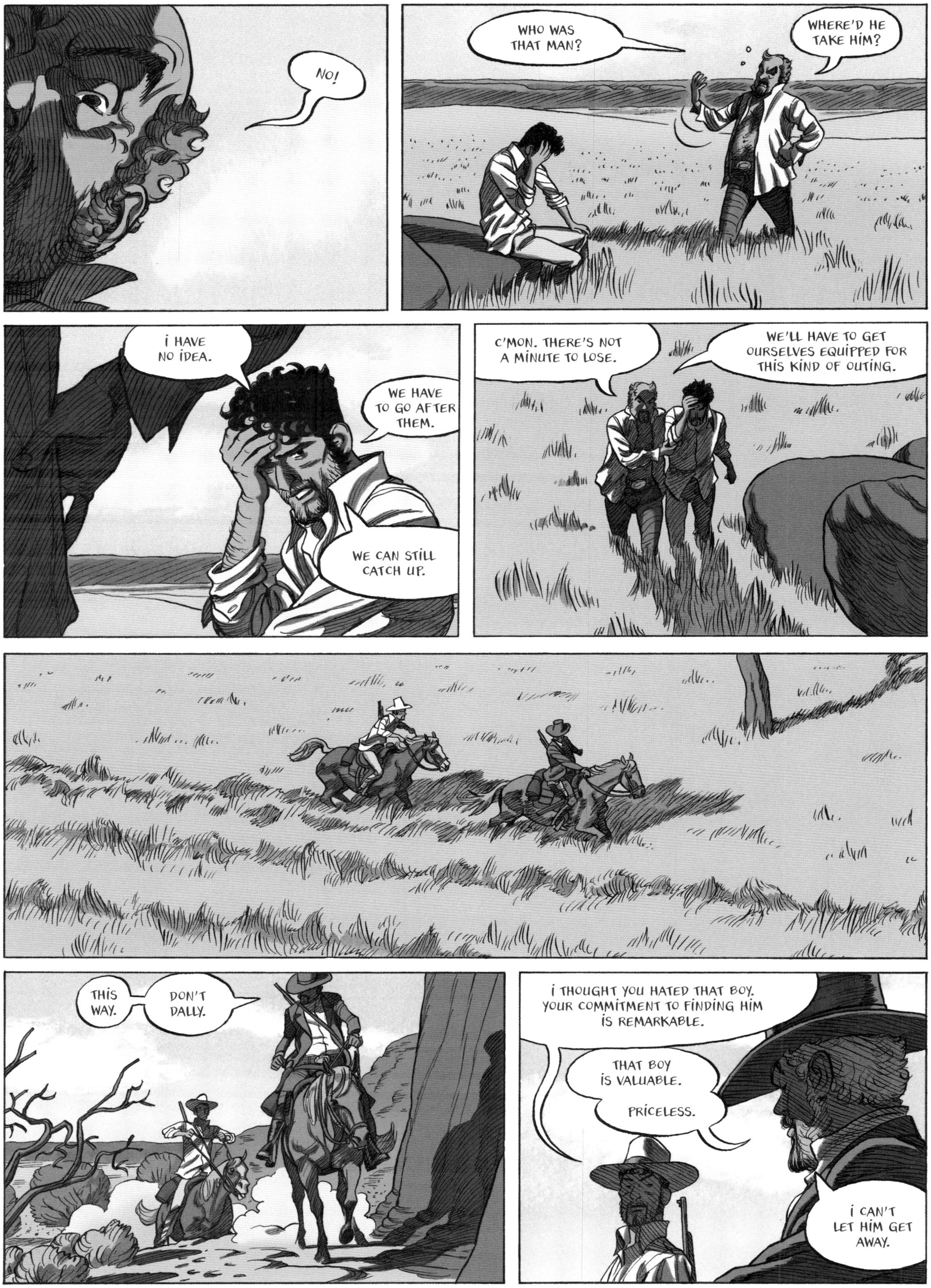
NO!
WHO WAS THAT MAN?
WHERE'D HE TAKE HIM?
I HAVE NO IDEA.
WE HAVE TO GO AFTER THEM.
WE CAN STILL CATCH UP.
C'MON. THERE'S NOT A MINUTE TO LOSE.
WE'LL HAVE TO GET OURSELVES EQUIPPED FOR THIS KIND OF OUTING.
THIS WAY.
DON'T DALLY.
I THOUGHT YOU HATED THAT BOY. YOUR COMMITMENT TO FINDING HIM IS REMARKABLE.
THAT BOY IS VALUABLE.
PRICELESS.
I CAN'T LET HIM GET AWAY.

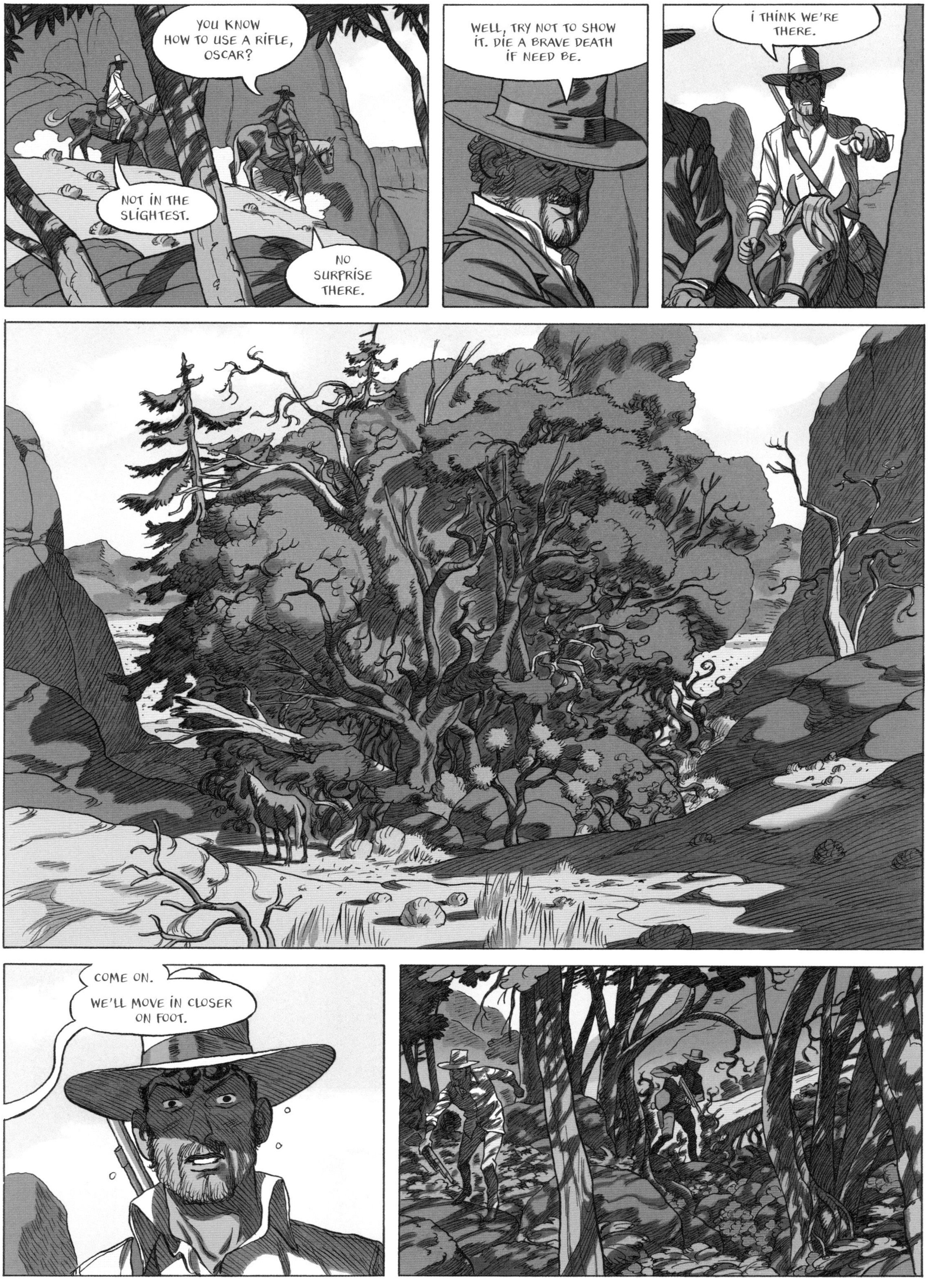
YOU KNOW HOW TO USE A RIFLE, OSCAR?
NOT IN THE SLIGHTEST.
NO SURPRISE THERE.
WELL, TRY NOT TO SHOW IT. DIE A BRAVE DEATH IF NEED BE.
I THINK WE'RE THERE.
COME ON.
WE'LL MOVE IN CLOSER ON FOOT.

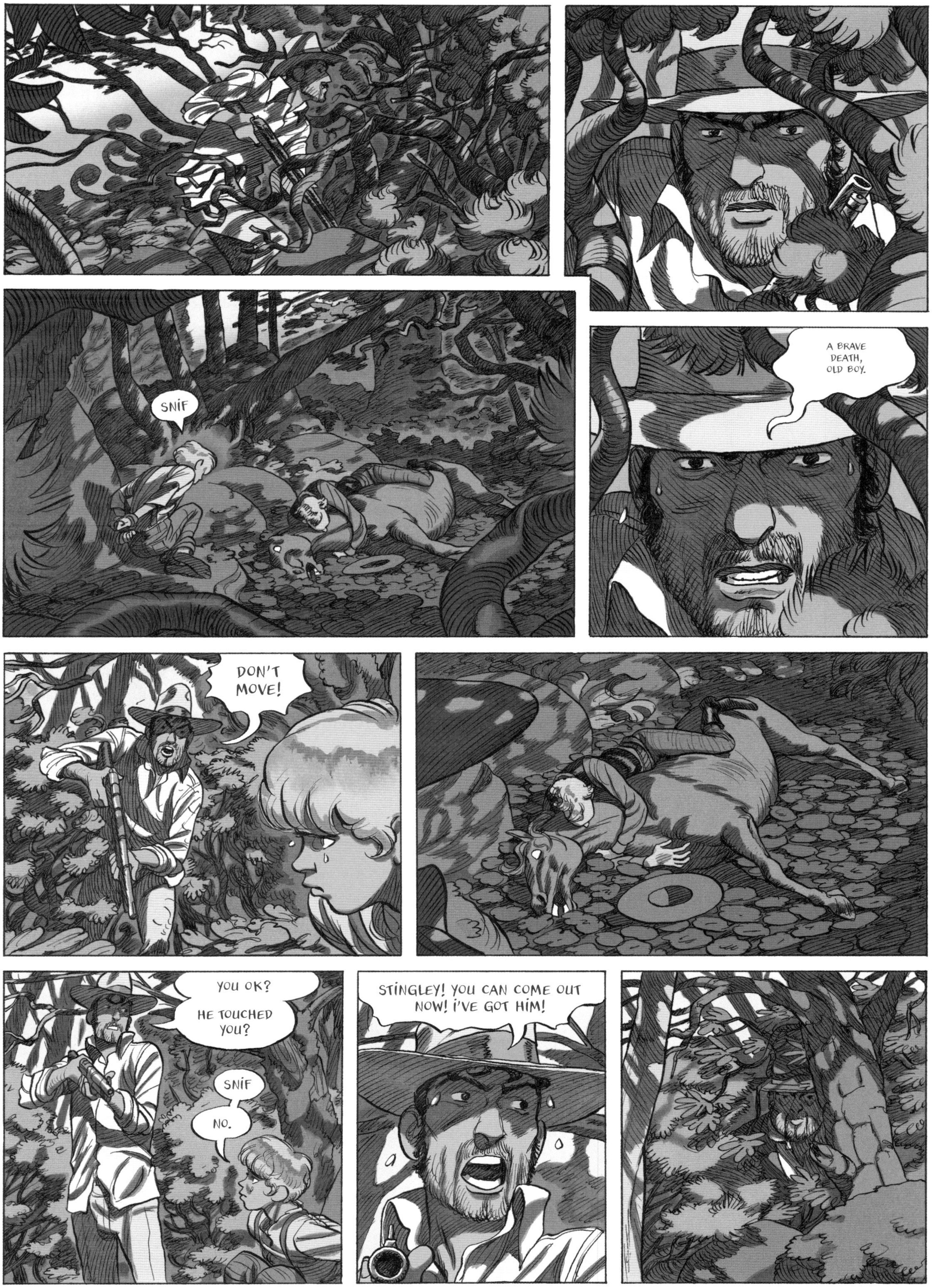

SNIF
A BRAVE DEATH, OLD BOY.
DON'T MOVE!
YOU OK?
HE TOUCHED YOU?
SNIF
NO.
STINGLEY! YOU CAN COME OUT NOW! I'VE GOT HIM!

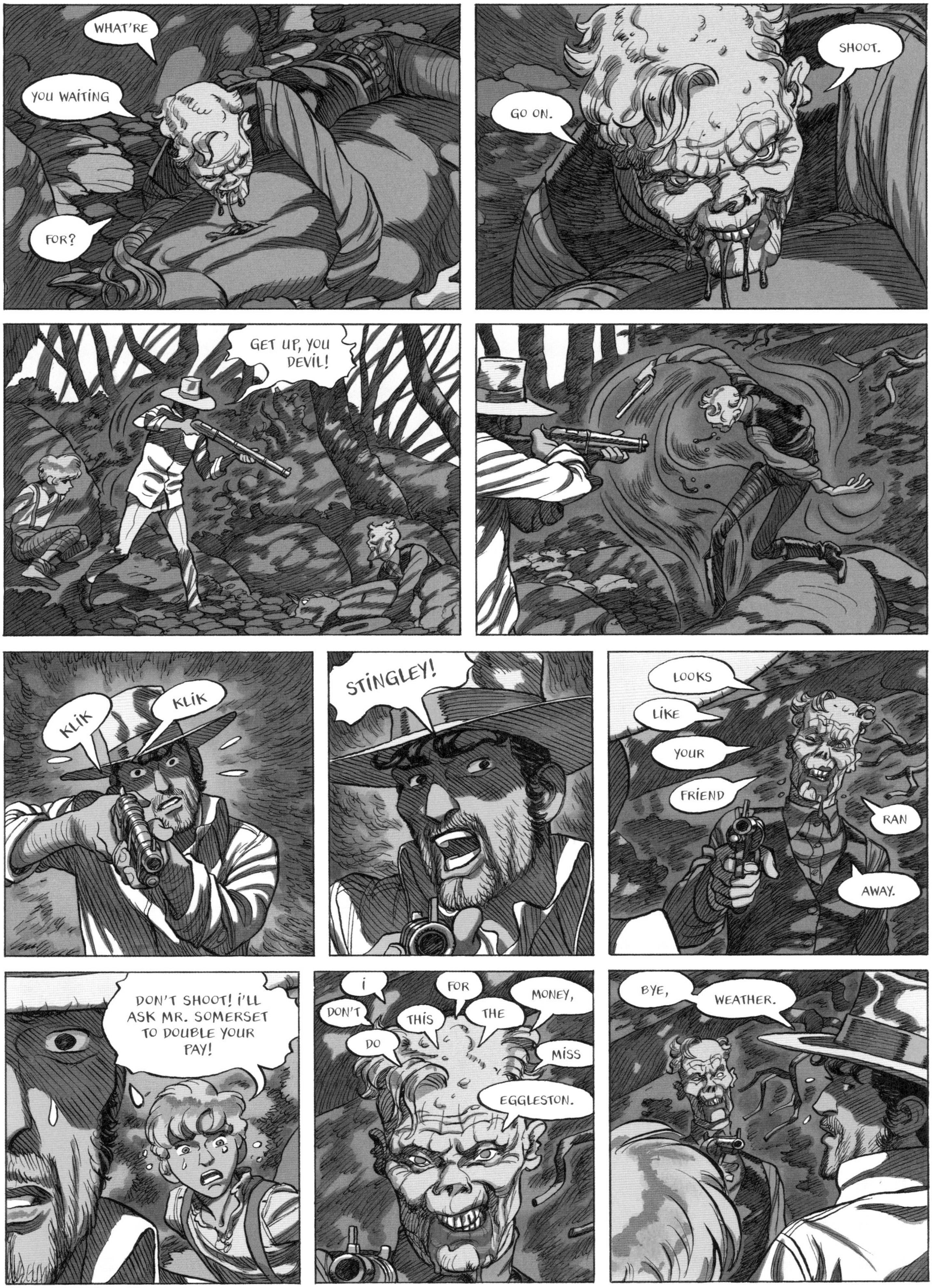
WHAT'RE
YOU WAITING
FOR?
GO ON.
SHOOT.
GET UP, YOU DEVIL!
KLIK
KLIK
STINGLEY!
LOOKS
LIKE
YOUR
FRIEND
RAN
AWAY.
DON'T SHOOT! I'LL ASK MR. SOMERSET TO DOUBLE YOUR PAY!
I
DON'T
DO
THIS
FOR
THE
MONEY,
MISS
EGGLESTON.
BYE,
WEATHER.

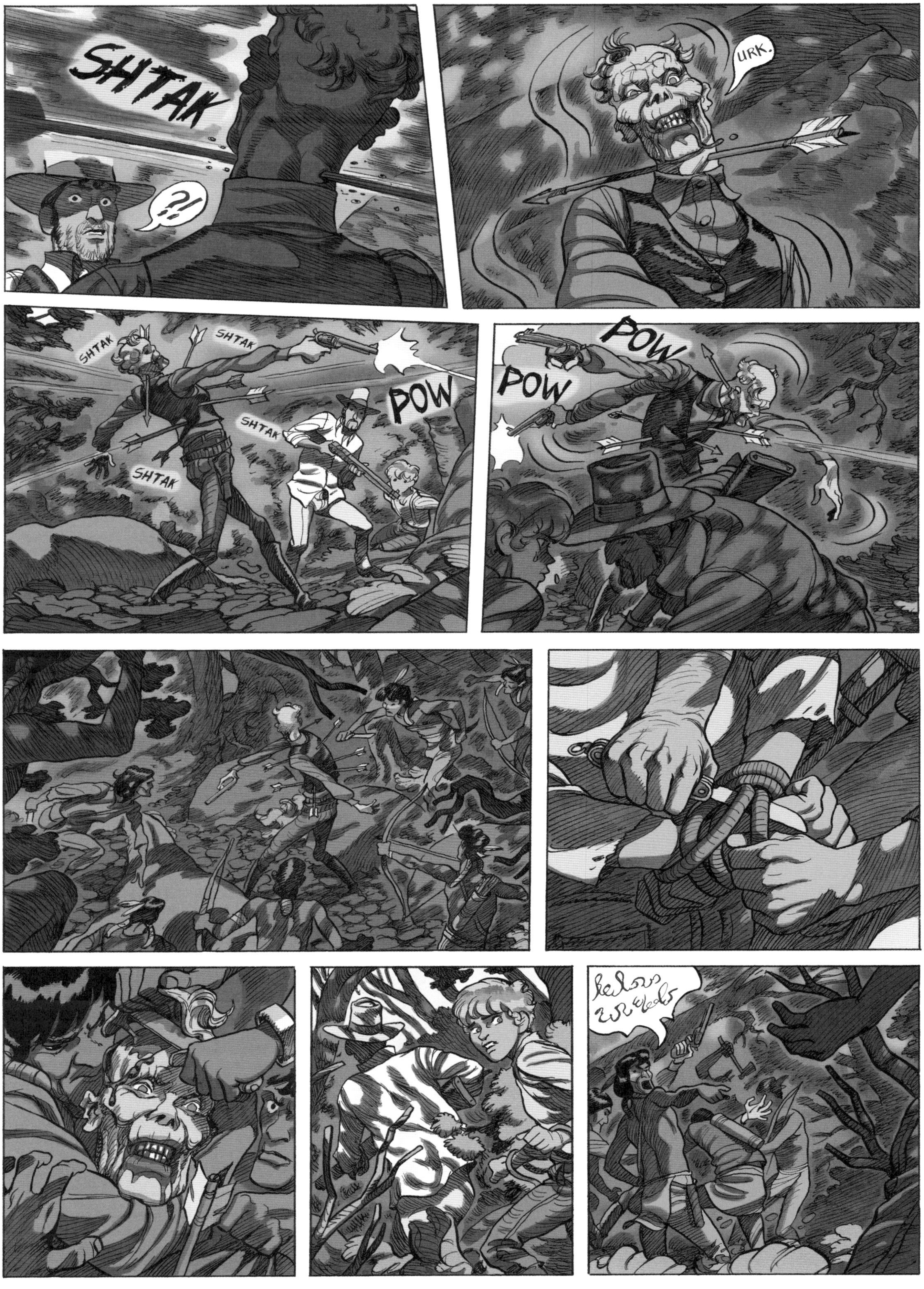
SHTAK
?!
URK.
SHTAK
SHTAK
SHTAK
SHTAK
POW
POW
POW

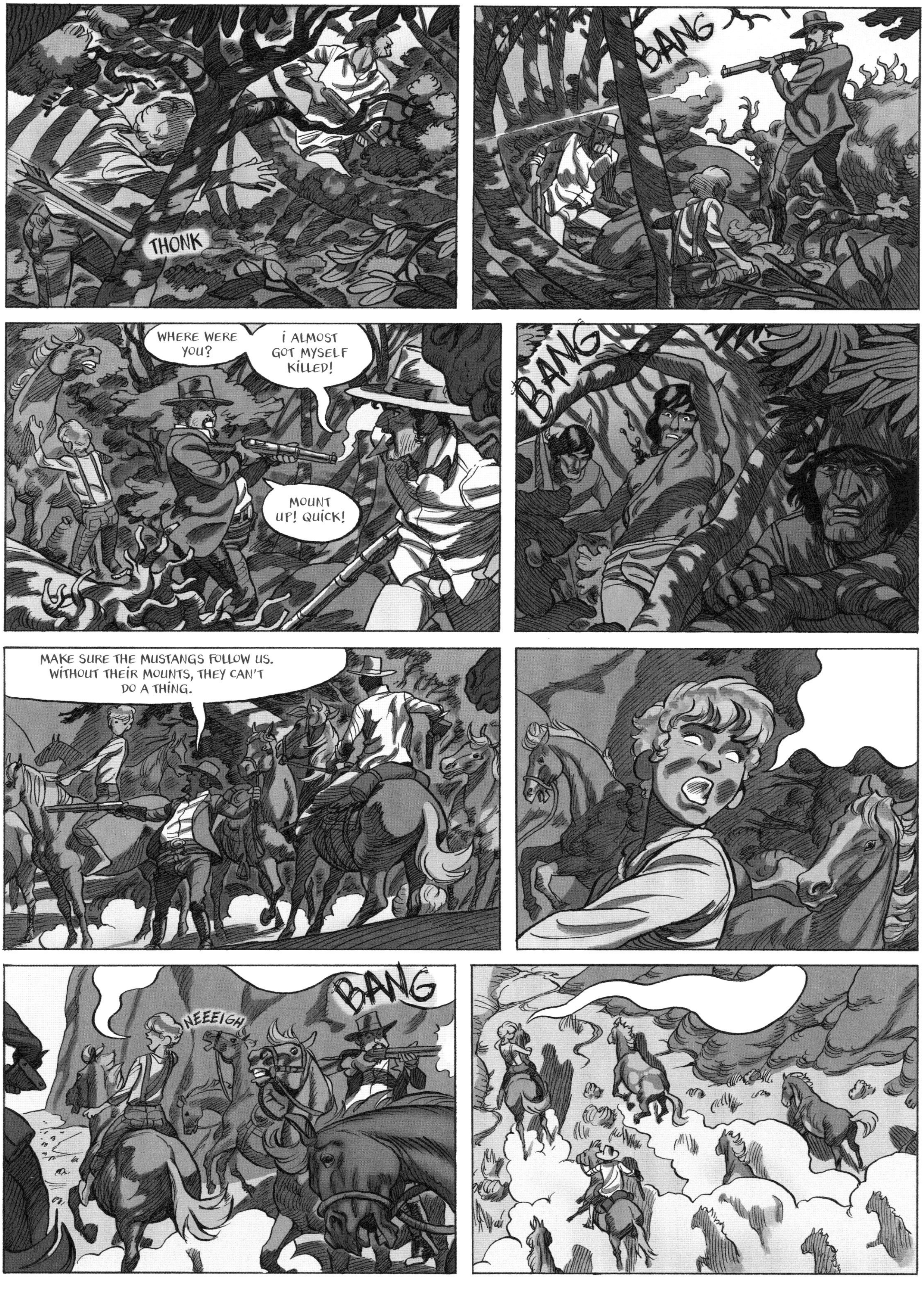
THONK
BANG
WHERE WERE YOU?
¡ ALMOST GOT MYSELF KILLED!
MOUNT UP! QUICK!
BANG
MAKE SURE THE MUSTANGS FOLLOW US. WITHOUT THEIR MOUNTS, THEY CAN'T DO A THING.
BANG
NEEEIGH

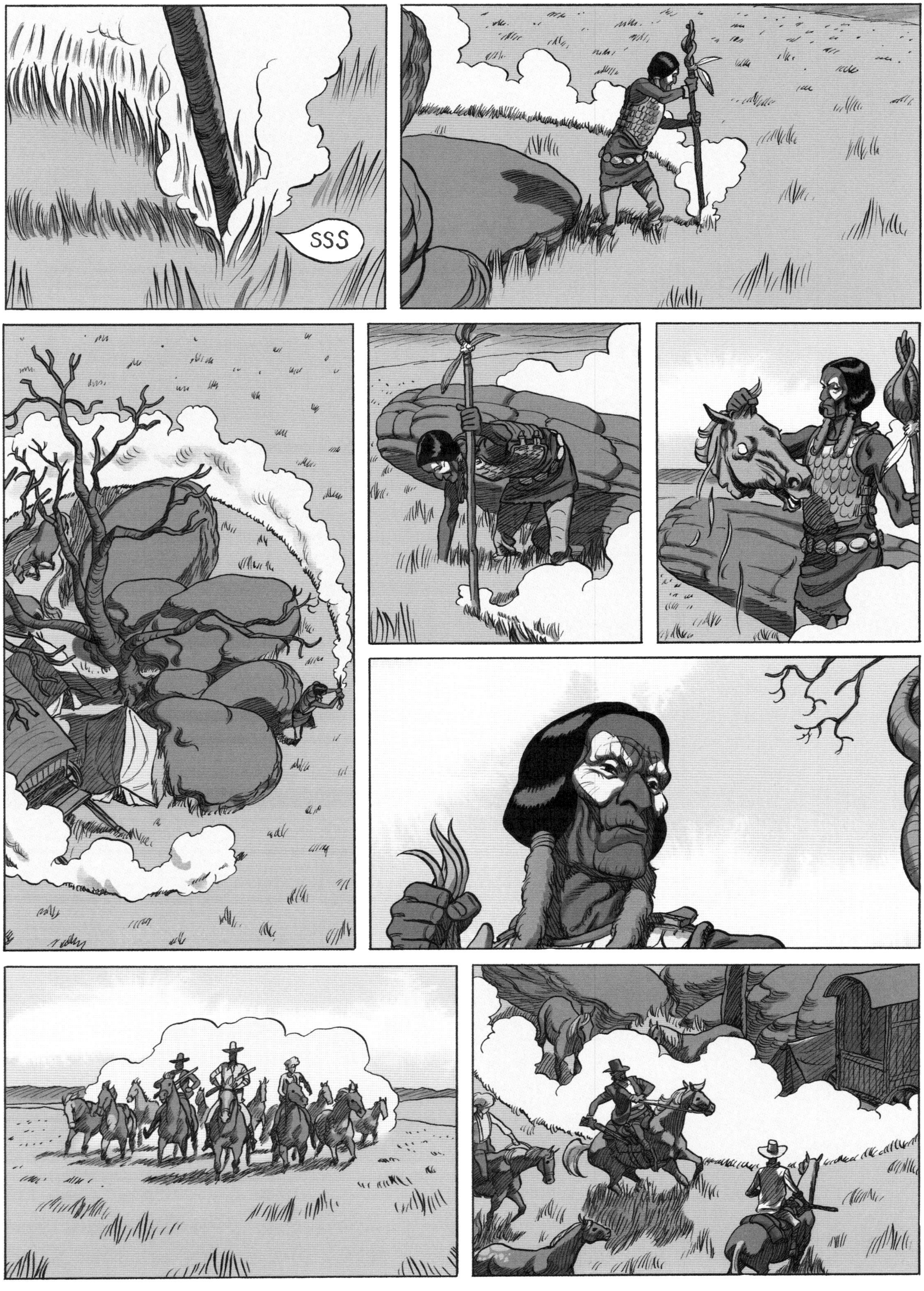
SSS

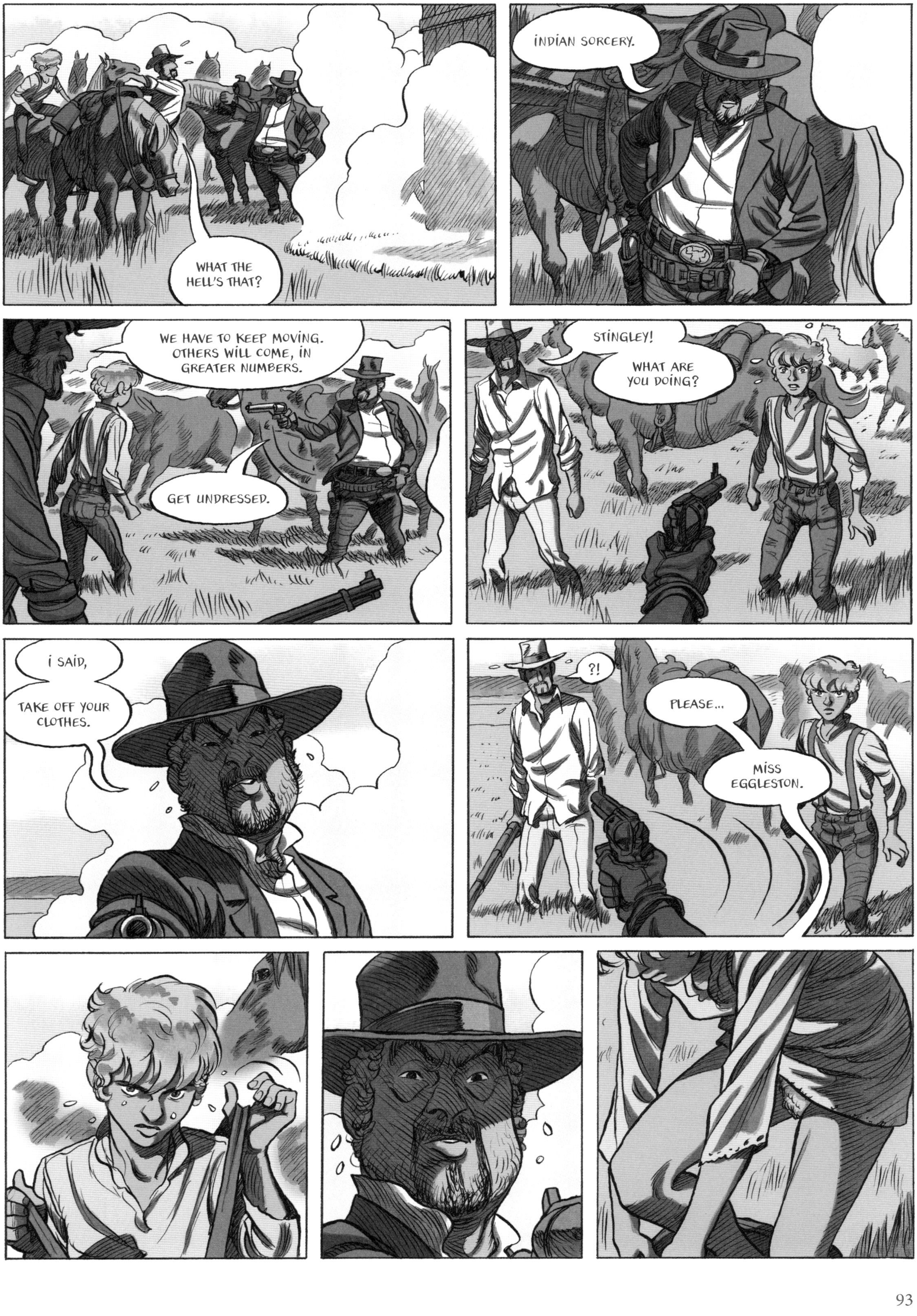
WHAT THE HELL'S THAT?
INDIAN SORCERY.
WE HAVE TO KEEP MOVING. OTHERS WILL COME, IN GREATER NUMBERS.
GET UNDRESSED.
STINGLEY!
WHAT ARE YOU DOING?
I SAID,
TAKE OFF YOUR CLOTHES.
?!
PLEASE...
MISS EGGLESTON.

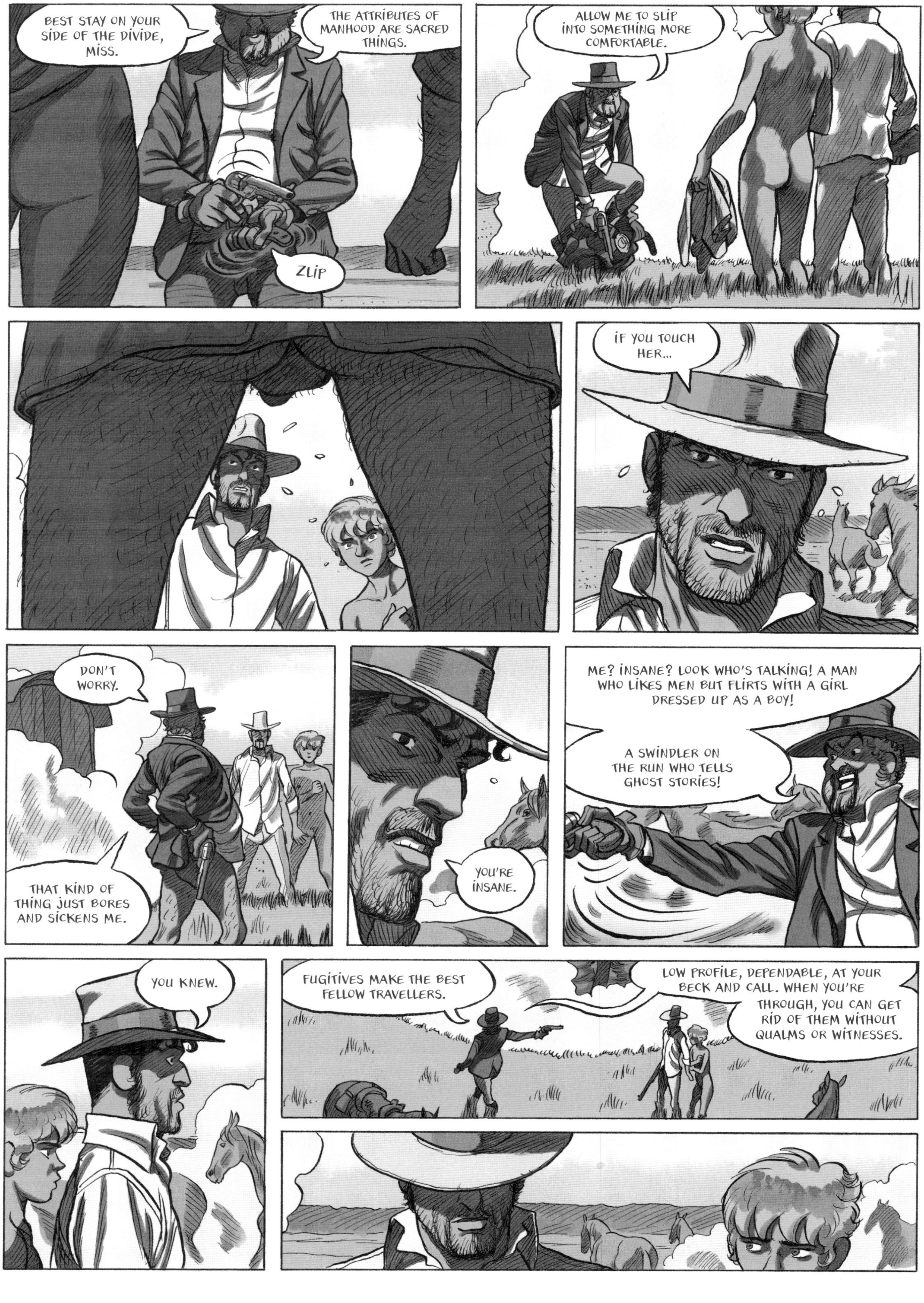
BEST STAY ON YOUR SIDE OF THE DIVIDE, MISS.
THE ATTRIBUTES OF MANHOOD ARE SACRED THINGS.
ZLIP
ALLOW ME TO SLIP INTO SOMETHING MORE COMFORTABLE.
IF YOU TOUCH HER...
DON'T WORRY.
THAT KIND OF THING JUST BORES AND SICKENS ME.
YOU'RE INSANE.
ME? INSANE? LOOK WHO'S TALKING! A MAN WHO LIKES MEN BUT FLIRTS WITH A GIRL DRESSED UP AS A BOY!
A SWINDLER ON THE RUN WHO TELLS GHOST STORIES!
YOU KNEW.
FUGITIVES MAKE THE BEST FELLOW TRAVELLERS.
LOW PROFILE, DEPENDABLE, AT YOUR BECK AND CALL. WHEN YOU'RE THROUGH, YOU CAN GET RID OF THEM WITHOUT QUALMS OR WITNESSES.

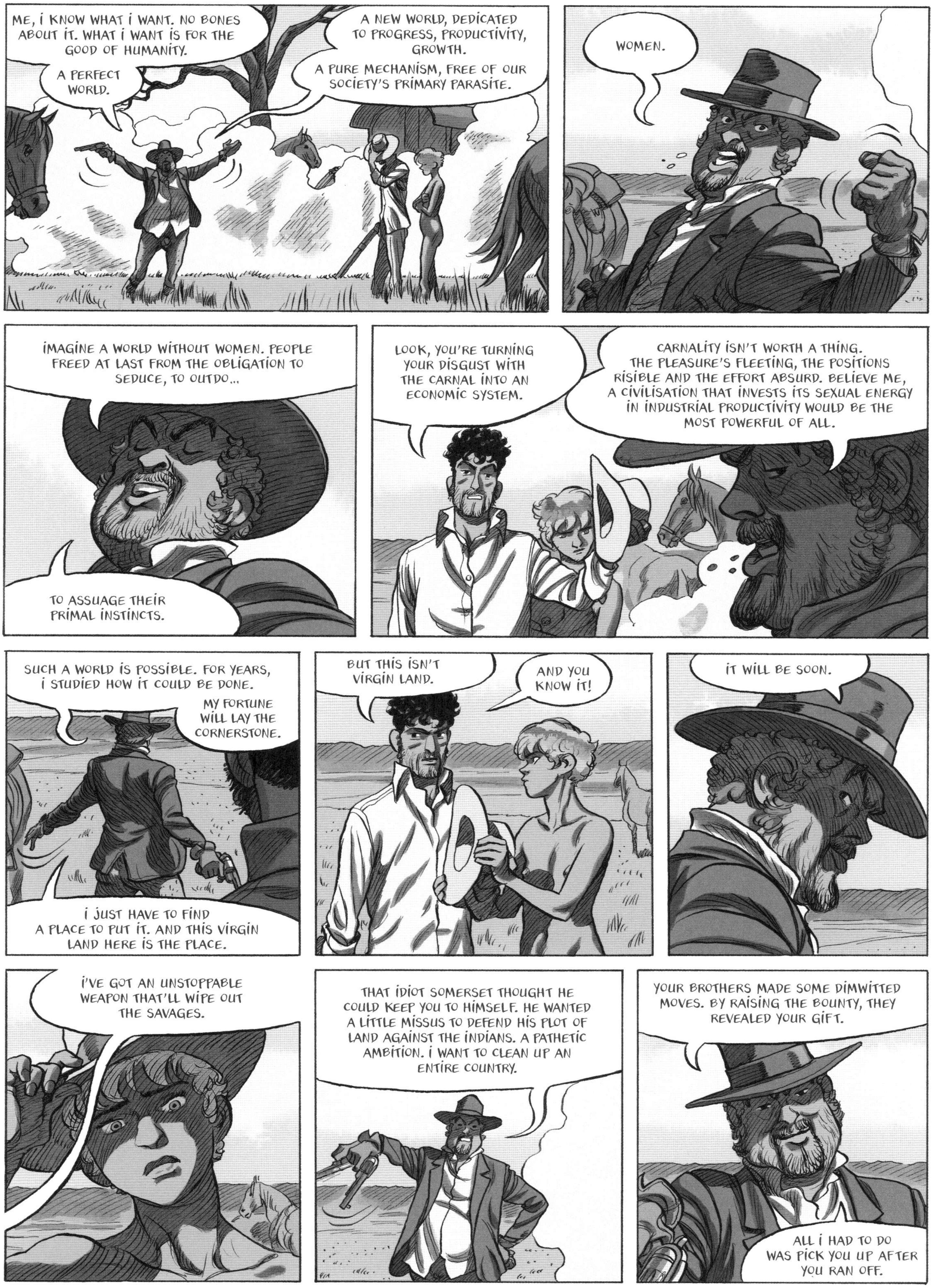
ME, I KNOW WHAT I WANT. NO BONES ABOUT IT. WHAT I WANT IS FOR THE GOOD OF HUMANITY.
A PERFECT WORLD.
A NEW WORLD, DEDICATED TO PROGRESS, PRODUCTIVITY, GROWTH.
A PURE MECHANISM, FREE OF OUR SOCIETY'S PRIMARY PARASITE.
WOMEN.
IMAGINE A WORLD WITHOUT WOMEN. PEOPLE FREED AT LAST FROM THE OBLIGATION TO SEDUCE, TO OUTDO...
TO ASSUAGE THEIR PRIMAL INSTINCTS.
LOOK, YOU'RE TURNING YOUR DISGUST WITH THE CARNAL INTO AN ECONOMIC SYSTEM.
CARNALITY ISN'T WORTH A THING. THE PLEASURE'S FLEETING, THE POSITIONS RISIBLE AND THE EFFORT ABSURD. BELIEVE ME, A CIVILISATION THAT INVESTS ITS SEXUAL ENERGY IN INDUSTRIAL PRODUCTIVITY WOULD BE THE MOST POWERFUL OF ALL.
SUCH A WORLD IS POSSIBLE. FOR YEARS, I STUDIED HOW IT COULD BE DONE.
MY FORTUNE WILL LAY THE CORNERSTONE.
I JUST HAVE TO FIND A PLACE TO PUT IT. AND THIS VIRGIN LAND HERE IS THE PLACE.
BUT THIS ISN'T VIRGIN LAND.
AND YOU KNOW IT!
IT WILL BE SOON.
I'VE GOT AN UNSTOPPABLE WEAPON THAT'LL WIPE OUT THE SAVAGES.
THAT IDIOT SOMERSET THOUGHT HE COULD KEEP YOU TO HIMSELF. HE WANTED A LITTLE MISSUS TO DEFEND HIS PLOT OF LAND AGAINST THE INDIANS. A PATHETIC AMBITION. I WANT TO CLEAN UP AN ENTIRE COUNTRY.
YOUR BROTHERS MADE SOME DIMWITTED MOVES. BY RAISING THE BOUNTY, THEY REVEALED YOUR GIFT.
ALL I HAD TO DO WAS PICK YOU UP AFTER YOU RAN OFF.

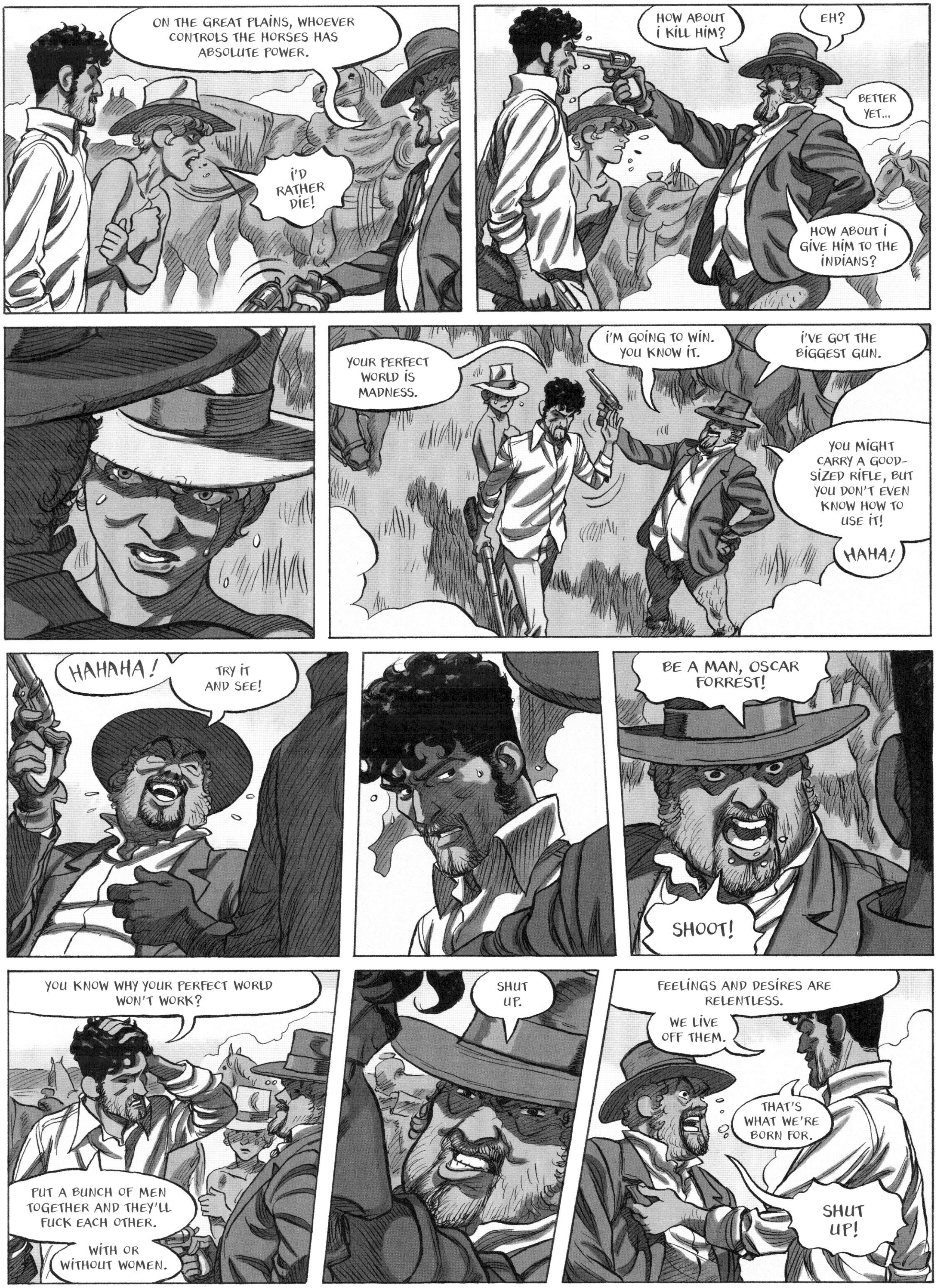
ON THE GREAT PLAINS, WHOEVER CONTROLS THE HORSES HAS ABSOLUTE POWER.
I'D RATHER DIE!
HOW ABOUT I KILL HIM?
EH?
BETTER YET...
HOW ABOUT I GIVE HIM TO THE INDIANS?
YOUR PERFECT WORLD IS MADNESS.
I'M GOING TO WIN. YOU KNOW IT.
I'VE GOT THE BIGGEST GUN.
YOU MIGHT CARRY A GOOD-SIZED RIFLE, BUT YOU DON'T EVEN KNOW HOW TO USE IT!
HAHA!
HAHAHA!
TRY IT AND SEE!
BE A MAN, OSCAR FORREST!
SHOOT!
YOU KNOW WHY YOUR PERFECT WORLD WON'T WORK?
PUT A BUNCH OF MEN TOGETHER AND THEY'LL FUCK EACH OTHER.
WITH OR WITHOUT WOMEN.
SHUT UP.
FEELINGS AND DESIRES ARE RELENTLESS.
WE LIVE OFF THEM.
THAT'S WHAT WE'RE BORN FOR.
SHUT UP!

LIKE IT OR NOT, WE'LL FUCK TILL THE END OF TIME BECAUSE WE LOVE IT SO MUCH.

THERE'S NOTHING MORE BEAUTIFUL THAN THE SMELL OF STARVING BOYS.

POW

NOOO!!

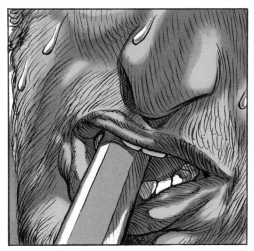

RUMMMMMBBBLBLE

?!

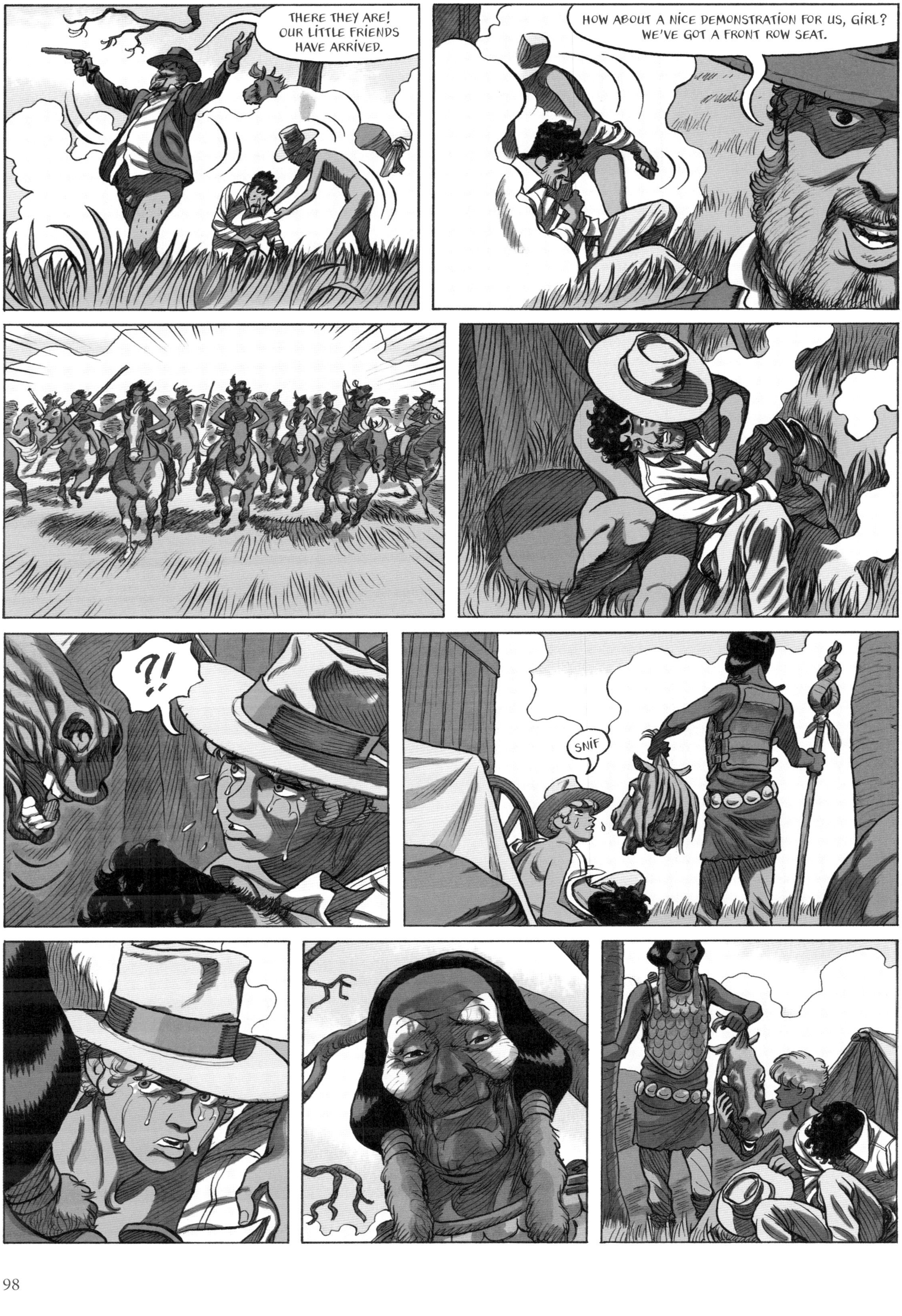
THERE THEY ARE! OUR LITTLE FRIENDS HAVE ARRIVED.
HOW ABOUT A NICE DEMONSTRATION FOR US, GIRL? WE'VE GOT A FRONT ROW SEAT.
?!
SNIF

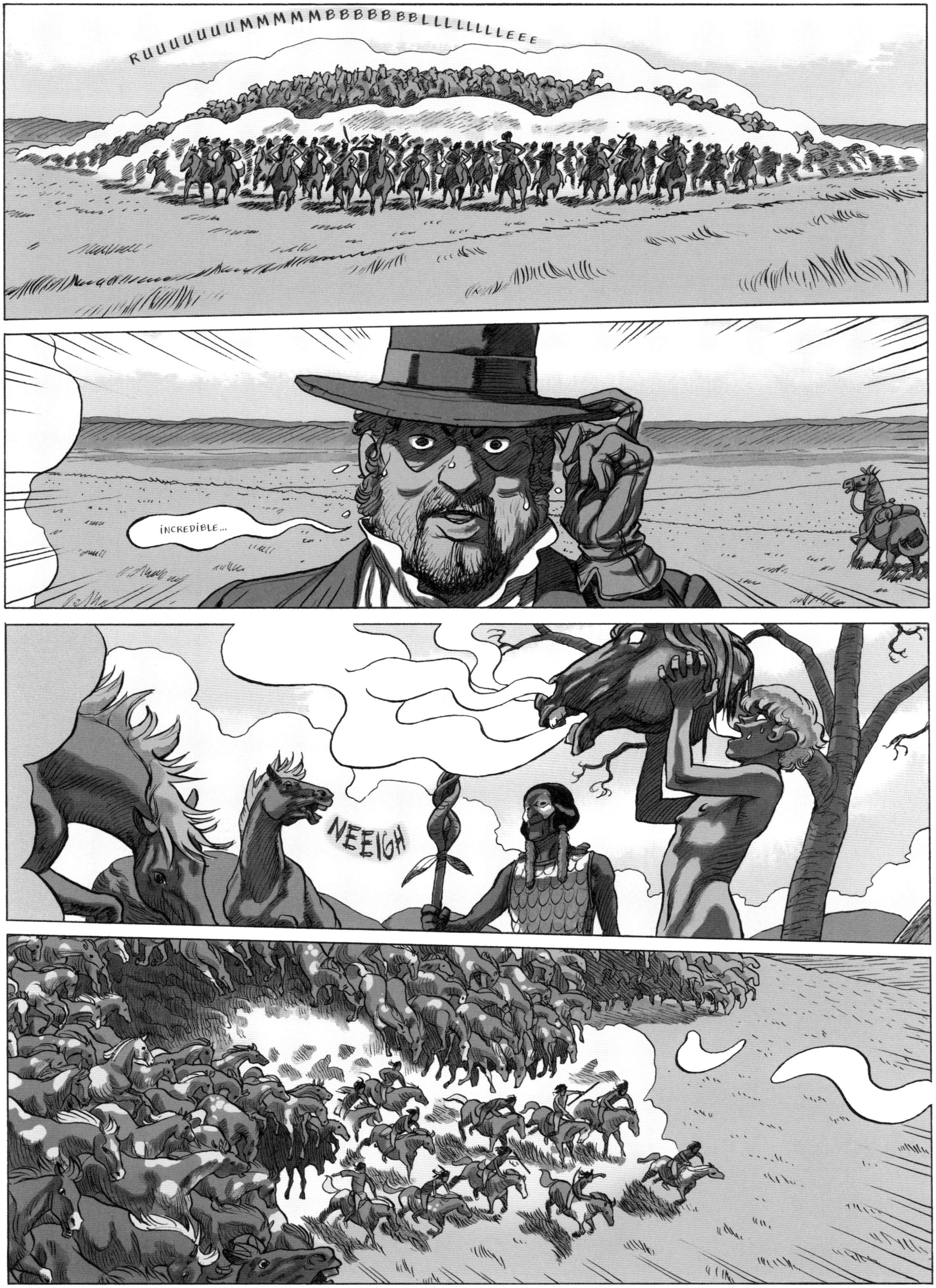
RUUUUUUUMMMMMMBBBBBBBLLLLLLLLLEEE
INCREDIBLE...
NEEIGH

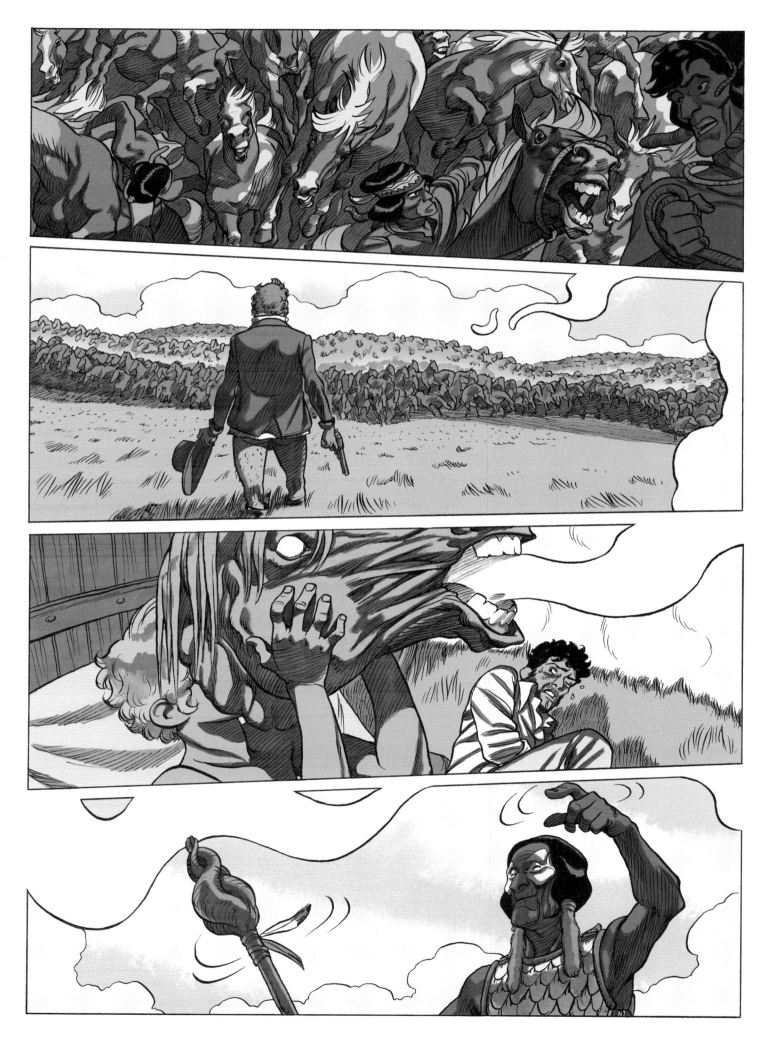

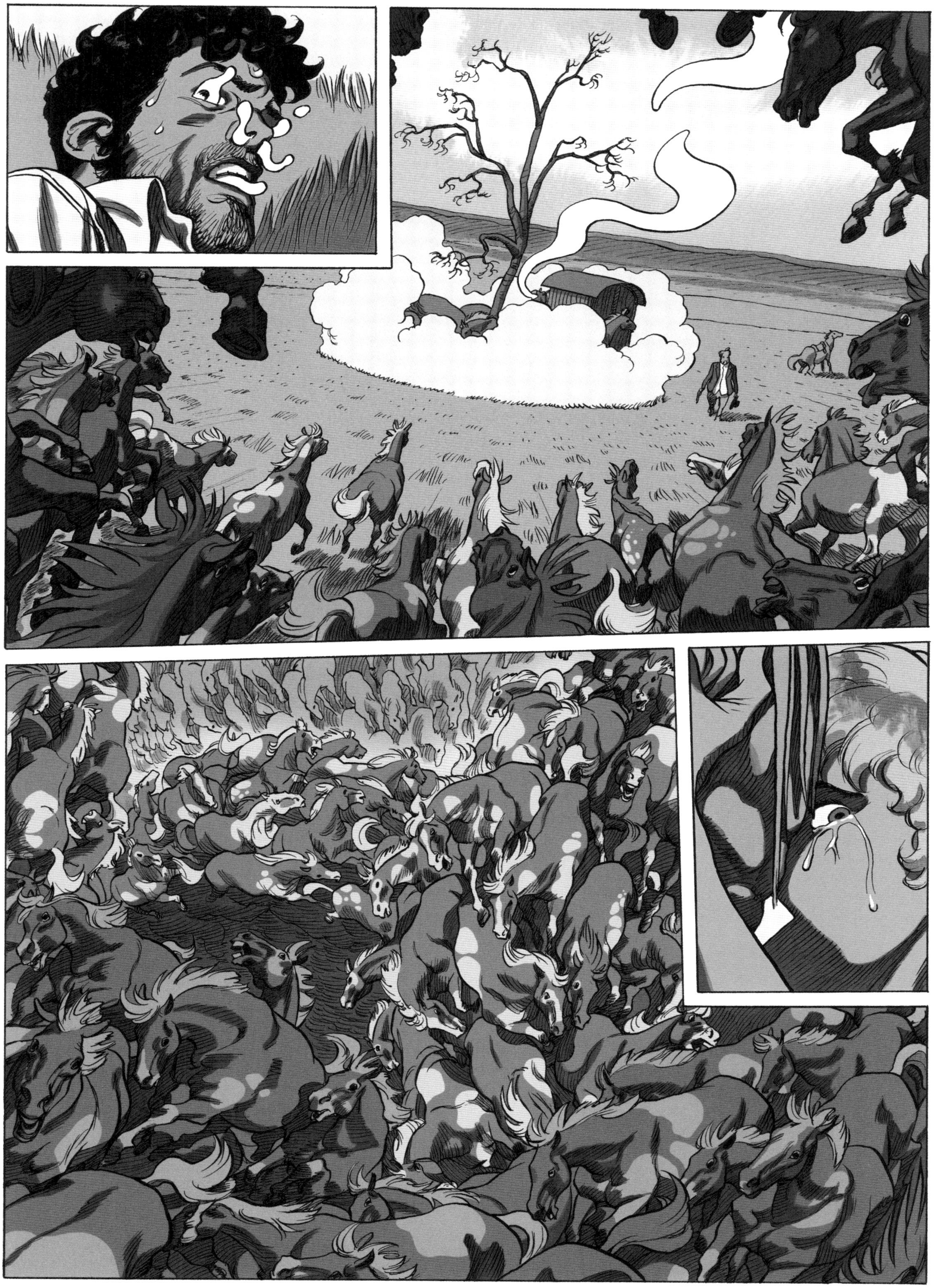

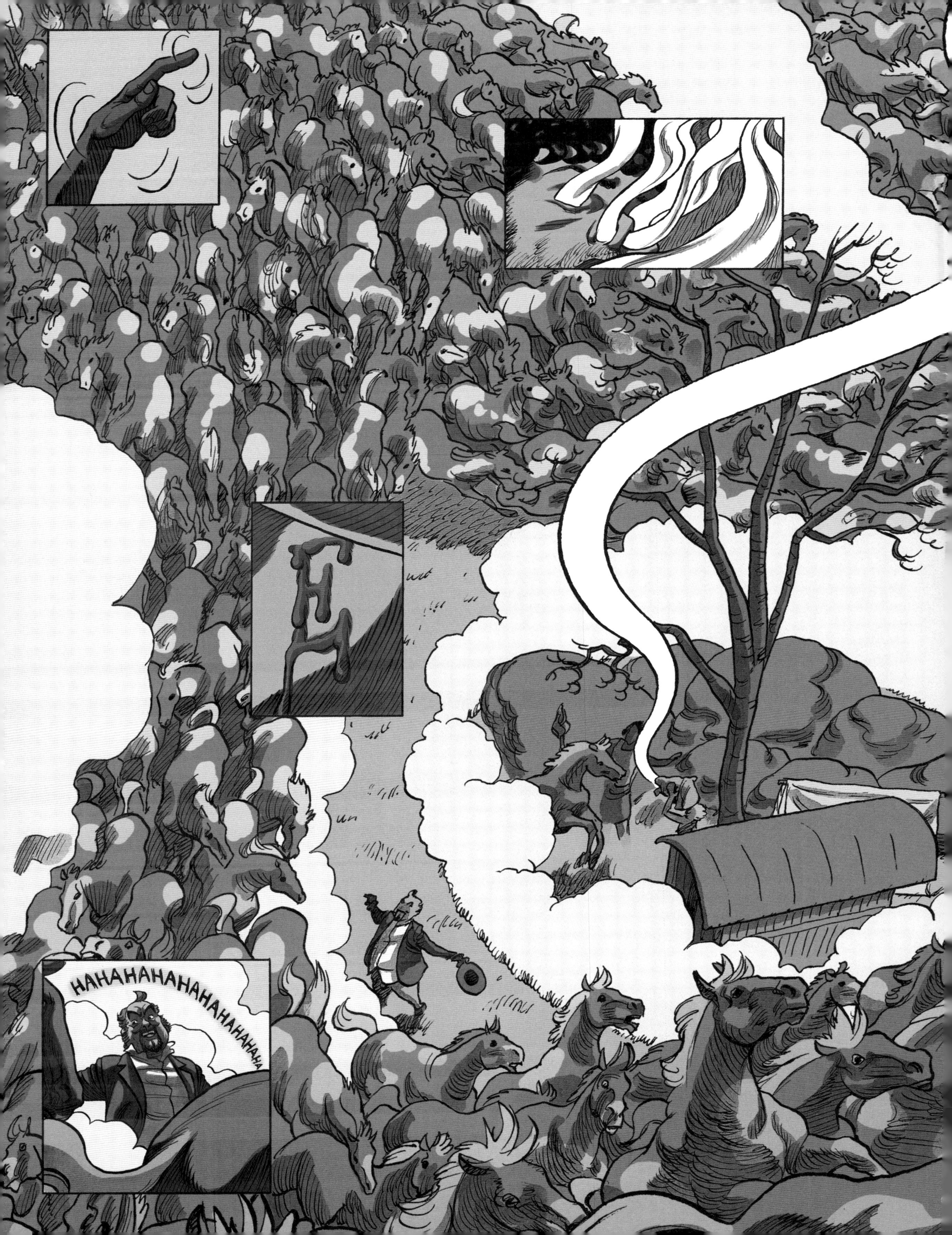
HAHAHAHAHAHAHAHAHAHAHAHA

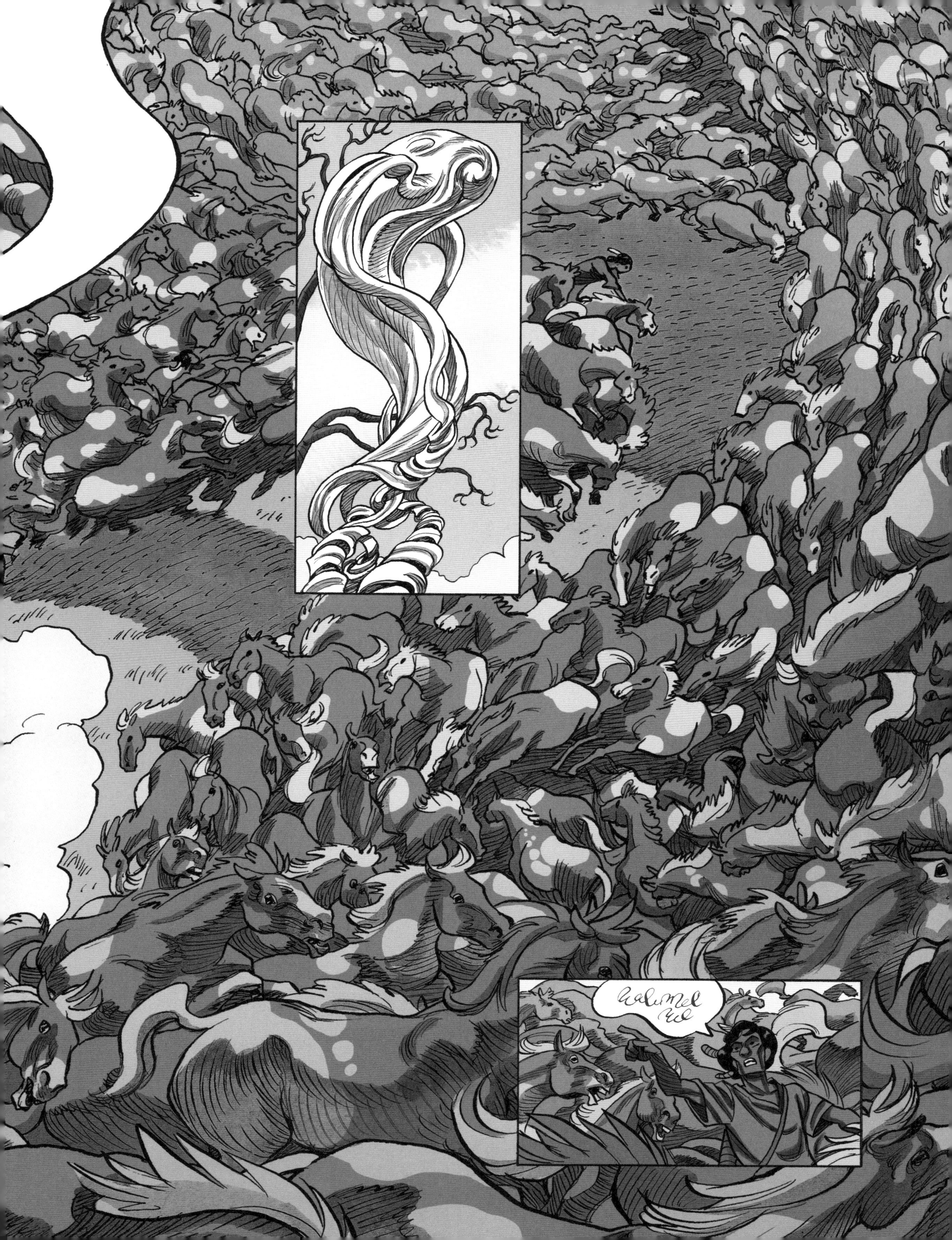

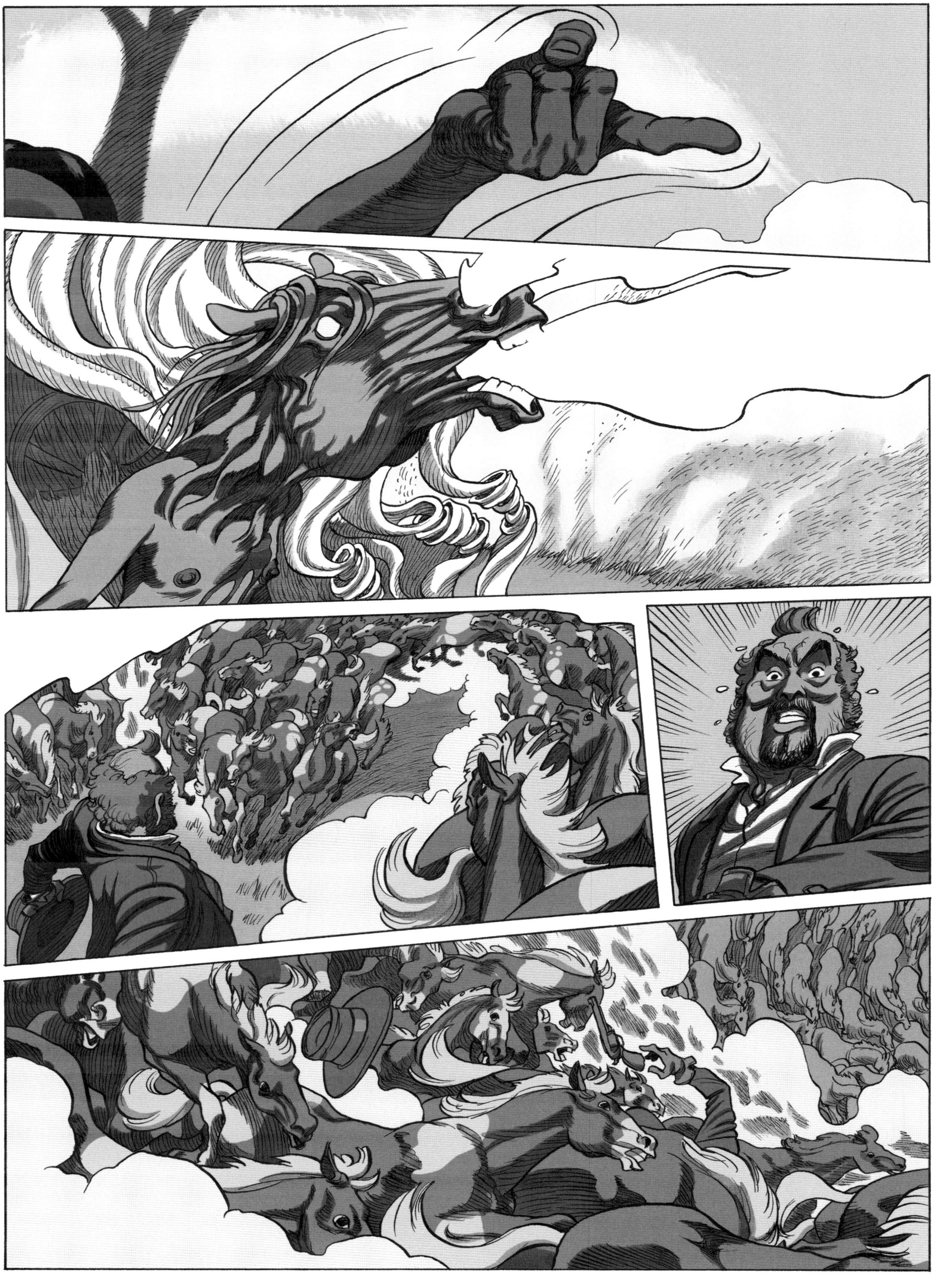

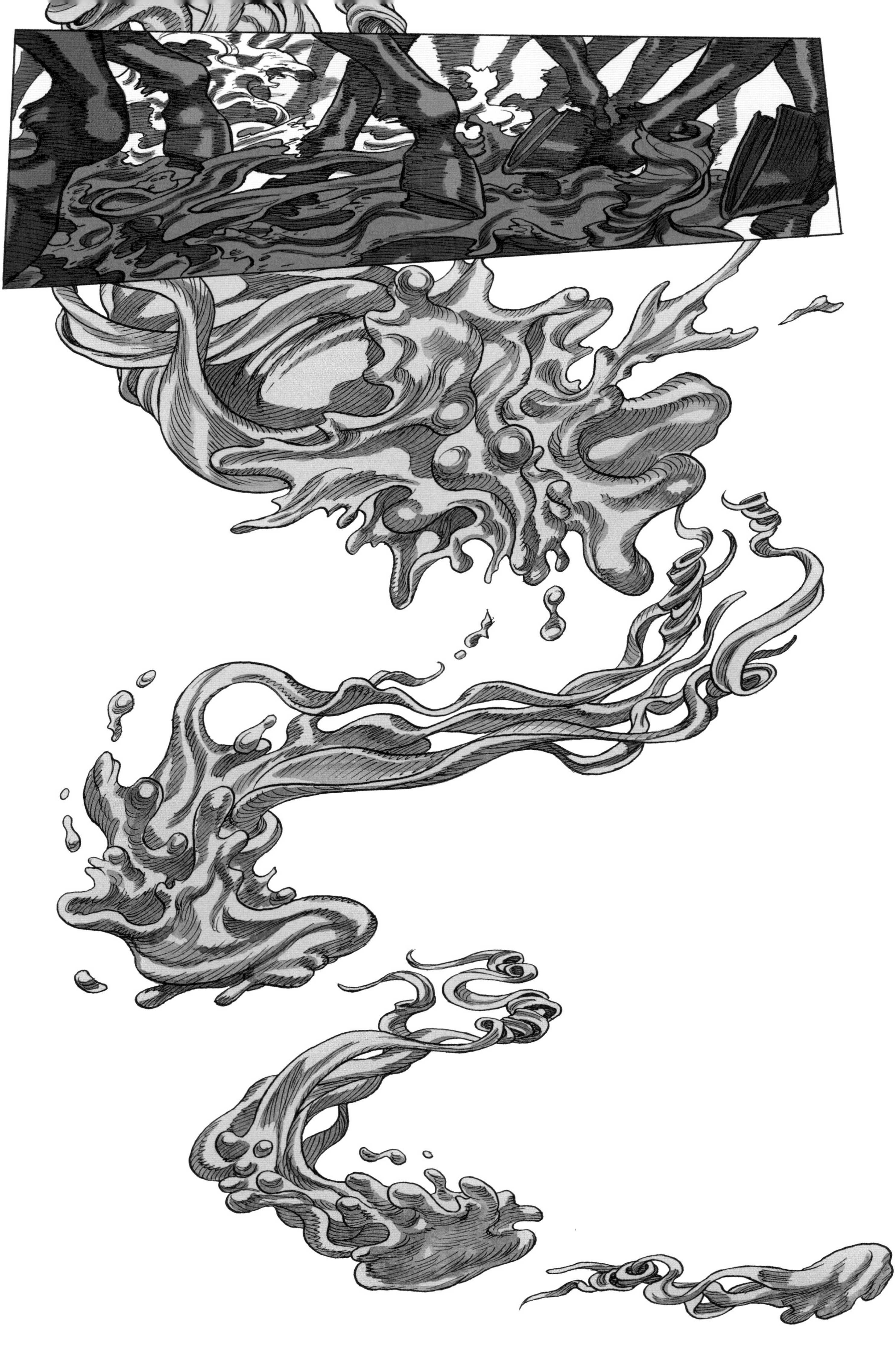

EPILOGUE

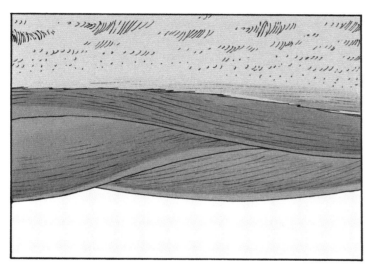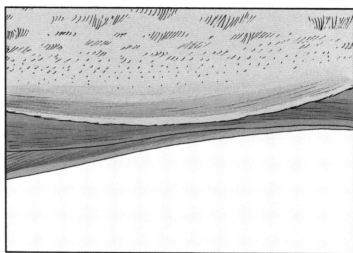

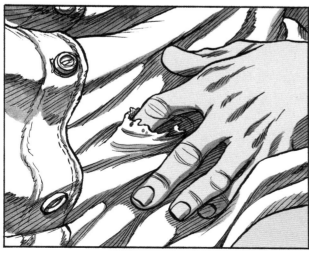

ARE WE STILL ALIVE?

MORE THAN EVER.

IT'LL BE OVER SOON HERE. WE'LL HAVE ALL THE TIME IN THE WORLD.

FUNNY, TALKING WITH SOMEONE WHO'S ALL DRESSED WHEN I'M BUCK NAKED.

EITHER WE'RE BOTH NAKED OR WE'RE BOTH DRESSED. IT'S KNOWN AS EQUALITY.

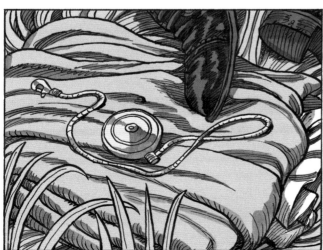

C'MON.

WE'VE STILL GOT A WAY TO GO.

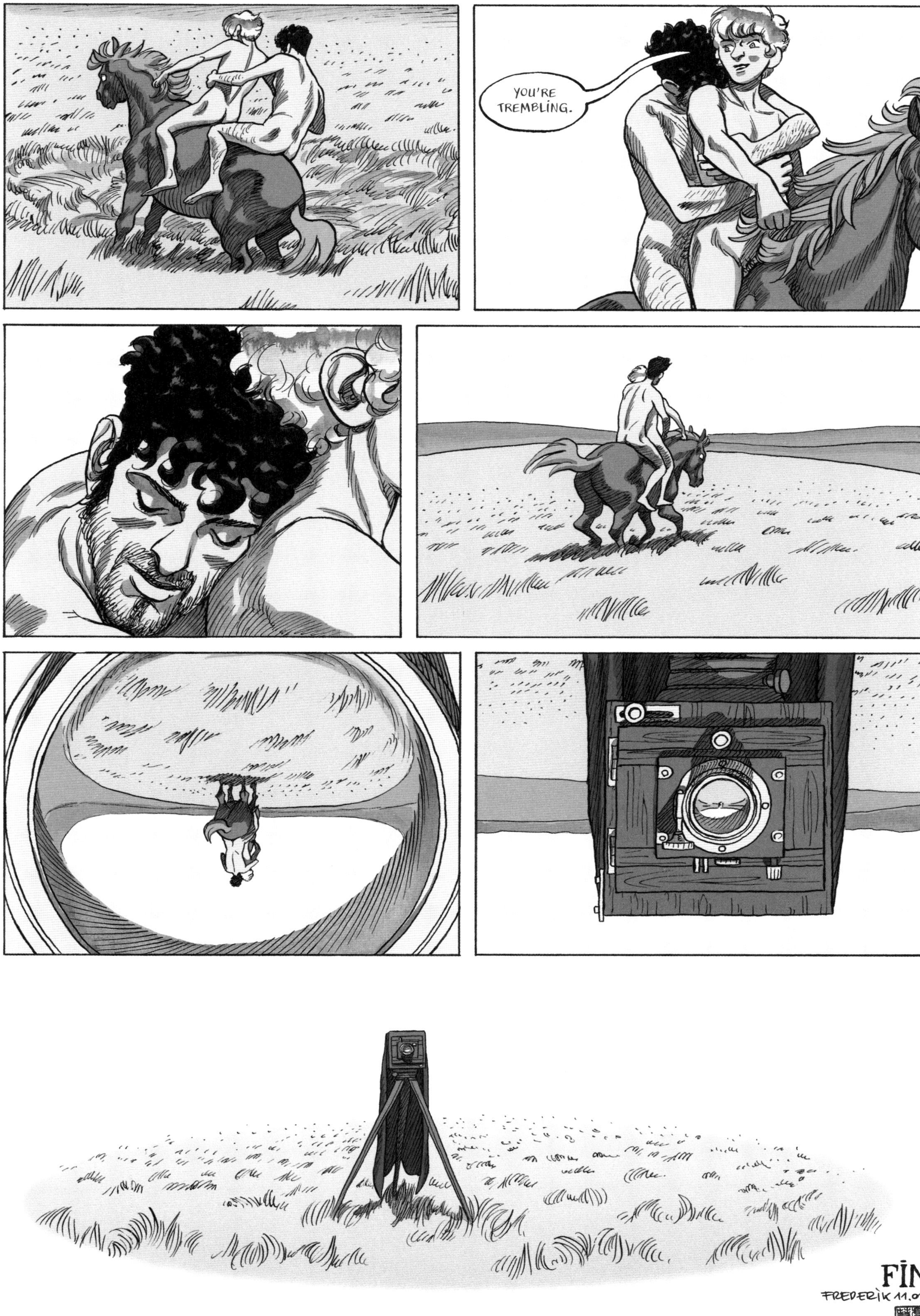
YOU'RE TREMBLING.
FIN
FREDERIK 11.015

LOO HUI PHANG

is the author of comics including *Panorama* (with Cédric Manche) and *Prestige de l'uniforme* (with Hugues Micol), and has also written plays, books, films, performances and installations, for which she has collaborated with renowned illustrators like Blexbolex and Ludovic Debeurme. Born in Laos, she grew up in Normandy.

FREDERIK PEETERS

is the author of *Blue Pills, Pachyderme* and *Aama*, among other books. He has been nominated eight times and has won three times at the Angoulême International Comics Festival, and has received many other prizes for his work. He lives in Geneva.